Linda Blair grew up listening to her grandfather read German fairytales from his homeland. He lived in a house that backed onto a wood wherein – he was fond of telling her – lived a number of fairies and elves, as well as the odd goblin.

She went on to become a serious student, achieving graduate degrees in psychology, clinical psychology and creative writing from Harvard, the University of London and Bath Spa University.

But her love of magic and possibility never left her, and after 40 years working as a clinical psychologist Linda began to wonder whether therapists should consider offering their skills beyond the human population.

After all, don't fairytale characters need therapists, too?

The Fairytale Therapist

To mom, in this, the year of your 100th birthday.

The Fairytale Therapist

Linda Blair

Jem Authors Agency

Published in the United Kingdom by Jem Authors Agency

First printed October 2023

A CIP record of this book is available from the British Library.

ISBN: 979-886-349-1509

www.jemauthorsagency.com

Contents

Have you ever had psychotherapy?

It depends on where you look of course, but it's estimated that somewhere between six *per cent* and thirty *per cent* of adults in the UK have had some form of psychotherapy, and many more have expressed an interest.

Why?

Because modern life is stressful. And because unless you pay for it, it's hard to find anyone who will listen to you when you go on and on about your problems; anyone, that is, who will listen fully and sincerely try to help.

I'll agree that therapists are united in their sincere desire to help – I've never met a colleague who's not interested in helping other people feel happier and more optimistic. But listen fully? During the entire session, without even one moment of mind wandering, not a second of trying to remember if we let the cat out before we left home? That's asking a lot. After all, we're only human.

I'll bet I'm making you wonder now how therapists deal with their own thoughts, and how they deal with their own problems. Because of course therapists have problems, too, just like everyone else.

Whenever therapists have a problem – I mean a big problem – they're advised to take time off work and seek out their own therapist to help them sort things out. But what happens if they don't?

That's why I decided to write this book. I thought you might like to listen in on some therapy sessions. You'll get to hear not only what both therapist and client are saying, but also what the therapist is thinking. And this therapist – totally fictional I hasten to add – is grappling with a really big problem.

It's time to introduce you to the therapist.

First, however, I had better warn you that you'll be meeting some pretty unusual clients.

Introduction

I've just gone back over what you're about to read, and I'm still not sure whether it happened. Really happened, I mean. Not just happened in my mind.

That's why there's so much detail. Any therapist would wonder why on Earth a colleague would take such extensive clinical notes, and why they would include all those personal asides. I had a good reason; I really couldn't believe what was happening, and I thought that if I wrote it all down, I could go back later and... verify it?

Because even now, I'm not sure. I checked for the straw, and it's still there in my top desk drawer, exactly where I put it after the Queen vanished. So surely the visits did happen?

Anyway, before you read my notes about those fairytale visits, maybe I should tell you a bit about myself.

My name is Helen Fisher. I'm a clinical psychologist. I used to be a mother, and I used to be married as well. But all that's over now. I grew up in the North of England, the middle of three. I have a sister who's four years older than I am. She's a consultant paediatrician with two perfect daughters and a surgeon husband. I never liked her much, because I could never measure up to her, never do as well as she did.

My brother is fourteen months younger than I am. He read philosophy at uni, but really he just wants to be an actor. To be fair, he does get occasional acting gigs. But most of the time he just hangs out with his thespian friends at my parents' expense. They don't seem to mind. They're convinced he's going to be the next Olivier.

My mum trained as a GP, but as soon as she gave birth to Nell she stopped working and she hasn't worked since. She's the eldest of six, and she used to say that all she ever wanted was to have children, like her own mum. But after Nell was born, she was told she wouldn't be able to have any more children – something about her diabetes. So, she stopped trying. She told me she didn't even know she was pregnant with me until she was twenty weeks on. I don't know why she told me that. Doesn't make me feel very important or wanted.

Mum probably got pregnant again so fast after I was born because she thought she was on a winning streak. Looking back, I realise that having a boy had always been her dream – she'd absolutely worshipped her older brother. So as soon as Will was born, I felt forgotten. No one seemed to care how well I did at school. No one made me play the piano or excel at sport. I suppose I should be grateful no one pushed me, but I didn't feel like that. It was more like I didn't much matter.

I don't really know what to tell you about my father, because I never really got to know him. He spent almost all of his time at the hospital. He was a surgeon, just like the man my sister married. Work was everything to him. I remember when I was in primary school, I used to wake up really early in the mornings, just so I could be with him before he left for the hospital. He and Mum got on okay as far as I could tell, but other than making the three of us I have no idea what they did together. They each had their own friends, and while Mum had lots of interests when she wasn't taking care of us, Dad just had work.

We were all expected to go to uni. No negotiating on that. In true drifter mode (at the start of my training we all took a personality test. I'm a 'drifter', apparently), I decided to read chemistry because it was my best A-level result. Besides, chemistry seemed like cooking, which was what I really wanted to do. But Mum said cooking wasn't a proper career. So, I read chemistry.

When I got to uni, I found most of the other students on my course wanted to become doctors or scientists. I had no idea what I wanted to do, so my tutor suggested I switch to something 'broader' and 'less demanding'. I asked her what she meant by that, and she just said there are lots of opportunities for psychologists, so perhaps I should read psychology.

So I did. I switched straight away, and found I was pretty good at it, especially the clinical bits. It felt like detective work, trying to figure out what was wrong with a person and what was really going on in their mind. Clinical psychology was the obvious career choice, and I even got a nod from Mum and Dad when I was accepted everywhere I applied – although Mum said she really wished I'd chosen a 'proper' medical career.

I met Theo during my clinical training. I'd mostly dated other psychologists before Theo, and although the sex was great, our conversations always felt very in-house, a little claustrophobic. Theo was someone different. He fascinated me. He owned a small art gallery and just loved every sort of art, especially watercolours. He was sharing a flat with my closest friend in my year, and she was the one who introduced us, said she thought Theo was just what I needed. We got on fine, and on graduation night he asked me to marry him. It was really romantic, and the timing was good, so I thought, why not? In true drifter fashion.

I got a job straight away, but that's not really saying much. It's really easy to get a job if you're a clinical psychologist. Everyone has problems, and there aren't enough of us. So, I always had a steady job, which meant I was the reliable one financially. Theo's income depended on art sales, so it was really variable.

I suppose things started to go wrong between us about three years after we married, when I started asking Theo when he'd like to start a family. I don't know why we never talked about this before we got married, but we never did. Like my mother, I wanted lots of kids, and I guess I just assumed Theo would want the same thing. I was married for five years before I started raising the subject with Theo – old enough, I thought. I didn't want to wait forever. But Theo wasn't so sure. He liked our easy life – well, especially his own easy life, with no obligation to earn or to care for anyone else. He was surprised, I think, to find that for once I was insistent. That's when we started arguing.

Then I didn't get pregnant. Month after month, wait after agonising wait. Nothing, not even a miscarriage to suggest at least fertilisation was possible. Our sex life was effectively ruined, dictated by ovulation charts and my temperature. I must have been a nightmare to live with. I felt frustrated and continually anxious. I was so desperate to see that blue line.

After a year, Theo agreed we could try IVF. That made our sex life even more of a nightmare. But on the third attempt I got pregnant, and we had Alex.

To me, Alex was perfect. Beautiful, sweet-natured, and, well, just... perfect. He had the longest eyelashes I'd ever seen on a boy, and his creamy complexion and strawberry blond curls were just like Theo's. He was an easy baby, then a carefree and daring child. He always had so much fun, and he was oh-so-self-confident, almost bullish. I adored him. I know Theo did, too, although I think he didn't feel like he could admit it after his ambivalence about having kids.

I can safely say Alex's birth marked the beginning of the best time in my life. I cut my work back to three days a week as soon as he was born so I could spend as much time as possible with him – while still making enough to cover the bills of course. Once he started school, I worked my three days as five short ones so I could always be at the school gates to meet him.

Even though I didn't get pregnant again, to my surprise I didn't seem to mind. Alex was enough for me. Alex was my everything.

When I think about it now, I can imagine how left out Theo must have felt. But at the time, I didn't let myself notice. Everything was just too perfect.

But then, the day after Alex's tenth birthday, my world went black.

Alex was cycling home from his best friend's house when it happened. Jack lived only a couple of streets away, so all four parents agreed to let the boys cycle between our homes – they were thick as thieves, constantly in and out of each other's houses. We all agreed it was sensible, because it encouraged their independence.

Alex was coming home when the car hit him. It was a direct hit at a junction, I was told. The driver said he hadn't seen him. I can't remember the rest. The driver wasn't charged apparently. They told me Alex died instantly.

The police came to the house. Theo was still at the gallery – well, looking back, maybe he was with Freya. He said he was at the gallery, but probably the affair was going on even then. Anyway, it meant I had to go to the police station alone. I had to identify Alex on my own. My perfect little boy.

Afterwards, I tried everything, I really did. I took antidepressants. I tried sleeping tablets. I saw a therapist. The one thing I refused to do was give up work, even though both my therapist and my supervisor suggested I take a break. I think I was afraid to lose the structure work provided, not to mention the feeling that people still needed me. After all, I was totally alone: Theo had left by then.

I really don't know what triggered the move – my escape, as my therapist called it. He tried to stop me; said I hadn't even begun to grieve. But I thought, if I go somewhere where I don't know anyone, not a soul, then I can start over and somehow everything will be ok.

It didn't take long to find a job – I already told you psychology jobs are easy to find. It was a sole practitioner post in a remote village in Wales. Ideal. No one would know my past. I could start over, just see what happened.

For the first month, things went well. I enjoyed my solitude, my little cottage with my cat. My receptionist – the only person I saw every day – just got on with her job, never asked questions or tried to be pally. I was sure I would defy everyone who'd warned me this wouldn't work.

But that's when the fairytale characters started coming through my office window, as you'll find out in the pages that follow. I've kept the content of my notes just as I wrote them – detailed 'objective' clinical notes – so I apologise if the narrative sounds a little cold and formal at times. It's because I wrote not as a storyteller, but as the clinician I believed those magical characters had come to see.

Most of the time it wasn't hard to guess who they were. But therapists are trained not to speculate, instead to regard each client as someone they've never heard of, never met. So, I pushed those thoughts away.

I also had to accept an odd way of working. I knew I couldn't suggest actions that would change these characters' stories, because their stories were already written, already well known.

Anyway, here are my clinical notes about those sessions. I'm happy to share them with you, because someday I might ask you whether you think the visits really happened.

I'm still sure they did.

Rumpelstiltskin

Tuesday, end of clinic. Thank heavens.

I sink back wearily into my worn leather chair, take off my glasses and close my eyes. So much suffering here! Identity crises, depression, phobias, sleep disorders. The same as in my London clinics.

When I chose to move to this quiet Welsh village, I was convinced I'd leave behind all those 'city problems', as I'd thought of them. I couldn't have been more mistaken. Mental illness, I was beginning to realise, has no respect for setting.

But enough. I just need to summon the strength to sit up straight and write my notes so I can go home, too, and leave this all behind. Eyes still closed, I lean forward, steeling myself for the last task of the day.

What was that? A scraping of chair legs across my consulting room floor? A rustle of some heavy material, silk perhaps? Not possible. There could be no one in this office now except me. Even my secretary has gone. I heard her close and latch the outer door only a few minutes ago.

I open my eyes in alarm and shove my glasses back on clumsily – rather askew now – and look anxiously around the room.

Sitting quietly across from me is a young woman. Long tight blonde curls fall to her shoulders. Perfect pale skin. Her wide mouth is closed and drawn. Her eyes are downcast, but I can see the long blonde lashes even from where I'm sitting. She is wearing a dress made from satin, I would guess, a soft grey. A long tight bodice draws in her delicate frame and is met at the waist by volumes of grey silk, a long skirt under which I detect an equally voluminous silk petticoat. The sleeves of her dress are full and loose, ending just beneath the elbows. Her hands rest in her lap, and in her left hand she's clutching a large linen handkerchief. Long pearl eardrops and a matching pearl necklace complete her ensemble, the latter plain to see above the low neckline of her dress. Clearly, a very rich woman. And equally clearly, not of our time. I wait, trying not to stare open-mouthed. Without looking up, she began to speak.

'You have to help me. I've been told you can help people. I don't want to lose my baby! You have to help me keep my baby!'

And with that, she began to sob uncontrollably.

I had no idea what to do or say, so I simply waited quietly – the therapist's safe fall back. Gradually, her sobs subsided. She wiped her eyes delicately with her handkerchief, and for the first time, looked up at me.

She was absolutely stunning. Perfect, delicate features. But oh, such fear, desperation and sadness in those pale blue eyes!

'You will help me, won't you?'

To my astonishment, I found myself smiling my professional 'I hear you and I care' smile and replying as I ordinarily would. I could only suppose that assuming my professional façade was more for me than for the 'patient' sitting across from me. Of course – it was my own attempt to cope, to regain a sense of normality. Because this certainly wasn't normal.

'I will happily try to help you, but in order to do so I need to know more about you, and what's gone wrong in your life. Perhaps you could start by explaining why you're afraid of losing your baby. Is this a baby you already have? Or one you are... expecting?'

She didn't look pregnant, but I needed to know if the baby was real, or whether this was a phantom pregnancy. At the same time, I was struck by the absurdity of the question. After all, was *she* real?

'Wilhelm is three months and a day. He is my life.' More sobs.

'And where is Wilhelm now?'

'He's safe in the castle with my servant girl.'

'In the castle? Are you, then...?'

She smiled through her tears now, a bitterly sad smile.

'I am the Queen. Yes, I am the Queen.'

She was silent again. I took off my glasses and wiped them with one of the tissues from the box I always keep in the top drawer of my desk. I put them back on, carefully this time. She was still there.

'Perhaps it would be best if you start by going back to the time when life was good for you... before you had... worries?'

'Good? Life is never good for a poor girl... I *was* a poor girl, and I don't remember ever being happy. Until Wilhelm was born.' She trailed off, gazing past me, far away. I didn't want to lose her attention.

'OK. Since we've not met and I don't know anything about you, perhaps it's best if you start at the very beginning, the first things you can remember.'

I opened the notebook I kept for case notes and picked up the biro beside it.

'May I take some notes?'

'Notes?'

'Is it okay if I write down what you tell me? So I can remember everything. The notes are only for us. I won't show them to anyone else.'

Definitely not, I thought. No GP to write to here.

'Yes, yes, of course. You go ahead and write it down.'

She drew herself up a little taller and dropped her hands to her lap, still clutching the handkerchief. She took a deep breath, fighting the corset.

'I was born a poor miller's daughter. Mother was always sad. I never remembered her smiling, not once. She wanted children, many children. But after I was born, she couldn't have any more children.

She never got over that. I had to do the housekeeping, cook the meals, do everything, because Mother was always too tired. My father...'

Those pale blue eyes narrowed as she held her breath and pursed her lips. For a moment I saw the possibility of an ugly temper tantrum. Mercifully, she took a slow breath instead, then continued.

'My father was so restless. So greedy. He always said he deserved a better life. Fate had dealt him a bad hand, he said. Except for me. He said my beauty would bring him riches.'

More silence.

'And did it? Did your beauty bring him riches?'

Her eyes narrowed again. I noticed she was now clenching the handkerchief tightly. Ugly streaks of red began to show on her slender neck as she leaned hard towards me and raised her voice.

'He lied about me. He made promises about me. Promises I could never fulfil. He didn't care what would happen to me!'

I could see she was fast warming to an outburst of unbridled fury, something that would definitely impede any chance I might have to figure out how to help.

'Can you slow down a bit here, please, for me? I need to understand, you see. I need to know what your father promised, and whom he promised. You have to explain these things to me, so I can understand. Otherwise, I don't think I can help you.'

Her shoulders dropped. She leaned back slightly and tried to breathe more slowly. The red streaks began to recede.

'I was fifteen. I was working hard. Every day, I worked so hard! Up before daylight. Sifting the grain, grinding it, putting the flour into bags, helping Father deliver it. But when I took the flour out with Father, when I delivered it in the village... men would stare.'

She blushed.

'I knew I was a pretty sight, even in my plain linens.'

She paused again, glancing down at her expensive silks.

'Tom was the worst. Tom would always watch me. Follow me everywhere. Every time I went out. Like a hungry dog, he would follow me.'

'Tom? Who is Tom?'

'Tom was older. No one knew for sure where he lived. People said he'd lost his wife in childbirth. The baby too. People said he was in love with me.'

'And your father disapproved?'

She tightened her grip on her handkerchief. 'Tom was poor. Father said he wasn't good enough for me. I deserved better, he said.'

Another pause. She stared ahead, the anger returning.

'The truth is Father wanted better for himself, not better for me. I don't think he cared much about me. Except for what I could get for him.

'One day – this is what I was starting to tell you about, the day before I turned sixteen – Father sat down to our evening meal all excited and happy. He said the King had asked for some of his flour. The King! Father was so happy. He said he had a plan. Now was our chance, he said. He told me he and I would take the flour to the King together.

'So, the next morning very early, we loaded the bags onto our cart and set out for the castle.'

'Is this the castle you live in now, as Queen?' She nodded. I saw a flash of something – wistfulness? Sadness? Regret? – pass across her face before she fixed her gaze back on me.

'When we arrived at the castle, Father told the guard we had to deliver the flour to the King ourselves. He said the King had commanded it. That was a lie. But the guard believed him. He took us into the King's day chamber.'

She looked away again, better to recall the scene.

'The King, when he saw me... I felt how he stared at me. But then he turned to Father, angry. "How dare you enter my private chambers!" But all the time he kept turning back to stare at me. That's when Father knew his chance. He wanted to make the King think I could be more than one night of pleasure.'

She paused, anger welling up again.

'Father set down the bag of flour he was carrying, and he nodded to me to do the same. Then he took off his cap and bowed low, all humble and pious.

'"Your Majesty, I bring my daughter here not just to help me carry the flour to you, but to tell you of her amazing power, a power she offers to Your Most Royal Highness," he said.

'He stopped talking then and looked up at the King. The King looked at me for a long time. So long I had to turn away, for fear he would see me tremble. What is Father saying, I thought. I have no amazing power!

'"Well, go on, man!" The King nearly shouted at my father, never taking his eyes off me. "Tell me of this power!"'

She paused again and closed her eyes, as if the memory was too vivid for her to bear. She went on, eyes still closed tight.

'Then my father said, "My daughter knows how to spin straw into gold."'

With this, her eyes flew open, glittering, fierce, tinged with helpless fury.

'The King looked away from me then and stared hard at Father. Was he lying? How could this be true? But even as I tried to understand Father's intent, the King must have been thinking of the consequences of such a power. If this poor girl can spin straw into gold, then she is not a poor girl. In truth, she might be so rich she could be a wife fit for a king. He began to smile. And then he laughed out loud and clapped his hands in delight, just like a little boy. He liked this story.

'"Well, then, miller," he said. "If what you say is true, this is fortunate indeed, for I as it happens, I am seeking a wife."

'He looked at me again, I suppose. I can't be sure, because I could only stare at the floor, trying my best not to tremble or faint. Then he went on.

'"Miller, you may leave now. Your daughter will stay with me. Go!"

'And Father left. I did not see him again until my wedding day.'

At this point I was leaning so far forward towards her, so engrossed in what she was telling me, that I knocked my water glass over. The water flowed freely onto my desk and notepaper. I dared not wipe it up, dared not break her narrative or look away from her. I wasn't taking notes anyway, and she seemed oblivious to the accident. I dropped my biro into the puddle on the desk and leaned back.

The water dripped slowly off the table.

'The King came over to me. He took my hand and commanded me to look at him. His face…'. She stopped speaking, shaking her head.

'What about his face?'

'There was desire. But for me? Or for the gold? I am still unsure, even now.'

She closed her eyes again, taking herself back to my room so she might continue her tale.

'The King led me to a small room at the back of the castle. There was only one window, high at the back. The room was bare.

'"Here, lass," he says to me. "I will call for a spinning wheel to be brought to this room, and my servants will fill the room with straw."'

She paused, reflecting.

'I am glad to say he is not a cruel man. He ordered his servants to bring me a plate of food and some water as well. Then he turned back to me. "Tonight," he said, "you must spin all the straw into gold. I will come back to this chamber at daybreak. If the gold is not here, and the straw not gone, then you must fear for your life." And with that he turned and left the room.'

I wanted to say something encouraging to this poor girl, try to show some sort of empathy. But every phrase that came to mind sounded trite or shallow. So instead, I decided for once simply to say what I really felt, while at the same time trying not to reflect the eagerness I felt.

'Please, go on, but only if you can bear to. This must be so painful to recall.'

She looked up at me gratefully.

'I never knew what alone meant until that night. I just knelt down on the floor and cried and cried. All the while the servants brought the straw, the spinning wheel, the food and water. I just cried. They never said a word. Then they left.

'I drank the water, but even to look at the food made me feel sick. I fingered the straw, wishing so much for its gold to be more than a colour. I even pushed a bit into the spinning wheel. The needle spewed it out. It was still straw.'

A tear ran down her cheek. She wiped it away absently.

'After a time, I must have fallen asleep. But then something startled me. There was a tapping at the window. I peered into the darkness. Tom! It was Tom's face at the window! He looked all broken up in the little pieces of glass. He was making signs that I should pull the glass towards me, so I could let him in.'

She looked directly at me once more, smiling, relief flooding through her at this memory. I smiled back and nodded, encouraging her.

'He was that nimble, he hopped straight in. I was never so glad to see anyone.

'"Now, what's the trouble, lass? You've been crying. What's the trouble here, lass?"

'I realised then I'd never heard him speak. I only knew him to stare. He had a coarse voice. But his words, they were kind.'

'So, I told him. Told him all.'

She looked to me for approval. Unsure why, I simply nodded and smiled again.

'And what did he say when you told him... all?'

'First, he looked at the straw, sort of measuring it like. Then the wheel. He tested it to see if it turned well. Then he took a big breath and turned to me, smiling and looking kind of... well, greedy? But still kind.'

'"I can spin this straw into gold for you."

'That's what he said. I thought he had gone wrong in his mind. No one can spin straw into gold. But I could see he meant what he said.

'"But lass, if I spin this straw into gold, what would you give me in return?" he asked.

'I knew I'd owe him my life. But what could I give? I had only what I was wearing. But then I remembered my necklace. "I will give you my necklace if you will spin this straw for me," I said.

'I was surprised that my small offer seemed to satisfy him. Boldly, he stroked my curls. I had to let him, didn't I?'

She paused and raised her eyes to meet mine. Again, that desperate need for approval. Why, I wondered, did she seek approval at this particular moment? But she did so, clearly. I nodded and smiled.

'Do, please, go on.'

'Then, he piled up all the straw beside the wheel, sat down, and began to spin. Big heaps of straw he pushed into the spinning wheel. And while I watched... mark my words! There was gold coming out the other side! Threads of pure gold! Tom never stopped, never looked up, until all the straw was gone. The gold was so beautiful! Then he stood up, held out his hand to me.

'"Your necklace, my love." I had to let him call me "my love", didn't I?'

I nodded again. My only desire was to hear more, but I knew she needed my approval rather than my eagerness to hear the rest of her story. 'Of course, you had to let him. Do, please go on!'

'Tom hopped right up to the window and jumped out, clutching my necklace. He was gone in a moment. I tried to see where he went, but it was still too dark outside. Then I pushed the window shut. I must have fallen into a deep sleep at once, because next I knew, I heard the servants talking all excited. They had come into the room I think, but upon seeing the gold, they'd run quickly out to fetch the King.

'I know him well now...' Here she dropped her gaze bashfully. But never have I seen him so delighted as when he came into the chamber that morning. He clapped his hands again and punched the air.

'"So, it's true! You can do it!"

'Best to say nothing,' I thought. I just bent my head respectfully and nodded yes.

'He danced – yes, he did dance round the gold, picking up strands of it and tossing them in the air. Then he kissed the gold in his hand, kissed the spinning wheel... and kissed me.'

Shy again. Demure, her eyes downcast. I was beginning to wonder now if she was telling me all that had taken place between her and the King that morning – and for that matter, all that had taken place between her and Tom earlier. If there had been intimacy, it would explain her desire for my approval. After all, if I'm placing her correctly, this happened long ago when sexual promiscuity was more frowned upon, and she hadn't been promised to either of them at that point. But then, did it matter? I wasn't sure. But I did wonder.

She resumed her narrative.

'The King went away, but first he ordered me to enjoy a bath, and that I be given the finest clothing. I was already being treated like a queen. I was so happy.

'That evening the King came to the bedchamber he had allowed for me. Though he looked at me with smiles, and though I knew he was pleased with what he saw before him, I feared my ordeal was not yet over. And I was right.

'"Miller's daughter," he began, putting me in my place, "You did well. But it might have been a trick. Tonight, I will ask you to repeat your magic, but in a larger room. If you fail, things will go badly for you."

'With that, he left me to his servants who took me to another room, larger than the one where I'd spent my first night. It was already filled with straw – so much straw! – and already the spinning wheel was in the room. Without asking, the servants fetched me a plate of food and a jug of water, and without a word, they left.

'I knelt down again on the floor. I had no idea how Tom had spun the straw. What was I to do? I looked out of the window hopefully, but there was no one there. I began to weep.

'After what seemed an eternity, I heard a tap at the window. I flew to it, and... yes! There was Tom's face! With haste I pulled the glass towards me. Tom hopped inside and looked at me kindly. I saw he was wearing my necklace beneath his old linen shirt.

'"My lass, was he not satisfied?"

'I shook my head.'

He looked around the room, thinking.

'"It seems he has set you yet another task."

'I nodded.

'"So, shall old Tom help you out once again?"

'This time I cried out for joy. "Oh yes! Please, Tom, please help me!"

'But he did not sit at the wheel. He turned to me first. Very close he was.'

She was pleading wordlessly for my approval again, her eyes searching mine, her hands clenching the handkerchief in her lap. I could feel that need plainly, and now I understood. Of course, there was more to the story than she was telling, more that passed between her and Tom. But that could wait. For now, I was eager only for her to tell me more, so I didn't question her.

'I understand. You must have felt so grateful to Tom, happy to do anything for him. Please, do go on.'

Her hands relaxed in her lap, and she let go of the crumpled handkerchief, shoulders dropping. A slow deep breath – more a sigh of relief.

'"If I help you again, what will you give me this time?" he asked. 'Well, I had a fine dress now, but I couldn't give him that, could I?'

For a moment she looked merry, child-like. She was actually teasing me! It was so good to see her happy, if even just for that moment.

'I had but one thing left of my own. My ring, the one my Mother's Mother gave me. So I told him he could have the ring. He must have thought it a fair bargain, for he sat down to spin at once. He spun it all, every piece of that straw. All of it he spun into gold. And so quickly! The room was filled with gold just as the moon had begun to fade in the night sky.

'"Now, give me your ring, and I shall be gone."

'And he was. Gone. Vanished into the night. I closed the window, and threw myself down – right there, on the gold – and fell asleep. I slept until I heard the King himself opening the chamber door.

'"She's done it!" he cried to his servants, though of course they could see with their own eyes. "We are rich indeed!"

'He kissed me again, several times.'

She paused, blushed again.

'Then he ordered the servants to give me whatever I wanted that day. I enjoyed another bath and a wondrous meal, and then I was taken for a ride in the King's carriage!'

Her face was alight with that memory – she looked so young and carefree, and so happy. But only in that moment. I recalled her desperate plea earlier. Much as I might wish it so, this tale was not to end happily, and I knew it even before her joy fell away.

'That evening, just as I was about to prepare myself for sleep, the King called me into his day chamber, the place where we first met. He had that look again, that greedy look. All my happiness vanished. I felt afraid again.

'"Miller's daughter, it is true that you have pleased me well. But still, you are not the richest of the women I may marry. Thus, I set you one final task. Tonight, you will stay in my largest chamber. It is filled already with straw. If you spin all that straw into gold, then it is certain you will be my wife."

'I was led away by the servants once again, this time to a chamber nearly as large as the King's day chamber. It was, as he had said, filled with straw. In the middle of the room sat the spinning wheel, and beside it a plate of food and a jug of water. Without a word, the servants left, closing the great door behind them.

'At once I located the window, ran over to it and sat down beside it. Tom was my only hope. But what could I give him? I had nothing left to give now.

'Time passed. How much I cannot say, but I think not much. If Tom could spin this straw, he would need most of the night to do it, I knew. Then soon enough, to my heart's joy, there was a tapping at the window. This window was large, the hinges heavy and stiff to open. But had it been the size of a mountain, I think I would have pulled it open, so great was my desire to let Tom in.

'"Aha!" he cried as he hopped into the huge room. "I see the King has grown greedier!"

'"Indeed, he has. But he has promised. This is the last test." I looked beseechingly at Tom. '"You can do this?"'

He laughed. '"Of course I can, my love!"

'But now he looked at me as the King had. With greed, with a hunger in his eyes. "And what will you give me if I do this task for you?"

'"You know I have nothing left to give you, Tom. Please help me anyway!"

'He stared at me hard and long. It seemed he was thinking what to say. But now... well, now when I think of that moment, I believe he had a plan prepared all along.

'"Well, then, my love", he began. "Well then. When your first child is born, you shall give him to me."

'Of course, I knew Tom had lost his own dear son in childbirth, and his wife as well. Of course, he would grieve the baby and wish for another. But of course, I knew also that I could never give up my child, especially to such an old and greedy man. But who was to say I would ever have a child? And what would become of me if I did not promise what he wished?'

She was looking at me hard, as if presenting me with a fresh dilemma. But I sensed the truth. She was only rehearsing an argument she'd had with herself countless times before.

'Of course, you had to promise,' I said. 'You had no choice. No other choice at all.'

Encouraged and relieved, she hurried on.

'After I made my promise to him, Tom hurried to the spinning wheel and began to spin. There was so much straw that on this night he needed my help. I had to fetch handfuls of it and carry it to him, so he never had to stop his spinning. He worked so hard. So fast.'

She looked away. Far away. Remembering.

'It was near daybreak when I handed him the last pieces of straw. He was so weary. He looked so old. Except his eyes were dancing with delight.

'"Your first-born child. Mine now! You will not forget, will you?"

'I nodded to him, not believing myself.

'"I will go away then. Until we meet again, my love, my Queen!"

'And with that he crossed over to the window and hopped through. I saw him heading into the woods. It was that light by then.

I pushed the glass shut with the last of my strength and sat down hard on the floor. There would be no time for sleeping that night, I knew. 'Only minutes later, I heard the King coming down the hall, talking loudly with his servants. He did not even knock but burst in through the door.

'"In God's name, she has done it! The gold! All this gold!"

'And he danced again, throwing handfuls of the beautiful strands of gold high into the air and catching it as it fell. 'After a time, he remembered himself and stopped dancing. He turned to me. He held my shoulders tightly and kissed me hard. Then he released me. At least he could see that I was exhausted.

'"Prepare the Queen!" he cried, and left the chamber.'

She paused. She'd stopped staring past me, and looked directly into my eyes once more.

'That was one year, one day past. I was married next day, and nine months later, came my child Wilhelm.'

Oh boy, I thought. This was getting complicated. If my calculations were right, Wilhelm could easily be the son of either Tom or the King. Who was his real father? I stopped musing, brought back to the present moment with a start. I was feeling the full force of my patient's angry penetrating stare. Clearly, I had underestimated this young woman. She knew my thoughts as if I had spoken them aloud.

'What does it matter who is his true father?' she accused me angrily. 'Did I have any choice in what happened? Do you imagine an old and poor widower could offer Wilhelm the life that a king could give him?'

Now it was my turn to blush.

'I am truly sorry. You will forgive my speculation. It's my job to make guesses from what has not been said.'

Stony silence.

'Please. I apologise. You are right. Wilhelm is a prince, whatever happened last year.'

This seemed to satisfy her, because she let out a sigh and relaxed. She paused for a moment, as if to let the air settle between us. A welcome pause.

'And now, here is where I beg your help.'

Another sincere, anguished look. By now I was hoping, far more than professional remit required – or for that matter, encouraged – that I would be able to give the help she craved.

'Two nights passed, when I was resting in my chamber, Wilhelm in my arms and sleeping so beautifully, my window was pushed hard open, and to my great dismay, in hopped Tom. The very same! He looked older than ever, but was smiling from ear to ear. At the sight of him, I felt no gratitude. Only fear and loathing in equal measures.

'"Hello, my love!" 'He stared at Wilhelm a long moment, as if transfixed. "I see my son is a fine strong boy."

'I clutched Wilhelm all the tighter. He woke and began to cry.

'Tom smiled at Wilhelm, then at me, then back at Wilhelm, with a look all greedy and cruel.

'"I made you a queen, my love! Now I have come to claim the debt you owe me!"

'And he reached out to take Wilhelm, who cried all the harder.

'"No, please!" I begged. "Anything but my baby! I will give you gold! Jewels! Land! Whatever you desire!"

'"We made a bargain. I desire only my son!"

'At that moment, I felt as if my life would end. My tears fell so hard and fast, and I begged Tom so. He began to soften. I could see – even through my tears – that he remembered how fond he was of me. He stepped back a pace and dropped his arms. I could see he was feeling torn in half.'

She stepped briefly out of her narrative to address me.

'Tom is not a cruel man. Not truly. He was still grieving his baby.'

I wasn't sure which baby she was referring to, but it didn't matter. I agreed with her. 'No, it doesn't sound as if he is a cruel man.'

We were both quiet again for a time. Then she continued.

'He was fighting with himself. I could see it. Like he was greedy and kind, both things, and they were fighting inside him. After a time, he spoke again.

'"My love, I will offer you a chance. Only this one chance, but I will offer it." He went on. '"My true name is not Tom. It is something else, something no one knows. The bargain I offer you is this. I will come back each of the three nights following, and on each occasion you may guess freely what is my real name. If by the third night, you have not guessed rightly, you will hand my son to me. If you do guess my name, you may keep him. Either way, I will leave and never trouble you again. Do you accept my bargain?"

'I knew he was struggling to offer me any chance at all, and had it been for any other reason, I would have loved him for his generosity. But I could not bear the thought of parting with my son. And of course, I had no choice really, so I told Tom I agreed to his bargain. Then he left.

'Next day early, I ordered the servants to nail up the window, which they did, so that with luck he could not return. But I had to prepare for the possibility that he would return, to do everything to keep my dear Wilhelm. So, I commanded all the servants to go out and search the neighbourhood and gather all the male names they could discover, and bring them back to me before nightfall, which they did faithfully.

'That night I sat in my chamber with Wilhelm. Too soon I heard the tap, tap on the window I so feared. I pretended not to notice. But then, in a twinkling, there was Tom, standing beside me. The window was still nailed shut.

'"I've played fair with you, my love," he said, true enough. "You should not try tricks with old Tom."

'I bowed my head in shame.

'"And now, my love, what is my true name?"

'And he sat down before me and Wilhelm, staring all the while at the baby. I drew out the list the servants had gathered for me.

'"Could it be that you are called Caspar?" I began.

'He smiled a gleeful smile.'

'"No, that is not my name. Pray, you may try again."

"Are you called Melchior, or Balthazar?"

'"No, those are not my names."

'And so it went, until I had read out all the names on my list. To say fair, he let me read them all.'

She trailed off, torn again between repugnance and pity for this man.

'When I had finished reading my list, he rose. He reached out and touched Wilhelm gently on his little arm before I could draw my baby to my bosom. Then he bowed – a mocking bow, I'll warrant – and said he'd be back tomorrow.'

She paused, obviously still in wonder at what she was about to say.

'Then he... vanished. He just... vanished.

'Yesterday, I did not order the window sealed or nailed shut. Instead, first thing, I called all the servants in my command to my chamber. I bid them search far and wide, wider than before, and gather names of every male in the Kingdom, and bring the names back to me before nightfall. They dispersed, and I was left alone with my son.'

She looked up at me, looking suddenly much older. 'It seemed such a long day, yesterday. Yet every moment with Wilhelm flew by too quickly.'

Large tears coursed down her cheeks, but then she drew herself up tall to steady herself so she could go on.

'My servants returned as instructed before nightfall. They gave me pages of names to offer, and I was hopeful.

'At exactly the same hour as the previous night, Tom appeared before me once more. I felt the cool breeze from the open window. I knew he would think better of me for not nailing it shut.

'"Thank you for not making my entry a complicated task," he began jovially.

'I felt only disgust that he had tried to make a joke. He sensed this at once and took on a serious expression. Then he sat down before me and Wilhelm.

'"And what names are you to suggest this night, my love?"'

'I drew out the list and began reading from it. "Perhaps your name is Shortribs? Or Sheepshanks? Or Laceleg?" But always, he answered simply, '"No, that is not my name."

'When at last, after I had read every name from my list, he rose. He did not try to stroke Wilhelm, though he looked longingly at my baby, now fast asleep in my arms.

'"I leave you now, my love. Tomorrow I shall return, and I believe I will leave then with my son."

'All night I lay awake, hearing his words: "Tomorrow I shall return, and I believe I will leave then with my son."

'This morning, when at last everyone was waking, I got up from my bed but did not know what to do. I had tried every name in my Kingdom. Where now, I thought, could I seek an answer?'

Now she turned the full force of her gaze on me. Begging, beseeching, pleading with me.

'I had been told of you, that you help people. I have ventured far from my Kingdom and my times to seek your help. Please, I beg of you! Tell me how to discover Tom's real name so I may keep my baby!'

Silence. She continued to search my face, although thankfully she respected my need for a chance to gather my thoughts. If indeed there was to be magic, I thought, I knew it must come from her world, not from me or mine, for by now I could no longer prevent myself knowing she had come out of a fairytale. Anyway, I was only an ordinary human being from a different time than hers. I had no magic to offer. But even if I had an answer, was it my place to give it to her? I remembered one of my professors reprimanding me early on in training: "Your job is not to sort out your patients. Your job is to make it possible for them to sort themselves out." With that in mind I felt ready to speak.

'When you seek the answer to a problem,' I began, 'you have to find it yourself. And you may well be surprised at what helps you most to find that answer. So please, open your mind to every possibility, every source. Listen, and trust yourself. If you do that, then the answer will come to you, and you will know it when you hear it.'

I wasn't sure I could believe myself, but no sooner had I finished speaking than we heard a harsh sound, a scraping or beating against the glass behind us. The Queen turned to stare at the window. I followed her gaze. The scraping sounds came from the only window in my office that faced the ancient woods at the end of the lane. I was astonished to see it was unlatched – I could have sworn it had been closed and locked all day. It was, however, unlatched now.

Listening more closely, it sounded like the beating of wings against the windowpane. A few more thrusts from those wings – if that's what they were – and the window flew wide open. In swept a little bird. It landed on the edge of the desk between us and perched there, flicking its tail and turning its bright gaze to each of us in turn.

It was a small bird, about the size and shape of a robin. The plumage was of soft silver grey with gold sprinkled on the underparts. It had a golden bill and a whitish throat. The colouring was unlike anything I had ever seen, but the eyes were what fascinated me most. They were large and black, encircled by pale silver eye rings, and although they looked not human, they seemed to exude a human intelligence. I felt as though this little bird was sizing us up, trying to make some sort of decision. We both stared at it, fascinated, as it appeared to make up its mind. Ignoring me, it turned towards the Queen and began to sing.

The song was most remarkable. The bird's register was far lower than I'd expected, a register nearer to that of human range than of a bird. It uttered four distinct notes, accenting the third. It flicked its tail, cocked its head at the Queen, and repeated the little song, sweet but to my ears meaningless. Then it rose abruptly and flew back out of the window. I watched it as it headed towards the dark and ancient woods, a silver streak disappearing into the twilight.

When I turned to face the Queen, I found the change in her appearance astonishing. Tears were coursing down her cheeks once more, but these were tears of joy. She dabbed absently at her face, tucked the handkerchief into her bodice, clapped her hands and laughed out loud in sheer delight.

'Thank you! Oh, thank you!'

'Whatever for?'

'You told me to listen, to listen to what matters to me, rather than to seek answers from others. That little bird comes from my world, and he has told me Tom's name! Now I know what I will tell him tonight!'

She clapped her hands happily once more, and then turned and regarded me. As if something had reminded her, she drew a small bag from the voluptuous folds of her skirt. She kissed it tenderly and held it out to me.

'Please. Take this. In gratitude for what you have explained to me.'

'Oh no, I couldn't—'

'But you must. The coins are made of gold that was spun from the straw.' She held it out determinedly, confident now in herself. It would be rude to refuse.

I thanked her, and set the bag down carefully on my desk, then lifted the flap of material that was folded over the top. A handful of the most beautiful, most delicate coins I had ever seen lay within the bag. They were made of pure gold I was certain, but that gold was the richest, deepest colour I had ever seen. There were delicate inscriptions on each coin, clearly marks of a language that no longer existed.

I looked up to thank her.

She was gone. Vanished.

I searched everywhere in the room. There was no sign of her, no sign of any change or disturbance, no clue. No evidence, in fact, that she'd ever been in the room at all. Nothing, except that the window behind me was now wide open.

Had this last hour really happened? Or in my exhaustion, had I fallen asleep and dreamt the most extraordinarily vivid dream?

Then I remembered the bag of coins. I hurried over to my desk to see if it was still there. It was exactly where I had put it down. The events of the last hour really had happened. I picked up the bag carefully and enclosed it tightly in my left hand.

I glanced at my watch. It was now precisely one hour after my clinic had been scheduled to finish. It was time to go home.

I rose, placed the bag of coins reverently in the left pocket of my jacket, dropped my wet biro and (blank) case notes into my briefcase, snapped the case shut, and headed for the door.

Then I remembered the window. I hurried back to close and latch it. Immediately as I did so, I felt a distinct tingling down my left side. Anxiously, I reached into my pocket to check for the bag of coins.

Instead of a bag, I felt something rough and dry. I drew it out.

It was a handful of straw.

Little Snow White

Did a fairytale queen from an age long gone really appear in my consulting room last week? Did she really sit down across from me and ask for my help? I'm beginning to doubt it. And yet... and yet... I open my desk drawer to check whether the handful of straw she gave me is still there, hidden at the back underneath some papers.

It is.

Time to go home. More than time, because it's been such a depressing day. Two patients didn't show up and one cancelled without offering any explanation. Am I no good? Do I hit too close to home too fast or speak too directly, causing these very private people to back away? Do my own concerns show through in my approach? Or has everyone just decided I'm an outsider here, someone who can't possibly understand or help them?

The five-mile cycle ride back to my cottage, especially on this wild Welsh night, feels like fitting punishment for my incompetence. I zip up my anorak, gather the day's notes into my backpack and strap it on as I head for the door.

A gust of wind nearly knocks me over as I reach over to

switch off the lights. I was sure I shut and latched the window facing the forest... I feel a delicious anticipation as I turn slowly around.

Someone is there.

A young man, in his twenties I would guess. Dark eyes set deep in olive skin, dark hair curling out from under his cap. His leather jerkin is well weathered, as are the loose trousers. A rough black tunic – wool, is it? – encases him beneath the outerwear. Thick leather boots, scuffed and damp, finish the ensemble. The smell of damp earth fills the room. I wait. He regards me intently, silently. Then, as if remembering his manners, he doffs his cap and gestures towards the chair across from my desk.

'May I beg your pardon to sit down?'

'Of course.' I drop my backpack, hastily unzip my anorak and drop it as well, retrieve a notebook and pen and sit down in my usual chair, never daring take my eyes off him. What if he disappears? Again I wait, hoping I look relaxed, calm and together. I don't feel it.

He studies his cap for some minutes, turning it round and round in his powerful hands, then slowly lifts his head to meet my gaze. 'I can no longer do my work.'

'Your... work?' I had no idea what his work might be, why it mattered.

'Oh, you cannot know my work, can you? For I am not wearing my knife.'

I had to suppress relief for that.

'I am a huntsman. One of the Queen's huntsmen.' He uttered Her Majesty's title as if it were poisonous on his tongue, then hurried on. 'My skills were once so fine. I could slit a throat as easily as...' his voice trailed off, right hand absently searching the tunic at belt level, presumably for the knife. Still unsure about his motive, I dearly hoped the knife would not materialise.

'I...I have lost my skills. And I can no longer sleep. I need your help.'

Familiar ground at last. Glad to divert him from throat slitting, I interrupted. 'You can't sleep? Not at all? Or do you sleep only in snatches?'

'I long for sleep, but I dare not allow it. If I sleep the dreams will come again, and I fear I may act on them.'

My unease revived as I remember I'm totally alone in this office. I need a safer topic of conversation to allow time to steady my racing pulse. He did say he wants my help, after all. Hardly likely to use me to hone his knife skills... yet.

'Perhaps if you tell me a bit about yourself it will be easier for me to understand your situation and help you.'

'Yes of course. Of course. We do not know one another. 'I am the fourth son of my father. My mother died when I was but three years. I am told of her, but I do not remember her.'

I wonder if this means he idealises women. Children who lose a parent at an early age may idealise not only the deceased parent, but sometimes everyone else of that gender as well.

'We all grew up together under father's care. We were lucky – we had a patch of land we could tend, to grow food and where we kept sheep and fowl. We had to work very hard, but we were never hungry, and for that I give thanks.' He paused to reflect on his blessings. 'One day when selling our goods at market, a member of the royal household approached my father. I saw him regarding me, and I remember his words exactly.'

'"Your youngest son is tall and strong. How old is he?"

'"He is seventeen years and indeed tall and strong, Sir," my father answered proudly but with respect.

'"Then he will do. The Queen is looking for more huntsmen. You will bring him to the castle gates tomorrow at sunrise and leave him in our care. If he is an able apprentice, he will gain the privilege of serving our Queen."

'This sounded like an honour, but I did not wish for it. I only knew my home and had no desire to leave it, and I told Father so. But he insisted that we must do the Queen's bidding.'

That same bitterness when he uttered her name. He certainly doesn't idealise all women.

'Next morning when it was still dark, we set out, Father and I. We arrived at the castle gates just as the sun appeared on the horizon. It was then I knew how little Father wished for this as well. He refused my gaze, merely shook my hand, then turned and walked away at once. He seemed older and more bent. I have not seen him since, a full seven years.'

The young man paused his narrative, lost in quiet sadness. I dared not disturb him, waiting as the minutes passed.

At last, he roused himself and looked across at me once more. 'Five others soon joined me in the courtyard that morning. The guards watched us suspiciously. No one dared speak. After some time, a trumpet sounded, and at once the guards turned to the great door. As it opened, they knelt and motioned for us to do likewise. The doors opened slowly, and from within walked the Queen, flanked by more guards.'

Another pause – I could feel him fighting his emotions.

'I will warrant, she was – she is – the most beautiful woman I have ever seen.'

He definitely regretted that admission, shaking his head and twisting his cap all the tighter. Perhaps he polarises women? Does he categorise women as either all good or all bad? If so, he clearly doesn't know where to place the Queen. I'm not sure why this is so important, but I feel it is.

'She regarded us coldly; I felt as if we were not human under her gaze. I will admit I was struck by her beauty, her raven hair and her milky skin. Even so, I saw something not beautiful in her dark eyes. After regarding us thus, she turned back to her guards.

'"Well chosen. Take them away and begin their apprenticeship at once." Her voice, like her eyes, was harsh, calculating.

'Having given her command, she turned and re-entered the castle, her guards closing rank behind her.'

Silence again. He was studying the cap, turning it nervously in his lap. Waiting for a prompt from me? But still unsure of his reasons for being here, I simply tried not to appear eager for more, and merely waited for him to speak again. Still, he remained silent. If I was to say anything it must be neutral, non-judgmental, so he would feel free to carry on in his own way. I still didn't have any real feel for his dilemma.

'And this was seven years ago? That's a long time. I suppose a great deal has happened since then?'

I hoped that wasn't too direct. But I might as well have not spoken. He seemed oblivious to anything but his own thoughts and remained silent for several long minutes more. At last, he spoke again.

'The training was difficult, but I am used to hard work. The six of us had to work together, but friendship was discouraged so we rarely spoke, neither when we hunted nor when we returned to our separate chambers each evening. I was never the best among the six of us, nor the worst.'

Of course not. He's the youngest child, never likely to lead, never likely to consider himself a leader or an expert. And he's used to teamwork not power games – no doubt as a child he and his brothers had to work together with their father on equal terms. Based on what I knew about the effects of birth order position, I also figured that as the youngest, his self-esteem would be easily threatened – hence the guarded self-assessment. I waited, hesitant to interrupt his thoughts. Better to wait until he felt ready to carry on.

'The days and weeks passed, the seasons and years. I no longer thought of any other future. But one evening, forty days past now, there came a knock on my chamber door. I opened the door to a guard I did not recognise, but I knew from his fine dress he must be of the highest rank.

'"The Queen bids you come to her chamber at once." He turned and walked away down the corridor. I had of course no choice but to follow, along wide stone floors and through the dark echoing hall passed rooms I'd never seen before, until we came to the Queen's chamber. The guard stood before it, I behind him respectfully. He knocked once, and the Queen bade us enter.'

Bitterly, now twisting his cap, 'I remember every moment of that encounter. The Queen dismissed the guard at once, without so much as a thank you. I was left to kneel before her, not daring to look up. But I felt her cold regard.'

Intense dislike now, his dark features tightened with disgust. Another pause as he wrestled with his unpalatable emotions, then taking a deep breath resumed his narrative. His shoulders had stiffened slightly, hands now twisting that poor cap mercilessly. I could tell he was reliving every moment. He seemed... frightened? Angry?

'Again, I recall her exact words: "Huntsman, you will not join your companions tomorrow morning. Instead, you will wait in your chamber until they have all gone out to hunt. Then you will hasten to the courtyard, and there you will wait. A guard will come and escort you here to my chamber once more."

'"I will be waiting... with my daughter. Tomorrow is her tenth birthday and I have told her that as a gift, she will be allowed to venture into the forest for a day of exploration. She has wished this for some time. I have told her she may have her wish as her birthday gift, although she must tell no one of it."

'"You! You will take her with you, deep into the forest, on foot the both of you. When you are far from the castle... when no one can hear her scream..." I remember how she regarded me. Emotionless. "Then you will draw your knife and you will slay her."'

He looked at me beseechingly. 'How could anyone be so cold? How could a mother...'

'"Do you understand, huntsman?" Her voice had risen, ugly and sharp. I hear it still in my dreams. "You will slay her. Then you will cut out her heart and bring it to me, that I may know you have done as I have commanded you."

'Those were her words. I swear I shall never forget them. Never.'

He was pleading with me to soften the memory. But of course, there was no way I could do that, though I wished I could. I knew I had to keep back, not open myself to his pain, or I'd never be able to help him. But it wasn't easy – he was so distraught. Poor man.

'I did not sleep that night, and I have hardly done so since. How I came to be back in her chamber the next morning I cannot recall.'

My mind was racing now. No wonder he was seeking help. He killed that poor child. He must have done! After all, he had to obey the Queen. Surely he did? But to carry out an order to kill an innocent child... no command could be more terrible, no reason great enough. Who could command such a deed? But I must stop these thoughts. I have not been asked to explore the Queen's psyche. I forced my mind back to the young man seated across the table, wretched in both grief and anger. I must stay with him. Wait as long as he needs to gather himself after reliving such a nightmare. At last, he raised his head and met my gaze once more.

'Do you believe I killed her?'

Impossible to answer that safely. I need a therapeutic sleight. I'll ask a question, that's what I'll do. Always a good dodge. 'Did you believe you had a choice?'

He relaxed and shook his head. Glad I got that one right.

'Next morning when I saw the child, my heart went out to her at once. She was just as her mother, raven hair, milky skin, dark eyes. But her eyes were not cold. They were full of joy, of anticipation, of curiosity and wonder. So much wonder.'

Could there be a greater contrast in the pictures he painted of these two females, the only ones he'd known until then? It did seem he polarised them.

'"May we go now, Mother?" she begged. She was so charming, her voice so soft and sweet! The Queen regarded me again, with a look such as I shall never forget. Black holes were her eyes. I swear she has no feelings. None. "You will take her now, huntsman. You will do as I have commanded."'

He paused once more. I had no idea now whether he'd killed the child. 'I remember our walk into the forest as a dream, only in fragments. The child... she was so happy, gathering flowers and berries, skipping more often than walking, a constant stream of chatter. So very, very happy. After some time, we chanced by a clearing. I knew the moment had come.'

I suddenly realised I was leaning so far forward I was about to fall off my chair. As discretely as possible I edged back and loosened my grip on my biro. I'd completely forgotten I was holding it. I dropped it – no need to take notes. I was not going to forget one word of this story.

'She asked me why we had stopped, why were we here. I unsheathed my knife, though my hand was shaking. But the moment I raised the blade to strike the fatal blow, there came a great crashing and clatter from the trees behind us. A young boar tore through the undergrowth, running heedless of me and of the child he would surely trample. I acted... there was no thought. I plunged my blade deep into the creature's throat. I gripped tightly as it writhed and twisted, blood spurting from the wound, eyes staring as it hit the ground, hooves flailing wildly, then slowing, the blood still letting, oozing now.

'I heard her screams, but I dared not turn around.

'"What have you done? Why did you kill him? What have you done? I hate you!"

'She was half sobbing, half shouting. I turned to face her, aware now of the gruesome scene before her. She recoiled, then turned and began to run, away from me, away from the castle, deep into the forest, the brambles tearing at her lovely silk stockings, though I am sure she was heedless of any pain. She kept crying out over and over, "I hate you! I hate you!" I remained as if frozen as her cries became fainter, until... until... she was... gone.

'I remember then I sat down heavily beside the dead and stiffened creature. What now? Surely I should run after her, save her from certain death alone in the forest. But then I remembered the Queen's words: "Cut out her heart and bring it to me, that I may know you have done as I command." Even if I could find the child, I could not bring her back alive to the castle. And where else could I take her? As for the Queen—'

Rage contorted his features at the mention of her. 'The Queen would demand proof of her daughter's death. I must give her some proof, to stop her looking for the child, to do... I knew not what to the poor innocent soul... and to save myself. Suddenly I realised that here before me was my salvation. I wrenched my knife from the creature's throat and rolled it onto its back. A deep thrust of my blade, dragging it straight from throat to belly, exposed the heart and lungs. I cut out the heart with great care, rolled the animal back onto its side and dragged it into the underbrush. It deserved that much dignity.

'This heart will be her heart. The Queen will not know the difference. I dared not think of the little Princess. A fine feast she would make for the wolves no doubt. But at least I had been spared the deed that would have been unbearable. I felt such gratitude towards the dead creature.

'I cannot remember the journey back to the castle, only that my ears strained at every distant sound, hoping not to hear a young girl's cries, and yet at the same time longing for them, as proof the Princess was still alive.

'Once in my chamber I wrapped the heart in a cloth, washed what I could of the blood that stained my hands, my tunic, my face, and tried – and failed – to sleep, still listening for the Princess. As if I could hear deep into the forest. Still hoping that somehow, she had managed to survive.

'Next morning still in my bloodied clothes, I sat on my bed and waited for the others to leave. Then, taking the heart in the stained cloth with me, I retraced the route to the Queen's chamber and knocked on her door. I did not have to wait.

'"Is that you, huntsman? Have you something to show me?" No greeting, only a horrible greedy eagerness. Without a word I held out the damp bundle. She grabbed it from me and tore off the cloth. Her joy...'

His voice trailed off, and I thought he was going to wretch. He needed support.

'You have done well to relive such a time. Many could not have recounted that tale.'

He looked up, back in the room with me now, grateful.

'Later I returned to the hunt – after a brief illness, or so the others had been told. Our usual silence and singularity was interrupted, for everyone was talking about the Princess. It was said she had died suddenly and mysteriously, on the very day of her tenth birthday. A funeral was planned for the following week, and all of us were required to attend.

'It was a lavish but mournful affair. The Queen....'

Venom, pure venom when he uttered her name this time. He paused to recover himself.

'The Queen was magnificent, dressed all in black. As the coffin was carried through the castle hall, I felt her eyes not on it but upon me. I thought I would faint, so strongly did I feel her silent warnings. My greatest fear was that she would somehow manage to discover what had really happened.'

He looked suddenly tired, as if he could not go on. I thought it best to wait once more, to sit with him in quiet companionship. After several silent minutes he sighed, looked up and brought himself out of his nightmare and into my room once more.

'Since then, I have not killed. Oh, it appears that I kill. I join with the others when we track our quarry. But whenever I raise my knife or load my bow, I imagine it is so that I may slay the Queen, to close those black eyes forever.'

His hand, curled into a fist, was searching his waist. Still no knife, thank heavens.

He was almost pleading with me now. 'At night, if I try to sleep, I see her before me, I hear her voice. When I hunt, she is my quarry. My desire to kill one who ordered the death of her own child has pushed away all other thoughts, all desires. And I am so weary! Please, can you help me?'

Who could blame him for wanting to kill her? But such thoughts were not going to help him, I reminded myself severely. Killing would only lead to regret rather than release. I must try to find a way to help him discover some peace within himself.

'Let us suppose you did find an opportunity to slay the Queen. What would happen then?'

'We could all rejoice. If she dies, then she would have paid the price for her cruelty.'

'Is that what everyone around you would think? No one but you knows what she asked of you.'

He reflected, shook his head regretfully. 'Of course. The crowds would simply turn on me. They would kill me, the Queen slayer.'

'Of course, they would. And they would then beatify the Queen, your victim, would they not? Do you really wish that to be her legacy?'

I could sense he was listening hard, rethinking, tasting hope. Time to press him. 'I wonder, do you think the Queen is happy now?'

He seemed startled by my question. But as I watched him revisit his memories, what I had hoped for, what I'd risked by asking that question, began to take form. I watched him as he silently relived the past forty days, remembering the time but realigning the memories, reframing the Queen's behaviour.

'She was happy. At first, she seemed incredibly happy. Although she still wore black, she walked tall and proudly, looking grave while trying to hide a horrible, satisfied smile.' Again his distaste stopped him. 'But not many days after the funeral, her demeanour began to change. Yes, she became different. Her skin lost its faint blush and... she began to appear drawn, anguished. Often, we would catch sight of her in the window of her sitting room, pacing back and forth, back and forth, clutching a looking glass.'

More clarity, new details emerging, things he'd overlooked or disregarded. He was thinking hard.

'She has three times disappeared for a full day since the funeral. This is most unusual for her. Each time she appeared elated upon her return. But then... then the pacing would resume. And she was never without her looking glass....'

'So, she is not happy?'

'Something troubles her deeply.' He seemed astonished not to have noticed this before. It was time to reinforce his new understanding.

'There can be circumstances that make us feel terrible, so terrible we might even long for death, don't you think?' I ventured. 'The endless torture of regret, or perhaps guilt – who knows what thoughts the Queen harbours – may be making her life so repugnant that she could be longing for it to end.' I waited for his reaction. He didn't dare believe me, wanting more reassurance that killing her was not necessary, that justice had already been served.

'I suspect the Queen is being punished already. If you killed her, you would only give her relief from the hell she has herself created.'

Good. I saw his sense of responsibility begin to lift. But I wanted him to look further, and I sensed he was now ready to do so.

'And think about the Princess. What if by some miracle she is still alive? She could be, you know. And if she is not, would you bring her back by killing her mother?' He shook his head. 'So let us leave the Queen to her own misery and consider the Princess. What proof have you that she is dead?'

'No child could survive alone in the forest.'

In my eagerness to lift his burden, I realised I was no longer thinking, or speaking, like a psychologist in the Twenty-first Century. Just as I had done with the Queen last week, once again I'd abandoned logic and embraced magical thinking instead. I so wanted him free from the burden of responsibility for a situation that was no fault of his own.

'But why do you assume the Princess is alone? Many creatures inhabit the forest. Who knows if some of those benign forest dwellers – elves, fairies, perhaps even dwarves – may have befriended her, cared for her and even now are looking after her? She could well be alive, you know.'

That did it. I could see hope returning, glimmers of a renewed zest for life. I could sense the heavy responsibility he'd felt so keenly slipping away. In his joy he jumped up and punched the air.

'The Queen suffers justly. And the Princess... the Princess may yet be alive!'

I smiled. His delight was infectious.

'I must go now, before my absence is noticed. I thank you. Oh, I so sincerely thank you.'

He stood up with renewed energy, waved goodbye cheerfully and hastened to the open window. But before he climbed outside, he paused and turned back. He regarded me reverently, doffed his now shapeless cap, and then to my astonishment, he bowed low.

'You are a true Queen. I thank you, Your Majesty.'

I felt tears welling in response to this completely unexpected accolade. I looked down, opened the drawer where I kept tissues and pulled out one of them to dab my eyes.

I'd only looked away for a few seconds, but when I glanced up again the room was empty, the window closed and latched. I could hear only the wind outside, and what I could have sworn was a young girl's distant laughter.

The Fisherman and his Wife

Tuesday, the day fairytale characters visit my surgery after hours. Or at least they have done twice now... well, I think they have. I'm still not sure what's happening, and I avoid the growing worry that I'm losing the line between reality and my fantasies.

I force my attention back to the road ahead. Although I've cycled the five miles to and from work every day for two months now, I'm still amazed every time I arrive safely. Compared to London these Welsh roads seem so narrow, twisting, vertiginous. Beautiful, yes, tall conifers rising up on either side of me instead of rows of tired terraced houses; birdsong instead of car horns and engines; the occasional battered four-by-four or motorbike ambling past instead of an endless stream of impatient cars and taxis. Clean air replacing car fumes.

I should be appreciating the beauty, but fairytale characters wander into my thoughts instead. I feel a childish eagerness to know who might materialise through the window tonight, but at the same time... what's happening to me? Maybe my therapist was right. Maybe I haven't processed the trauma that triggered my escape to Wales as well as I'd thought. I still remember the look of astonishment on his face – before he could hide it – when I told him I'd decided to move to a small village in Wales. Other than instantly replacing that astonishment with the usual therapist's concerned and caring mask, he just sat there, silent. For what seemed like hours.

Then carefully, 'Are you really sure you've given yourself enough time to work things through? To accept two such enormous personal losses in less than a year?' I never liked a direct challenge, and he knew it: no sooner had he spoken those words than he backed down. 'What's your new job then? Tell me what you'll be doing, and why you chose that particular spot.'
But I knew what he was really thinking...

A strident blast from a car horn jolted me out of this reverie and almost off my bike. I'd been cycling in the middle of the road. What an idiot! Apologetic wave; the driver passed me quickly, shaking his fist and head in annoyance.

Focus, Helen. You made your decision, now you have to make it work. This had recently become my mantra when the doubts crowded in and refused to go away. I redoubled my efforts up the last hill before turning left into the surgery car park.

Only one car in the small makeshift plot as I cycled in, still pedalling hard. No matter how early I arrive, Emma is always there ahead of me. I love her for it. Instead of a cold empty entrance hall it means I'm greeted by the aroma of strong French coffee and the sound of the ancient heating system kicking into action. She nods and smiles as I shut the door on the autumn chill. Never one for conversation, she merely hands me the surgery list on my way to my office. Another thing I love here; handwritten client lists.

Okay, layers off. Jacket out of my backpack, smoothed and shaken to give the air of a professional who knows what she's doing. Am I already madder than anyone I'll see today? I try to brush away the thought by reading through my list and putting a face and a dilemma to each name. Once clients start arriving it will be fine. There will be no time for the thoughts to creep in. Thank heavens I'll have other people's narratives to engage me. Emma brings me a mug of steaming black coffee – great coffee – and informs me my first client has arrived. Good.

The day flies by and there are no cancellations. Maybe, maybe I'm beginning to tune in appropriately to this new, more taciturn population? Are they beginning to accept me? I write more notes than I know I need to write, to fill time, hoping...

Emma must be leaving. The shaft of light from reception disappears from under my office door and I hear the front door close quietly. I keep writing, glancing around too often to the window behind me, the one that opens onto the old forest. And then...

I smelled him before I saw him. A gust of wind scattered my papers, carrying with it a powerful salty, fishy odour.

'Begging your pardon, may I come round and sit down?'

Gruff voice, older male.

Without daring to turn around, 'Of course, do make yourself comfortable.' I try to sound like this happens to me all the time.

I can track him by the stench as he walks respectfully around my desk to the client's chair opposite. I would guess he's in his late fifties, greying heavy beard and moustache, weather beaten sun-darkened skin, hands rough, nails dirty. And boy is he smelly. He's wearing some sort of oilskin that he takes off and drops beside him. A heavy black woollen sweater, long woollen leggings under wide waterproof trousers, a vest of some rough hide, flat cap, and heavily weathered boots encrusted with salt complete the ensemble. He holds a smoking pipe in his left hand that he must have been topping up recently, but once he's sitting down, he tamps it out with his finger and tucks it into a trouser pocket. Next the cap, which he removes and drops on the oilskin. When he looks up at me and smiles nervously, I'm reminded of a malodorous Father Christmas.

'You are the one who helps us?'

I suppose I am. I nod.

'Well then. Good then. How do we do this?'

I had to fight the urge to burst out laughing. Despite the rough appearance of someone very much my senior, he was charmingly childlike. I liked him instantly.

'Well, this is your time, so you can tell me whatever you think is important. Just remember that I don't know anything at all about you, so you'll need to fill me in before you describe your prob... before you tell me what's troubling you.' He still sat there expectantly, unsure. 'I mean, I need some background – where you live, who you live with, what you do...' (no guesses there). 'Then when you talk about... about... the reason you've come here, then it will be easier for me to figure out how to help.'

Apparently, this suited him. He relaxed, leaning back gratefully into the soft leather chair.

'I am a fisherman, as was my father before me and his father before him. My father did well, and after some years he was able to purchase a boat of his own. Every day he left the house long before sunrise and returned with the setting sun. He seemed to have a way about him – everyone wanted his fish. He always sold all his catch, every day.

'It was as well he was so successful, for he had many mouths to feed. I am the sixth of nine, with five brothers and three sisters. All the boys joined our father at sea as soon as we were able. I was so young I cannot recall my first voyage. My sisters were all older. They stayed at home to help Mother. But they were married off early, so I hardly knew them.

'We brothers, we loved the sea, and we worked well with our father. However, Father always said only I and my eldest brother had the gift.'

This could be important. I interrupted his narrative. 'The gift? What do you mean, please, by the gift?'

'We have the gift of calling the fish. We can stand with our nets open, and Father said the fish willingly jump in.' He said this without pride or arrogance. It was just a fact. Then he sighed. 'But my brother, being the elder... Father gave him the boat when his old arms could no longer cast and retrieve the nets. The rest of us, we were told to find a wife and make our own way, to find a place to cast our nets from the shore, to claim a place that was to be our own.'

It was clear he would have preferred a life at sea rather than on the shore. Could this be the problem? Was he consumed by jealousy of his brother, because he was given the boat? He hadn't shown any strong indications of jealousy, at least not yet.

Silence. I looked up from my notepad to find him regarding me, as if he could read my thoughts. Clearly, I had underestimated this 'simple' man. I was ashamed when I realised my prejudice: simple job, no formal education, the man must not be very clever. Wrong. It was clear he could read other people, just like he was able to read the sea and know where to cast his nets. He was doing a better job of guessing my thoughts than I was of understanding him. I needed to redress my mistake, rebalance our relationship.

'I'm sorry. I was racing ahead with my thoughts. Please forgive me. You were explaining that you needed to find a wife and a place... a place of your own to fish?'

He smiled sweetly, forgivingly. My respect for him was growing.

'A good place to fish, that was easy. I had walked the shores many times. I knew which headlands held promise and which did not.'

He smiled broadly as he imagined himself by the sea, but then the smile faded, and he paused. Whatever was coming next was difficult, but at least I'd learned my lesson. This time I kept quiet and just waited.

'But how to find a wife? I did not know. I prefer the sea to talking to people, and I had no clever talk for women, like my brothers. Three years passed, and by that time all my brothers were married, even the youngest. My mother was displeased with me. She was often displeased.' He paused, reflecting. 'She was a strong woman and neither kind nor tolerant. One evening she called me to her and told me she had waited long enough to be free of us all, and that since I seemed unable to find a wife myself, she had done so for me. And that I was to make do with her choice.'

Now we were getting somewhere. A relationship problem. I absolutely *must* stop trying to guess the problem before my client tells me – one of my faults. Patience, Helen. Listen and wait.

Another long sigh. 'There was a woman, some years older than I. An only child of older parents. She was not beautiful, and had never been... chosen, and now it was past her time of childbearing. But Mother said she would do. And so, she became my wife.'

Resignation. Poor guy. I could tell we'd arrived. An unhappy marriage to an older woman, and no kids to take his mind off his unhappiness. Only his work to distract him. I wondered if he'd known that from the day he married. This reminded me I'd neglected to ask a key question, *de rigueur* during a first therapeutic interview. Why is the client seeking help *now*? I interjected gently into our shared silence.

'How long have you been married?'

'Just gone fifteen years.' Another sigh.

'I see. But perhaps... am I right in saying you haven't found life too difficult... until now?'

I was rewarded by a gorgeous smile. 'You see to the heart of a problem, just as I know where to fish.'

High praise. I smiled back.

'Yes, it's true. When we first wed, she seemed happy enough – well, for the first few days. Then the complaints began. She had been so much happier, she told me, when she was living with her parents. They understood her. They doted on her, fulfilled her every desire, even before she had to ask.'

What a lousy way to raise a child, I thought. But I said nothing.

'But I... the mornings were not so bad. I rose before her, prepared my nets. But no matter how quietly I tried to be, she always managed to hear me, and would call out, "Bring back more fish today. We are too poor, and I never make enough money when I go to market with your catch. Try harder!"

'But despite the bad start every morning, my mood would always lift as I walked away from our cottage towards the sea. I would watch the sun rise, note the weather, smell the clean air. It is always so beautiful by the sea. Some say it's always the same, but I know differently. Each day the sea and the sky, even the path I walk, have their own new beauty. Each day holds new promise.'

This man will definitely never need instruction in mindfulness. He knew how to live in the moment, how to appreciate his surroundings just as they present themselves to his observant eye, without wishing them to be more or different. What a contrast to his unfulfilled wife!

'Fishing alone by the sea – I tell myself every day what a lucky man I am. I knew, too, I had chosen my location well. The sea is always generous to me.'

A shadow crossed his face now. 'But then, as soon as I stepped inside our cottage... no matter how many fish I brought home to her, no matter if they were all large and fat, she was disappointed. "Is this all? How can we ever escape this hovel when all you bring home is this?" Often, she would work herself into a proper rage, and every evening I would be told that her parents knew how to make her happy but that I did not.'

I wondered if Theo had seen me like that, carping, never satisfied. Is that why he left?

Helen! Stop it! This isn't about you. To regain my focus, I interrupted inappropriately with a question. 'Do you think perhaps there was another reason for your wife's dissatisfaction? After all, you did bring home fish every night, didn't you?' He nodded. 'You always provided her with something to take to market, did you not?'

He looked slightly hopeful, considering.

'Well, now you ask, I did think perhaps there might be something else... that if she had been able to bear a child... I, too, would dearly have loved to have a child. If we had been blessed with a child, perhaps she would have been fulfilled. I did often think of that.' Then after a pause, revisiting his memories. 'But she never spoke of a child...' He looked up, his thoughts clarifying. 'I think now a child would have made life worse for her. She wanted all the attention...'

'I think you're absolutely right,' I said. 'It was bad enough – to her way of thinking – that she had to share you with the sea, and that she could see how satisfied and happy you were after a day's work. That was something she could not achieve. A child would have fulfilled you perhaps, but for her a child would only represent competition, someone else with needs of their own.'

I waited for that to sink in, to see if he agreed. After a few quiet moments I still wasn't sure, but I felt it time to press on. Going by the last two visitors, I had only one opportunity, one session, to do all the work I would normally do in five or six.

'You were not at fault for her unhappiness.' I stated. 'Please don't blame yourself. Happiness is something we must seek within ourselves, by deciding how to think about what we have. I think you know that. It's lovely to share our happiness of course. But if you rely entirely on others to make you happy... that's a happiness that doesn't last.'

He was thinking hard, reworking his vision of his marriage, unloading some of the responsibility for his wife's state of mind off himself and onto her. Good. I allowed this silence happily. Then, when he looked up, I said, 'It sounds like your wife's parents raised her to expect happiness to be provided by others and – when she was younger – by them. If only they had encouraged her to find her own joy, her way.'

He was still trying to take in this new way of thinking, and to grant himself permission to be free of the responsibility for his wife's unhappiness. 'Do you think she may learn to find happiness?' he said. 'Is there any way I can help her do that?'

There he was again, taking responsibility. 'You can show kindness, and you can listen to her without judging. But you cannot help her discover where to find joy. She is not a child. This is something she must discover herself. You cannot make her know it. Even if you made suggestions, tried to come up with ways you think she might find happiness, it wouldn't work. She must discover it herself.'

He considered, and I could see he was conflicted. 'So, I cannot change her unhappiness... or our unhappy marriage?'

'No. I'm sorry. You can't. But you can resolve to make the best of the situation. You can decide not to let her anger make you sad or destroy your own moments of happiness. For now, you must accept her as she is.' I saw his disappointment, so I hurried on. 'You can hope she will learn to find happiness. But if you keep trying to please her she won't have any need to seek for sources of happiness herself, will she?'

This apparently made sense. With the realisation that he needn't be responsible for his wife's state of mind – in fact that trying to do so inhibited her chances of finding it herself – he began to cheer up. The years almost fell away, and I was rewarded with another melting smile.

'Then I may find my joy beside the sea each day, and... just wait?'

'And hope. Always hope. She may learn to find joy, in her way. It's always best to be hopeful.'

We sat for what seemed a long time in a companionable silence as he reflected, rearranging his thoughts and looking at things in this new more comfortable way. Then recalling the question I'd put to him earlier on, 'But I asked you why you have come to me now. For some years, it sounds to me that your life together was bearable... although I grant, not joyful. Something must have happened to change that.'

He stepped away regretfully from his thoughts and prepared to resume his story.

'You are right. Each day was the same, it began and ended unhappily. But for much of the day I was very happy. And yes, you are right. I had found contentment... until this midsummer's day, when I discovered the King in my nets.'

Good heavens! There were men living in the sea during his time? But I supposed if I could accept that a character from a story that's more than two hundred years old is sitting across from me, I should find it easy to accept that men once lived beneath the sea. Even so, I needed some clarification.

'The King?' I exclaimed.

He smiled mildly, surprised at my ignorance. 'Yes. The King. The King of the Fishes.'

I waited, still obviously lost, so he went on.

'For every creature there is a king of their kind. By terrible misfortune, I had captured the King of the Fishes in my net. And when I saw him, I was afraid. How dare I rob the sea of its King?'

There he was, taking responsibility again for something unintended and not his fault. I was about to interrupt, but happily there was no need. He saw that for himself.

'But I did not mean to catch the King, did I? And before I began my apology, the wise one spoke. "Dear fisherman, I was asleep when your net entrapped me. Please, have mercy on me. Allow me to return to the sea." He did not see my actions as deliberate.'

My credulity was overstretched. 'This fish could talk?!'

He smiled, pitying me. I really didn't know much, it seemed. 'Of course he can talk. He is the King. He is a magic fish, the cleverest fish. All kings command all tongues. It is part of their vast wisdom. No doubt they laugh at human 'wisdom', so small is our knowledge compared to theirs. That is why I could not imagine how I found him in my net.'

I nodded. I was still feeling a bit lost, but I wanted him to continue. It was inappropriate to interrupt yet again.

'So of course, I picked up the King carefully, cradled him in my arms and placed him back in the water. He swam away at once, joyful, breaking the water in a curve to show his gratitude. 'When I returned with my catch that evening, my wife seemed angrier than ever. "Why so few fish? This is worse than even your usual catch! So few to take to market." And on and on she raged.'

I noted with quiet satisfaction that he had already become more detached from his wife's emotional turmoil. She was angry – but that was not his doing. Her anger, her distress, these were not his fault. Progress.

'Even at supper she would not stop. "You still have not explained to me why you brought home such a meagre catch. Did nothing else happen today?"

'That was when I made my error.'

I had to interrupt, even without knowing what was coming. Once again he'd taken responsibility. It would take a bit of time before he would automatically reframe, change his self-talk, and avoid pointless self-recriminations. 'Might it be better to say, "that was when things changed"?'

He smiled, remembering. 'Of course. That was when I said something that made her angrier, although I did not intend to inflame her mood still further. I explained my small catch was because, among the ordinary fish in my net that day, I found I had caught the King of the Fishes. Thinking it only right, I added at once that of course I set him free. 'But if I had thought she was angry before, it was but a mere shadow of what happened next. "You simply let him go? Just like that?" She snapped her fingers. "Why did you not wish for something first? He owed you his life, and you just let him go! Without obligation or recompense?"'

He looked directly at me now, his face reddening. 'She surprised me; perhaps that is why I replied without thinking. But instead of remaining quiet, I made another mistake. I told her I did not seek repayment for an act I considered only respectful. And besides, I ventured, "what could I have wished for?"'

He paused. A slow smile spread across his face. He didn't have anything to wish for. Only she did. Her dissatisfaction was not his fault. He was able to understand this now.

'I remember her very words: "Oh foolish, foolish man! Do you not think it terrible we live in this... this hovel? You should have wished for a proper house! Go back and call the fish. At once. Tell him we want a nice cottage with a proper garden. He owes you his life. He is sure to grant your wish and we are owed a wish. Go!"' I tried to ignore her, but she carried on and on, late into the night. She even woke me over and over again. No peace was possible, so at last I promised I would do as she demanded. I rose early the next morning and returned to the sea with my nets. But before casting them I stood on the shore and called to the fish. Almost at once he appeared, rising up through the waters and asking simply, "And what does your wife wish?"'

He stopped, reflecting. 'He knew why I had come. He knew it was my wife who had a wish, not myself. He is indeed wise. 'I told him what had passed between us, and no sooner had I finished speaking than he said, "Go back to your wife. Her wish has been granted."

'I did not stay a moment longer but hurried home straight away to give her the news she wanted. When I arrived at our house, my first thought was that I had lost my way. Where our home had stood only hours before there was now a fine cottage. Scarlet and pink roses twined up and round the door, and there was a lovely garden filled with vegetables and fruit trees where several fat brown hens scratched happily.

'Inside I found my wife chopping fresh salad in a gleaming

kitchen. Fine furniture filled the house. There was even a soft bed for us, with new linen mind you. It was perfect. Who could ever wish for more, I thought, and I remember saying to my wife, "Now we can be truly happy."'

He paused, no longer feeling guilty, just relating his tale.

'I recall that she was happy. For some days. But then I began to sense her restlessness. The criticisms crept back. She no longer smiled.

'One night, less than a fortnight after we had been given the cottage, she woke me to say she was finding the house too small. "I have decided. I want a castle, a large castle," she said. "This house no longer suits me. Go back to the fish. Tell him we must have a large stone castle."

'I did not wish to trouble the fish, nor did I wish to leave the wonderful cottage. But I knew there would be no peace at home if I did not go back. So, the next morning I returned to the shore and called to the King, and once again he appeared immediately as I called to him. "And what does your wife wish for now?" I told him she wanted a large stone castle. He replied merely, "Go back to your wife. She has her wish." Then he dived deep into the water and swam away. I noticed the sea was no longer calm and inviting. The waters were disturbed and murky, and a cold wind had blown up.

'I hurried home, and instead of our lovely cottage,' He paused, wistful. 'Instead of our lovely cottage, in its place stood an enormous stone castle. My wife was at the entrance, waiting in a large courtyard. When I accompanied her inside, I found the furniture was made of gold. Pure gold! I had not known it was possible. Everywhere I looked there were large murals adorning the walls. Bustling servants stepped respectfully around us keeping everything in order.

'I went outside to see what else was different. There were stables round the back, and behind that a large deer park. It was beyond my imagination, this vast estate. I returned to my wife, lost in wonder. "Surely," I said, "we can be truly happy now!" He shook his head sadly. 'But this time she only replied, "We shall see."'

I could sense what was coming.

'It was but two days hence when my wife woke me early, pushing and prodding me until I had to sit up in bed. "Wake up!" she kept repeating. "Look outside! Look at all this! You should be King now!"

'I knew not how to reply, so I said nothing, hoping either she would allow me to sleep again, or that I would awaken from a bad dream. But she only took my silence as a sign of yet more weakness. "Fool! If you do not wish to be King, then I shall. Go! Go at once. Go to the fish and tell him I wish to be King of this land."

'This was indeed madness. But by then I was so weary, and I knew it would be pointless to resist. I dressed, gathered my nets, and left the castle. She called after me as if I might forget her demand, until at last, thankfully, I could hear her no longer.'

His self-confidence was growing. He looked at me and grinned. 'I was so glad when I could no longer hear those greedy demands.'

I suspected that was the first time he'd ever criticised his wife at all, let alone out loud.

'This time when I approached the water, however, I had to stand some distance from the shore, for the sea was in turmoil. Waves bucked angrily, and the water was dirty, disturbed. I called for the fish, and of course he appeared at once. '"And what does your wife wish for this time?"

'Oh fish, King of Fishes, I am so sorry, but my wife says she wishes to be King of the land. Again, a simple reply: "Go then. Go home. Your wife is now King." Then the waves appeared to swallow him up, the swells rising ever higher, the growing storm ever wilder. I hurried away.

'As I approached the castle, I noted rows and rows of soldiers at the outer gate. When they saw me, they raised their trumpets and beat their drums to herald my arrival.'

He reddened again. Clearly the memory was distasteful, all that fanfare and attention.

'The gates to the courtyard swung open and I walked across and into the castle. The entrance hall was made of marble and gold, with swathes of velvet draped across finely brocaded chairs. And there… there before me sat my wife, high up on a golden throne. She was wearing a great crown of gold encrusted with rubies, diamonds and I know not what other jewels. I bowed before her, and she smiled. She smiled! I felt hope rising. "Please, wife", I remember pleading, "let us now be content."

'But no. Of course not!' He was reconstructing this memory even as I watched. 'Of course, she would not remain content. She did not even stop to consider or enjoy her new position I do not think. It was only hours before she commanded me to appear again before her, demanding I go back to the fish and ask him to make her Emperor.

'This time I did not even stop to plead with her or consider the arrogance of her demand. It was now late afternoon, but I walked straight back to the headland.

'The water was by that time completely black, and a cruel wind was blowing across it. The waters curdled and roiled and leapt up in crashing waves. I had to shout, certain the fish would never hear me. Yet he did. At once he rose out of the angry waters, towering above me. I felt his anger and I was so afraid. "Oh fish, now she wants to be Emperor!" I cried out as loudly as I could. His only reply, "Go then. She is Emperor already." And with a mighty leap and a twist he dived deep into the blackened waters. I turned and fled towards home for fear the next wave might engulf me and carry me away.'

He paused for breath. This memory was clearly disturbing, even with his new powers of insight.

'Can you imagine the castle of an Emperor? There was now a drawbridge into a towering edifice which was surrounded by a wide moat. Guards, richly adorned, were positioned everywhere. When I stepped inside, my eyes were dazzled by a thousand tall candles that lit up the vast chamber. Richly embroidered cloths adorned gilded chairs. And high above, there sat my wife on a throne made entirely of gold. She was so high up I could barely recognise her. Her heavy golden crown, encrusted with jewels of every shape and hue, reflected the candlelight and dazzled my eyes.

'I stood there, unable to speak. But when she spied me, she

called out: "Husband, this is not enough. I must also be Pope!"

'Of course, I felt utter dismay, and on this occasion, I did plead with her, heedless of all the servants and the soldiers who regarded me suspiciously as I called up to her, begging her to accept the extraordinary gifts she already enjoyed. But of course...'

He realised he was staring at the ceiling of my office, as if his wife was seated there on her throne. He lowered his gaze, took a deep breath, and took himself back into our shared space.

'Of course, you know what happened. And although I could not even approach the furiously raging seas or hear any noise but that of the storm, I saw the fish rise out of the waves briefly when I shouted out my request. When I returned, my wife was Pope.

'That was yesterday.' He reflected for a moment, shaking his head in disbelief. 'Only yesterday. But at last, at long last my wife seemed content.'

He smiled conspiratorially at me, 'Not that I could imagine there was anything left for her to wish.

'That night we were able, for the first time in many days, to enjoy the fine meal we were offered. I hoped now I might resume my fishing life; that perhaps the sea would have calmed now; that I might return in the evenings to someone who would at last be content. However, when I woke this morning, I found she had already risen. She was standing by the window watching the sunrise. Hearing me stir, she turned and addressed me thus: "There is something more, husband! Yes, there is something more I could have. Something more I demand. Yes, there is more waiting for me. I wish to command the sun and the moon and all the stars above. Go to the fish. Go at once. Tell him it is not enough for me to be Pope. Tell him I wish also to command the sun and the moon, all that we see about us day and night. Tell him...tell him I wish to be like God!"

'This request was beyond arrogance. It was sheer madness. I could never ask this of the fish, nor of anyone else for that matter. I would not be able even to utter the words. But she never ceased demanding, ordering, wheedling, pleading, repeating herself over and over again. It never occurred to her, I think, that I wouldn't give in to her.' He paused, seeing her anew. 'And despite all she had, even despite the granting of each new demand... oh how desperately unhappy she was still!'

He looked at me again, understanding dawning on his face. 'With each wish, she only becomes more miserable, only greedier. I'm not helping her find contentment by returning endlessly to the fish to ask for yet more, am I?'

I shook my head but said nothing, not wanting to break into his narrative nor steal his insight. He'd figured this out himself. It was his to claim.

'Finally, late this morning, I could stand it no longer. I told her I would go and talk to the fish. I left the palace and fought my way towards the headland, but it was not easy. A great storm had arisen. All the trees were bending deeply in the mighty wind, and the sky was almost entirely black. Towering waves rose higher than mountains. It took me twice as long as usual to reach the sea, fighting those winds. I stood as near to the shore as I dared and prepared myself to shout for the fish. But suddenly I knew...I saw the unending folly of my behaviour. Instead of calling out, I turned and ran away, far from the sea and into the woods, to... here.'

He stopped, regarding me, waiting for a reaction.

'So, you stopped trying to make your wife happy, did you? Because you realised you weren't helping her. Acceding to her demands seemed only to make her more miserable. Is that what you came to understand?'

He shook his head sadly. 'Yes. I failed. So badly.'

I realised I needed to slow down, to be more gentle – otherwise I would lose him again in a morass of over-responsibility and self-blame. I needed a new direction, at least temporarily, to steady him.

'Have you ever wondered why the weather became wilder each time you visited the fish?'

The change of tack surprised him – and it did the trick. Jolted out of self-pity, he thought back. 'The fish... perhaps he commands the weather as well? Perhaps the rising storms were a sign of his increasing displeasure with me?'

'No, not his displeasure with you. He was not displeased with you at all.' He regarded me doubtfully, but I pressed on. 'I believe he was displeased not with you but with your behaviour. He did not like to watch as you kept taking responsibility for your wife's happiness, rather than stepping back so she might look for fulfilment within herself. When at last you did cease trying to please her, then I suspect he was glad. And I think, if you go back now, you would find the weather clement and the sea calm.'

He liked this. 'And my wife? Is she now God?'

'What do you think?'

For the first time he laughed out loud. 'The fish would never allow it. No one can be like God. Anyway, he knows that granting her wishes doesn't make her happy. Or at least, it had never done so before.'

'And if you find – when you find – he didn't grant her that wish, you might wonder why. Do you think it might be because you... finally... realised you had to step back? Because at last he saw that you – her husband, the person with whom she shares her life – has realised that the only way to give her a chance to find peace and contentment was for you to stop trying to fix things for her?'

At this he jumped up from the chair, almost dancing with delight. 'Of course! I understand now. I can be happy whatever my wife decides! But she could be happy as well, as long as I stop taking responsibility for—' he saw my stern look, and corrected himself '...as long as I give her the chance to find her own sort of happiness. And if she does find her way... we could enjoy so much, wherever we live, whatever the conditions.'

He picked up his cap and oilskin, putting both on hastily as he headed back towards the window. 'I must return now, return to my wife and to my home.' He threw me another grin – 'whatever home it turns out to be.'

Then suddenly, apparently remembering a courtesy, he stopped and turned around. 'I wish to thank you. But how? I have only a fish to offer you.'

With that he drew from the large pocket of his oilskin an extremely odorous, very dead fish whose variety I could not begin to identify. He started to hand it to me, then stopped to sniff it. 'This is not fresh. I cannot give you this.'

I laughed. 'Don't worry. I'm in no need of fish. Honestly. Your gratitude is more than any material gift as far as I'm concerned.'

Just then the window flew open, and a gust of wind rushed in, scattering my notes. I leaned down to pick them up. When I sat up again the fisherman – and the stinky fish – had vanished.

The Companionship of the Cat and Mouse

'You're going straight home tonight, just as soon as your last client leaves.' So I kept reminding myself.

Truth was, I didn't want to go home right away. I wanted to stay, just a little while, just in case...

A gentle knock disrupts my thoughts. Emma, letting me know my last client of the day has arrived. Her steady calm demeanour helps me refocus. I get up, compose my caring mask and walk briskly to the waiting room to escort my client into my office.

Fortunately, the hour is not without interest... although all too soon, I'm reminding her we have only a few minutes left. Is there anything else she wants to discuss? No? We book another appointment, same time next Tuesday.

Alone again, the thoughts that have been haunting me all day flood back. No one came through the window last week. I'd waited over an hour, pretending to myself that I needed the time to write up my notes. As the minutes crawled by, nothing. No unusual sounds, no gusts of wind blowing the window open, no fairytale character taking a seat opposite me to ask for help. Once or twice I thought I heard a sort of scratching at the window, but nothing came of it. My imagination, I expect. After another twenty minutes I'd packed up and cycled home, feeling totally dejected.

And then the dreams returned – well, perhaps not dreams so much as flashbacks – waking me throughout the night. I'd thought they were over, those flashbacks. But there I was, back at the mortuary. How I got there and how I got home afterwards I will probably never remember. The police officer, asking if I'm ready, carefully lifting the sheet that covered his face... 'Is that your son?' His sweet, perfect face. The long lashes I'd always adored. The only difference was the pallor. And, of course, the mangled body that I knew lay beneath the sheet below that beloved face. Mercifully the officer simply stood quietly beside me, near enough for me to lean on if I felt faint, a silent support. I nodded. It was Alex. The officer must have led me out. I don't remember...

I knew why the flashbacks had returned. The greatest loss of my life, my precious only child. My boy. And well before I'd fully faced my grief I'd run away, here to this village where I knew no one, where I'd never even visited, in the delusional belief that if I left it all behind, I would be able to forget the pain.

The new job and the new place kept me occupied during waking hours, and cycling to and from work left me so tired that even the flashbacks stopped after the first week. But the leaden feeling remained. It was such an effort to do anything...

Until last month, when the fairytale characters started coming in through the window. Suddenly, once more I had something to look forward to, creatures who challenged me more than I'd ever been challenged.

Until last week, when no one came.

I told myself firmly that no one blew in last Tuesday, because no one had *ever* blown in through that window. It was my imagination in overdrive, my desperate wish for something magical to come back into my life. And now I'd lost that magic, just as suddenly as I'd lost the magic that was Alex.

And yet – how embarrassing, I think now – I'd found myself nosing around the back of my surgery last Friday, on the pretence I'd dropped a glove when closing the window before I cycled home the day before. Despite Emma's raised eyebrows – no comment of course; she's too tactful for that – I'd continued to nose around out there, checking the ground underneath the window meticulously.

There was nothing, apart from quite a lot of large mouse droppings.

The front door closed quietly, taking me out of my reverie. Emma leaving. Right. Time to cycle home. Anorak, scarf, gloves (never really lost), backpack...

There it was again, that scratching noise at the window, just like last week. Distinctly scratching. Then a thump, as if someone had thrown a clod of earth against the glass.

I turned round in time to see something – a dark shape – hit the window again. Frightened or not, I had to investigate.

No sooner had I lifted the sash than the dark shape, now discernible as brown fur with a tail following, launched itself through the open window and sailed underneath my left arm. Whatever it was hit the floor with a dull thud, seemingly dazed, although it quickly appeared to recover itself.

I could see it now. It was a mouse. And it was growing fast. It remained perfectly stationary while it... grew. And grew. Until it was about the size of a large dog. Then it let out a sigh and looked directly at me. And smiled.

It definitely smiled. Even more remarkably, it addressed me in perfect English.

'Could you please show me where I might sit down? I need your help.'

I tried but failed to say something in response, so I simply pointed to the client chair.

'I thank you.' He scampered over, climbed into the chair, turned to face me and adjusted his position. Little legs sticking straight out, front paws on the arm rests. Another smile.

Still dumb, I walked back to my desk and sat down opposite, not daring even to blink in case he disappeared. I waited.

The creature cleared his throat once or twice, flicked something off one arm, shrugged his shoulders several times, stared at me. He was clearly waiting for something. Maybe I need to kick off the conversation?

'Would you like to tell me what's... brought you here?'

'Of course, yes, very much. Thank you, so much I thank you.

'But wouldn't you be more comfortable if you took off... discarded some of your outer garments?'

How unprofessional I must have appeared! There I was, sitting in the therapist's chair still wearing my anorak, thick scarf and gloves, and leaning into my backpack. He'd tried so politely to give me hints, flicking at his arms, shrugging his shoulders, staring at the anorak zip. I'd missed them all. I quickly removed the unnecessary baggage and dropped everything on the floor beside me without even glancing down.

'Thank you for reminding me.' Weak smile. 'Now that we're both... comfortable, would you like to tell me a bit about... yourself?'

'I do thank you. I thank you so much for giving me your time. I count myself very lucky.'

I'd already learned some important facts about this creature. He was extremely sensitive to others. He was polite and had an excellent command of language. And he had a very strong desire to please. He was almost obsequious – or at least he needed to be seen as incredibly caring and concerned. On this occasion I could only rely on my patient's comments to gather that all-important first impression information therapists are trained to pick up. The body language of mice is not my strong suit, which was why I had to rely entirely on what he said.

'It's my room-mate. I've come to speak to you about the companion I live with.'

A relationship issue. Good. I should be able to handle this, even if we are talking mice rather than people. I offered a concerned smile. 'Do go on,' I said.

'Nobody approves of him.'

That was definitely unexpected. I was preparing for relationship counselling, not ostracism. I needed a moment to recalibrate.

'Nobody at all?'

He shook his head vehemently, whiskers twitching.

'Nobody. Not even my sister. Definitely not my mother. And since we moved in together none of my friends will visit, nor will anyone in my family.' A large tear formed, and plopped unnoticed onto his lap. Another clue about him – easily emotional. But what could be wrong with this other mouse? Must be something pretty bad. I needed more information.

'What reason does everyone give for staying away? Or does everyone offer different reasons?'

He shook his head. 'No, same reason. Everyone says our relationship is unnatural. My sister even says it's definitely dangerous.'

Good grief! Unnatural? What could he mean? Was he in a gay relationship? I didn't know mice could be gay. But what a prejudiced community if that was the case!

'So, you're cut off... from everyone?'

Another vigorous nod. 'Everyone.' He began tapping his paw on the arm rest, clearly agitated. Then, without warning he jumped down and started running wildly, round and round his chair. I held my breath, dared not move. Was he going to run back to the window, leap out and disappear?

But no, after about a dozen laps he hopped back into the chair, breathing heavily.

'I am so sorry. So very sorry. Excuse me.'

It must be his way of self-calming. Relieved to see he was still here, I made another mental note – be on the alert for the tapping – it's the sign that his anxiety is about to spiral out of control.

'No one likes him. They can't see how wonderful he is to me. They don't understand. They don't even try.' The tapping resumed.

Clearly this wasn't a good topic. We needed to go somewhere less distressing. 'In what ways is your... partner wonderful to you? Do tell me. I'd love to hear.'

Good question. The tapping stopped and he looked across at me eagerly. That lovely smile again.

'Felix loves the food I make, how I go out every day and find food for us both, and how I keep our cottage neat and tidy. It means he has plenty of time to relax and rest.'

I should think so, since it didn't sound like his partner lifts a finger... a paw... in the house. I wasn't sure I was going to like Felix very much.... Still, this little creature clearly adored the lazy so-and-so, so I'd better show my approval. I would need that to gain his trust. And it wasn't my brief to pass judgement on Felix anyway.

'So, Felix is really appreciative of your efforts?'

He beamed. 'He tells me every day how lucky he is.'

I wasn't sure where to go next. If the problem was everyone else's opinion of Felix, there wasn't much that could be done. I remembered one of my professors chiding us sternly. Never encourage a client to think other people will change for their sake, he used to warn us.

'Maybe... I suppose... do you think it might be possible for you just to try to accept that your friends and family can't see the wonderful qualities you see in Felix?'

I could see in his eager face (I was getting better at reading a mouse face already) that he so wanted to do what I suggested. But something was holding him back. Was there some doubt here? Does he really believe Felix is totally wonderful, or does he need to believe it, lest he's forced to accept he made a bad choice? I needed more information about their relationship.

'You know I've never been to... where you live. So, I can't visualise how you and Felix organise your day. What's a typical day like for the two of you?'

That lovely smile again. Thank goodness.

'I get up first, to forage for food and make us a tasty breakfast. Then I clean the cottage and do the laundry while Felix relaxes.' He paused, considering. A bit less happy now. 'During the day I used to gather more food, to stock up. But now is not the season when I can do that.' He looked up at me, another big tear welling up. 'We're very short of food.'

Come to think of it, he did look rather thin... for a mouse. Poor thing. I needed some more context – he didn't seem the sort who would let stocks run out.

'Is that usually a problem at this time of year? The shortage of food, I mean.'

Uh oh. More tapping.

'I mean... you seem such a conscientious creature.'

But my attempt to soothe came too late. He was overwhelmed again. Down he went, more laps. I waited, less worried this time that he'd run away. This was obviously his release valve. I made a mental note to talk to him about some more adaptive ways to release anxiety... but not now. That was for later. I still hadn't clearly formulated the problem. I waited for him to finish letting off anxiety.

Panting, he finally dropped back into the chair. 'We shouldn't have run out of food. The jar should have been full to the top. But it was empty. Completely empty.'

'The jar? I don't remember you mentioning a jar. Could you perhaps explain a bit about this jar?' He was starting to cry again, so I carried on. 'Did you have some food stashed away in... this jar? But when you went to retrieve it, you found it was empty? Is that right?' Floods of tears now. I handed him a tissue from the box sitting ever ready on my desk. 'I'll tell you what. Why don't you take a minute, catch your breath, and then go right back to the... beginning? To when things began to be... unclear?'

This suited him – a smile through the tears.

'Yes, yes... okay. Good. I am so sorry. Silly me.' Deep breath. 'Last season was harvesting time, when everything is so rich and luscious. It was the time to prepare stores for the leaner months, so I gathered all I could from the fields, dried and stored all of it. But best of all...' He looked up, smiling broadly. 'I prepared the jar of fat.'

'Fat?' This sounded faintly disgusting.

'Yes, Felix loves fat best of all foods, especially the top skin.' He reflected fondly for a moment. 'I always make a big jar of fat, because if everything else runs out it lasts such a long time, while we wait for the spring and all the new growth.

'When I'd finished filling and sealing the jar – lovely it looked – I asked Felix where we should store it, so it would be safe for when we really needed it.'

I nodded encouragingly.

'Felix suggested we hide it in the church. He said no one dares steal anything from a church.' A wave of sadness, then determined brightness. 'So, we did. Late that night we went to the church and hid the jar under the altar. You couldn't see it, no matter which angle you looked from. I was so proud of that jar. My best one ever.' Another tear.

'But you just said it was empty. Did you go back to get it, is that when you discovered it was empty?' He nodded. Lots more tears now. This time I handed him the entire box of tissues. 'When did you make that discovery?'

'A week ago.' He was sobbing now. Poor hungry creature. I dearly wished I had some cheese...

'Was Felix with you?' He nodded, the sobs abating now. 'Did he... did he have any ideas about who might be responsible... who might have stolen the fat?'

Vigorous head shake. 'No, we just had to go home... hungry.'

'So, you must both be pretty hungry by now?'

More tears. 'We're hungry, yes... and I'm so lonely.'

My ears pricked up. 'Only you are lonely? Is Felix able to see his friends and family then?'

'Well, he's had some wonderful celebrations to attend.'

I felt we might be getting somewhere, although I wasn't sure yet where. 'Perhaps you'd like to tell me about these... celebrations?' Clearly he did. Another lovely smile through the tears.

'The first invitation came only a few days after we hid the jar. Felix was very excited that morning. When I came back from foraging, he told me he'd heard from his cousin, and that this cousin had just brought a little son into the world. He said the child was brown with white spots, and that he was thrilled – he'd been asked to be his godfather. "You wouldn't object, would you, if I attend the christening tomorrow? I am sure to be allowed to hold the little creature." That's what he said.

'Of course, I was delighted for Felix. It must have been a wonderful occasion, for he didn't return until late that evening. He said the christening feast was delicious.' A wistful sigh. 'I had hoped he might bring home a piece of christening cake for me. Just a small piece... but of course he was far too busy to think of that.'

It sounded pretty selfish to me, and thoughtless. It was

getting harder and harder to find anything likeable about Felix. But I mustn't allow my attention to wander – he was still talking.

'When Felix arrived home, I asked him what everyone had to eat, and what they'd decided to call the child. The food sounded... so lovely....'

He started tapping. I'd better intervene. 'And what did they name the new arrival?'

'Oh, yes. The name. Felix said they named him Top Off.'

'Top off? 'That's... a very unusual name, don't you think?'

'I tried to ask Felix about it, but he started twitching his tail, so I knew he was irritated. Perhaps it is a secret family name...'

Tail twitching? I'd never heard mice twitch their tails. It wouldn't be sensible to chase that lead right now, however – I wanted him to continue with his narrative. He was clearly in the flow, reliving the memory. I dared not risk side-tracking him at this point. 'So after that, everything returned to normal?'

'Well, yes and no. A week later Felix burst into the kitchen while I was trying to think of a way to make something interesting out of the few seeds and fruit peel we had left. He seemed very happy. He told me his cousin had given birth to another child, and that again he'd been given the great honour of becoming its godfather. He said the child had a white ring around its neck, and that was a special sign, so he couldn't refuse. Could I spare him again while he attended the christening the next day?'

This was extraordinary. Surely mice don't give birth on a weekly basis? But I reminded myself that it would not be wise to interrupt while he was in full flow. 'So, of course, you encouraged him to attend?'

'Yes. Yes of course I did. And when he returned... oh it must have been a rich feast, for his whiskers were shining with butter or oil...' A sad sigh once more. 'When he returned, I asked him what they'd named his new godchild.'

'And?'

'He said they'd called the child Half Gone.'

Top Off. Half Gone. My suspicions were alight. That's how you might describe what happens when you eat the contents in a container full of food. It seemed pretty obvious to me that Felix had been eating the fat in the hidden jar. But why did he feel the need to torment his partner like this?

'Did you ask Felix about the origins of that... unusual name?'

'I thought I had better not. Felix told me he was tired and that he needed a long sleep after... all the food...' A tear plopped loudly onto the table.

Oh, how I felt for this poor gullible creature! Love can be so blind! Felix sounded not only dishonest, but mean and insensitive. How dare he go on about the food? But then I reminded myself I'd never actually met Felix. I could be misjudging him. Anyway, I was meant to be helping my client, not passing judgement on his partner.

'But then things got back to normal after that?'

Well, yes, for some ten days all was as usual. But then last Saturday, Felix bounced into the kitchen again. I was just sitting in my chair, for I'd found nothing edible that morning so there was nothing for me to prepare. I could tell what was coming by the look of excitement on Felix's face, but I didn't let on so he could enjoy passing on the good news. He said he'd been asked to be godfather yet again, and that this was the most special child ever born he was sure, for it had not one white hair on its entire body. Felix said that only happens once every few years. Surely, he begged, I would let him attend the christening next day?'

'And I'm sure you did.'

Nod. 'Of course. I only wish... well, if only... Felix had thought to bring me back a crust from one of the sandwiches...'

I thought I better divert him – the tapping had resumed. 'Was the child as wonderful as Felix thought it would be?'

That question seemed to do the trick. He stopped tapping and smiled. 'Oh yes, yes indeed. Felix told me they called this child All Gone. And it must have been a wonderful christening party. Felix didn't even ask me whether there was any food in the house for two whole days.'

'But I thought you'd already run out of food?'

'Yes... but Felix forgets sometimes.' Then he looked at me directly – the first time in a while, I realised. I wasn't sure, but I thought he looked a bit frightened. 'But then, three days after he returned from that christening, Felix started asking me why I hadn't prepared him a meal. He seemed angry and upset, no matter how carefully I tried to explain we'd run out of ingredients. I became so desperate that yesterday I went out and tried to find something, anything, even though I know full well there's nothing growing right now. Nothing at all.' He looked straight at me again, eyes wide, nose twitching. I could sense his fear.

'And now Felix seems so different. His tail twitches almost all the time, and he keeps circling round me when I'm trying to do the cleaning. And the way he looks at me... it all seems so different... and that's why I've come to see you. I need to understand what I'm doing wrong... I know I must be making Felix angry. Please, please tell me what I can do to make things better, to stop Felix acting so... strangely!'

He was pleading now, frightened and desperate. I really wished I knew more about the habits of mice. I also needed a moment to put together everything he'd just told me, and to figure out why Felix posed such a threat.

'I hope you don't mind, but I'm a little surprised about the... tail twitching... and the... the circling. Is that something mice do often?'

He looked at me in total astonishment. Was I a complete idiot?

'Felix? Felix a mouse?' Then he laughed – a loud nervous laugh, but good to hear anyway. 'Surely you can see that Felix is a cat?'

Oh my God. The circling, the taunting, the deception. Of course Felix is a cat, and that means this poor mouse is in untold danger. I absolutely had to stop him returning to his home. Forget therapeutic interventions, I told myself. Just save his life.

I tried to sound calm, measured. 'No, I guess I missed that detail. Silly me. Of course Felix is a cat. How could I not have realised?'

He was tapping furiously now. I desperately needed to keep his attention before he launched into another set of chair laps. And I had to keep him from going back home. Without bothering to compose my words I dived in.

'You know what I think would help most? A break. I really think you two need a little break in your relationship. Don't you think that would be nice...' He was tapping with both hands now. Most unprofessionally, I could hear myself pleading with him, my voice sounding ever shriller and louder in my desperation.

'Wouldn't it be nice for Felix... for Felix! Wouldn't it be lovely if you gave Felix the chance to enjoy some time on his own?' I could hear myself shouting now as I tried desperately to regain his attention. 'How about if instead of going home, you go straight to your sister's house – right now – s and spend a few days with her? Wouldn't it be great for Felix to enjoy a little own time, so...'

But he wasn't listening. He was literally bouncing up and down in the chair.

'Of course! It's so obvious! I know now what I need to do! I just need to talk to Felix! We've always been able to talk. How could I have forgotten? All we need to do is talk about the fat...disappearing. About how I'm trying to help us both, trying to find food. He'll understand everything. Felix is really understanding. And he'll stop... he'll stop staring at me like that...'

'Please! Please hold on! Just for a minute, so we can think this through together...'

But even as I pleaded, even as I begged him to stop and reconsider, he launched himself from the chair and began scampering towards the back wall, shrinking with every step. I paused for breath and watched helplessly. And then, just before he reached the window, he stopped, as if remembering something. He turned around and addressed me, smiling once more.

'Thank you. Thank you so much for listening to me. Now I just need to have a good talk with Felix. Of course. That's all I have to do, then everything will be fine. Thank you! You've helped so much!'

And with that he gathered himself, leapt into the darkness, and was gone, the window slamming shut behind him.

Off to become a cat's dinner.

Cinderella

I woke this morning with such energy! And optimism. I'd almost forgotten my old self – this is how I always used to feel. But of course. It's Tuesday.

I thought I managed to stay well focused today. But now at last my clinic is over, and I just heard Emma leave. It's magic time – at least I hope it is.

I'd unlatched the window facing the old forest earlier in the day. Absurd, I knew, because none of the fairytale characters to date had encountered any problems entering my office through a closed window.

That's when I catch myself, when my sensible self speaks. Whatever am I thinking? I really, really must be having a breakdown. Believing that people – and a mouse – from two hundred years ago have been visiting me, seeking my help? I know what I'd think about someone who told me that...

A gust of wind blows the blank sheet of paper in front of me onto the floor, and I hear a cry of dismay. 'Oh no! I'm stuck!'

Whipping round, I see a mop of brown curls topped by a white linen day cap pointing directly at me and two arms flailing wildly, blue silk to the elbows ending with double-flared cuffs. A young woman has tried to launch herself through the window, and apparently has indeed become 'stuck'. And she is not happy about it.

'Why does everything go wrong for me?' Then, craning her neck up and catching sight of me, 'Well don't just stand there! Can't you see I need some help?'

I knew four things about this young woman already. Judging by her dress she's rich. She's large. She's rather clumsy. And she's extremely demanding.

'Of course.' Standing in front of her upturned scowl, 'If you'll take hold of my hands perhaps I can pull you...?' Without waiting for an answer, I take hold of the still flailing arms at the wrists, straighten and start to tug. Then pull. Then heave. She is clearly stuck fast. Maybe some part of her outside the window is the problem? I've never had much spatial sense.

'The panniers! Dratted panniers! Go out there and untie my panniers will you!'

She rode here on a bicycle? And she needed to bring things with her? They had bicycles in the Eighteenth Century? This is too strange. 'Sure thing!' As if I know what I'm doing.

The cold night air is sobering. What *am* I doing? But I keep walking, round to my window at the back.

It is half open, but... I feel a creeping cold on the back of my neck. There's nothing there. Nothing holding the window open. But the window is definitely open. The panel is suspended halfway up, trembling slightly. I know the contours of the building so well that I'd not turned on the torch, but I do so now, shining it on the window frame. Empty space. Just a half-open window. I switch off the torch and feel a wave of dizziness, the beginnings of a panic attack, as the possibility that I'm experiencing hallucinations suggests itself. Will I be admitted as an in-patient?

But then I hear her howls of indignation. She's real! Well, at least half of her is real. Thank heavens! I rush eagerly back and into my office.

She's there all right.

'What *is* the matter with you? Why didn't you untie the

dratted panniers?'

'I... I couldn't see them in the dark. So sorry!' With that I took hold of the top frame and heaved it upwards with renewed energy. She fell unceremoniously onto the floor in a heap of linen and silk petticoats, her day cap now askew.

All of her. From the waist down as well as up. All there. Do they only materialise once they're inside my office?

The petticoats had hitched up and bunched around what looked like a roll of rubber tubing round her waist. That must be what she meant by panniers. She was trying desperately hard to look nonchalant as she re-adjusted the layers and layers of silk and linen. Beautiful gold ribbon garters tied over each knee holding ivory silk stockings in place.

But only one shoe, the left, black leather with a dull silver buckle. A thick wrapping of white muslin hid most of the right stocking from toes to calf – no shoe could fit over that. The muslin was stained in varying shades of dirty red. Must be a nasty wound on that foot or ankle – and recent, too, judging by the bright red blotches amid the deeper reds. She stood up a little unsteadily and regarded me, assessing me shrewdly, less angry now.

'I need your help. Is there somewhere I'm supposed to sit down?'

Recovering myself, 'Yes. Yes, there is. Just... there,' gesturing to the chair at the far side of my desk. I didn't dare offer to help this proud young creature as she hobbled over, carrying her head high. Once she'd adjusted the gown and petticoats to her satisfaction she looked up. I waited expectantly.

'It's Mother. And Christine. Things have just gone too far.'

Mother and daughter problems, one of the two relationship hotspots in my work; that and couples. I can do this. But, 'Who's Christine, please?'

'Christine is my big sister. And I hate her. And she hates me.'

I nodded. Not that surprising. The elder is usually jealous of the baby of the family, while the younger envies their older sibling's sophistication.

'So it's just... the three of you at home?'

'Oh no! There's my... stepfather.' Look of distaste. 'And...And

I suppose I have to mention Cynthia.'

'I see. So, Cynthia is your...'

'She's my stepfather's daughter. Cynthia! What a stupid name. Who would name someone like her after a goddess? Really! Wishful thinking there!'

Although she spat out the words, it felt rather like an automatic habit, that dismissal. I sensed an ambivalence, wondered what she really thought of her stepsister. But maybe it wasn't wise to ask her just yet. I needed more general information right now.

'Is Cynthia younger than you?' Nod. 'And how long have you all been... been a family?'

Oops, hit a nerve there. She reddened, shook her head, curls bobbing furiously. 'Never! It's never worked! We're no family!'

Keep quiet, I tell myself, no leading questions, no directing. She stared hard at me, as if needing to bore her statement into my head. I waited, keeping eye contact but trying not to suggest confrontation. After a moment she lowered her eyes, shoulders sagged. Shook her head sadly.

'I wish Mother had never, *ever,* remarried. We were happy enough as we were! But Mother... Mother never has enough. More, more! I see that now. Everything, everything is about how she can get hold of more wealth, more status... even... even.... That's all I am to her. A chance for more.'

She looked up, big tears welling in her hazel eyes. Poor unloved creature! This is a delicate moment, I tell myself. No standard responses, no nods, no handing out tissues. Let her recover herself, then stay quiet so she can decide where she wants to go next.

She remained bowed, crying a little but quietly. After a few more long moments she looked up, wiped her eyes with the back of her hand and took a deep breath. 'Do you have some way I could... rest my foot...'

I'd forgotten that poor bandaged limb. 'Of course. I should have offered.' A grateful look. I was beginning to like this overgrown child. I fetched one of the two other chairs and placed it to the right of her, seat facing her.

'Thanks.' Slowly and carefully, wincing but clearly determined not to cry out, she lifted the bandaged leg up and placed the foot on the chair seat. Heaved a sigh of relief.

'My father died when I was six....' Reconsidering, 'No. My father disappeared when I was six. Mother told us he died fighting for the King, but recently I have come to doubt that story. I think he could no longer bear my mother's constant demands... and....' More tears. 'And the fact that she bore him only daughters.'

Poor child! This time I did hand her the box of tissues with genuine compassion. Did no one love this girl?

As she dabbed her eyes, I found myself feeling that familiar stab of pain as I thought of my own ambitious, cold mother. Then sharply to myself, 'No, Helen! This is her story, not yours! You know the rules. Keep yourself well out.' Deep breath, refocus.

'We lived alone for nearly twelve years. It was a pleasant life. Father had left us well provided.'

Father had a heart then. Good. At least there was one parent who didn't always demand to have their own way. One decent role model in her life? Maybe.

'But Mother was always looking... looking for a better position. When she heard Baroness Reinhardt died in childbirth, she was determined to marry the Baron.' She looked up, a wry smile. 'And my mother always gets what she wants.

'At first we were very excited, Christine and I. Our new home was so grand, and we had more servants, so many more. Mother ordered fine gowns for us all. And we had our own chambers...

'But now we had a new sister as well. Cynthia is three years younger than I am. Mother loathed her from the first moment she set eyes on her, and encouraged us to do so as well – rather, she demanded we do so. She would act kindly, oh so kindly towards Cynthia when her new husband was present. But I remember that first day after the wedding, when Baron Reinhardt went out hunting. We were finishing breakfast when Mother suddenly turned to Christine and me. Pointing at Cynthia, "What's this terrible useless thing doing in our rooms?" Then addressing her, "Off with you to the kitchen! Whoever wants to eat bread in this house must first earn it. You will be our maid!"

'Then Mother ordered the servants to take away Cynthia's fine gowns and burn them, and give her an old grey smock to wear instead. And Cynthia had to work with the servants, do all the same things they did – get up at dawn, carry water into the house, make up the fires, cook and wash. Mother would encourage us to pour peas and lentils into the ashes of the hearth, so Cynthia had to spend all day picking them out. Then at night, because she no longer had a bed of her own – I learned later Christine's chamber had once belonged to Cynthia – she had to lie down beside the hearth, in the ashes, to sleep. Mother told her husband Cynthia had chosen this new life, that after she lost her mother she wished to live the life of a servant, repentance for her mother...' Anger flooded her, stopping her narrative. My chance.

'How did you feel about... what was happening with Cynthia?'

She shook her head guiltily. 'That's the terrible thing.' Her eyes, pleading forgiveness. 'I just joined in with Mother and Christine. I was just as cruel. They loved tormenting her, and I... I must admit, I was so glad no longer to be the object of their cruelty. So, I pretended to love taunting her as well.' Long pause. 'That was wicked, I know that now.'

I was fast warming to this young woman. Of course, she would be attracted to bullying. It's what she'd experienced, and I could hear my professor telling us that the bullied are highly likely to become bullies themselves, in an attempt to regain the sense of power they'd lost. Yet something had caused her to change – or at least to want to change – I wasn't sure which yet. But either way, it was pretty impressive. And it could have a lot to do with why she'd come to see me.

'Do you know, can you remember, what made you start to think differently? What was it, do you think, that made you realise bullying Cynthia was something you no longer wished to do?'

'Well, it didn't happen all at once. At first, just sometimes I would stop, realise I wasn't happy. In fact, I was even more unhappy than when Mother and Christine used to tease me so badly. But the real change, the big change – why I left to come here – it happened after the Prince's Ball, I think.'

'The Prince's Ball? Can you tell me a bit about that?'

She beamed. How attractive she was when she smiled like that, free from worry and remorse.

'Oh, I would be so glad to tell you about the Prince, and about the ball. Everyone says the Prince is the most handsome man in our Kingdom.

'Last month his father, the King, announced that the time had come for his son to choose a bride, so in the Prince's honour he was going to organise the most magnificent ball ever. It would last three nights. Three nights! Can you imagine?'

What a smile!

'The King said the purpose of the ball was to allow his son to find his bride, and that every young woman in the Kingdom would be invited. It was all so wonderful, so exciting! The best thing ever! Mother ordered new ball gowns to be made for us specially, for Christine and me. And we had new silken dance slippers fashioned for us as well.

'Christine said it would be good fun to make Cynthia really jealous, because of course Mother said she could not attend the ball. So, we made her comb our hair, fasten our petticoats and brush our silk slippers, all the while saying how wonderful it would be when we had our turn to dance with the Prince at the ball. We'd remind her she had to stay home, because, "if anyone saw her and knew her to be our sister, we'd be ashamed". That's what Mother told us to say.' She paused, looked directly at me. 'We really were cruel to her.

'Then, just before we left on the first night, Christine thrust a bowlful of lentils at poor Cynthia and told her that they all had to be sorted before we returned.' Big tears, shaking her curls sadly. 'However could I have been a part of that?'

It was hard to know whether to reply, to reassure. I decided against it. It would be better if I could help her find a way to forgive herself.

'The ball was like the best dream anyone could have. There must have been a thousand chandeliers! And the Prince, so handsome, dancing with everyone, each in turn… though he smiled little, and he never spoke.' She was lost for a moment, transported back to that splendid evening. 'And when we returned, do you know? Cynthia had sorted all the lentils! I wanted to praise her, but Mother said it would only make her lazy. Instead, the next afternoon after she had dressed us in our dancing gowns and put up our hair, Mother gave her an even bigger bowl of peas and told she had to sort the good from the bad, every one, before we returned from the second night of the ball.'

She paused, reflecting on something – happy or sad? – I couldn't tell, but she stayed silent so long I felt I had to ask, 'And the second night? Was the ball just as it was the first night?'

Her body language made it clear that it was not.

'It was so different! So very, very different. Oh, it all began in the same way, the silent Prince dancing with each of us in turn. But then, late in the evening, a carriage pulled up in the courtyard. It was driven by six of the most magnificent black horses I had ever seen. Each one had feathers in their bridle, and there were servants dressed in blue silk with silver braiding. The carriage was so extraordinary that someone even ordered the music to stop as it arrived in the courtyard, and everyone left the dance floor and hurried outside to take a look. But then, when the servant opened the carriage door... oh my! Out stepped the most beautiful princess – she must be a princess – her silver gown and slippers sparkling so brightly in the light of the chandeliers. When he saw her, the Prince started smiling. And he kept on smiling. For the rest of the evening, he would dance with no other partner.'

She looked up at me, her face alight with joy and generosity.

'She was more beautiful than anyone else, and her face so full of kindness. She deserved to dance with the Prince.

'When we returned at last – it was nearly dawn – we found Cynthia asleep on the hearth, all the peas sorted. I felt so sorry for her, all alone that long evening and night. Watching her sleeping there, I realised for the first time that she was actually a very pretty child. Had she been allowed to clean herself up and wear a gown, I thought, no doubt she would have looked wonderful.' Tears flowing again. 'I wanted to stop tormenting her, I really did! But I was so afraid Mother and Christine would turn on me again.

'The next night, the last night of the ball, Mother gave Cynthia an entire sack of peas to sort. I didn't think she could possibly manage to sort them all. Then off we went, leaving her standing alone in the courtyard, the heavy sack of peas beside her.' Looking up at me again, she paused, reflecting. 'That's when I knew I would be happier if I could be kind to Cynthia, instead of treating her so badly. I don't know why it happened then, but that was the moment I knew. But I was still too afraid of Mother and Christine...'

Her thoughts were drifting, her thinking confused. I waited quietly.

'The last night of the ball was the most amazing of all. More chandeliers than anyone could count, and the most delicious food on silver platters, all manner of sweetmeats and delicacies. Everyone was wearing the most beautiful gowns, everyone looked so beautiful. It was truly magical.

'But the Prince... the Prince would not choose a dance partner. Whenever his father encouraged him, he replied simply that he was waiting. For what? For whom? We all knew. And at last, the carriage drew up, drawn this time by six white horses adorned with plumes of red and gold. And the servants who drove the carriage and opened the door for the princess wore red silk with gold braiding. And the princess...This time she was dressed all in gold. I think the threads must have been true gold. Her gown was studded with precious gems, so that she glistened – really, she glistened – as if she herself were the midday sun.' She looked up at me again, eager to share. 'If only you could have seen her! It brought such joy to all of us – except Christine. She was white with envy.' She paused, dropped her eyes, ashamed of her sister.

'Once again, the Prince would dance with no other but the mysterious princess. But later, just before the stroke of midnight, I saw the princess glance up at the clocktower, and when she saw the time, she turned suddenly and began running to her carriage, without a word and heedless of the Prince's pleas for her to stay.

'She leapt inside the carriage, a servant closed the door at once and jumped into the driving seat, calling to the horses. As the carriage sped deep into the night, the Prince simply stood in the courtyard looking heartbroken, unmoving, oblivious to everyone around him. Then, looking about as if in a dream, he espied something glistening brightly at the bottom of the stairs. He hurried over and picked it up, and as he did so his face brightened once more. It was a golden slipper – her golden slipper. In her haste it must have loosened from her little foot.'

She paused, looking down sadly at her own bandaged leg, allowing another tear to fall. 'Her feet were so small and dainty.'

I knew it wasn't wise to interrupt, but I couldn't bear that she'd become aware of the pain in her leg again – in her eagerness to describe the ball, she'd momentarily forgotten. But now the pain must be raging... would she feel able to return to her story?

'Does that mean the Prince has no bride to this day?'

'No... well, not yet.'

'Not yet? So another ball is planned?'

This, I was glad to see, made her laugh.

'Oh my goodness no! Not even our King could afford another such sumptuous occasion in the same season! No, no more balls. But the next day there was a proclamation that the Prince would personally visit every household in the Kingdom, and that every maiden in each household would be invited to try on the slipper he had found. The maiden whose foot fit the slipper, read the proclamation, would become his queen.

'Can you imagine the excitement!' Her eyes shone. 'Everyone hoped they could fit the slipper!' Smile fading. 'Especially Christine, encouraged by our mother of course.' Fixing her attention back to me and trying to summon up kindness, 'You see, Christine has very small feet. She's always been so proud of her tiny feet. Mother said now was her chance.'

What a generous soul!

'At last, five days later, it was our turn. Late in the morning we heard the Prince approach our house with his entourage. Our chance had come, and Christine was trembling with excitement.' She paused, sighed. 'Mother was trembling as well. But I soon realised she was not excited for Christine – or for me, if I would be given the chance to try on the slipper. No, Mother wished this possible good fortune only for herself. She wished to become the mother of a queen.'

She looked so hurt, so dejected. But I knew to keep quiet. She had more to tell.

'Mother greeted the Prince with so much praise and bowing, it was not pleasant to watch. But the Prince didn't seem to notice. "He was in a hurry," he said. "Are there any maidens in this household who attended the ball, who wish to try on the slipper?"'

'With more bowing and curtsies, Mother assured him there was a very special maiden waiting to try on the slipper. The Prince nodded impatiently. She called to Christine, who came out almost on tiptoe so as not to put weight on her feet, to keep them dainty.'

She laughed to herself, the memory amusing.

'When the Prince handed her the slipper, I could feel Mother's keen gaze, measuring up that slipper against Christine's foot. "Your esteemed Majesty, my daughter is so delicate! She will need to be sitting down and alone to put back on the... *her*... slipper. May we take it inside the house?"

'Thinking about it now, the Prince obviously knew Christine was not his bride, so he merely nodded. "But be quick with you!" he exclaimed.

'The three of us hurried indoors, Mother clutching the precious slipper. Once she closed the doors, she became rough in her greedy excitement, and thrust the slipper at Christine. "Well, put it on, Daughter! Get on with it! I wish to be the mother of the queen!"

'Poor Christine pushed and struggled and wiggled, but try as she might the slipper was too small. And that's when I knew for sure Mother loves no one but herself. She ran to the kitchen and fetched a sharp knife and handed it to Christine. "Cut off a piece of your heel. Then the slipper will fit. It will hurt, but what does that matter? The pain will pass. And it will be worth it, for then you will be Queen!"'

She paused, extremely angry but also clearly distressed.

'Can you imagine? A mother who would encourage her own daughter to cut off part of her foot?' She shook her head sadly now. 'So of course, Christine did as she was told – she, too, fears our mother. I hadn't been aware of that before. Her heel was bleeding badly – it was horrible – and Christine went quite pale. But Mother shoved her foot in just the same, "That will stop the blood flowing. Mind you, don't let him see what you have done!" And she almost pushed Christine over in her eagerness to get her back to the waiting Prince.

'When the Prince saw that Christine was wearing the slipper, he sighed. I know he didn't believe she was the real owner, but he had to keep his public word. So, he escorted her into the carriage and they drove off. Mother was mad with greedy joy. It was so... ugly.'

New tears.

I waited. After another few moments she looked up, took a deep breath and repositioned herself. There was more to this story.

'But even before Mother could settle herself in the house so she could begin planning our move to the castle, we heard the carriage returning. We both ran to the window – there was the Prince, shaking his head sternly as he helped Christine out of the carriage. As she began hobbling towards the house, Mother rushed out. "What did you forget, darling? You could have sent for anything!" But I could sense her foreboding. The Prince addressed our mother coldly. "Your daughter is a false bride. She has cut her own foot to fit the slipper."'

She stopped her narrative abruptly – reflecting on her mother's behaviour must have overwhelmed her and struck her temporarily dumb. But then, instead of carrying on with the tale, she appeared to lose self-control and throw what I can only describe as a mini tantrum, bashing her fists on the desktop in fury and kicking her good leg up and down. Then remembering me, she shook her head in embarrassment, drew a deep breath, relaxed in her chair, and resumed her narrative.

'And what did Mother say? Did she welcome Christine? Did she thank her for her sacrifice, for trying to do her bidding? Did she offer to bathe her foot? No! She ignored her daughter completely. Instead, she turned her full attention on the Prince. '"Your Majesty, I beg your Majesty's forgiveness for such a false daughter. She insisted to me she was the one. Such a liar!"

'I could see Christine turning ever paler, poor thing.' Again, I marvelled at her generosity. '"Your most wonderful Majesty," my mother carried on, "your true bride is my other daughter, standing here beside me. I wanted to tell you earlier, but she" – throwing a sharp glance towards Christine – "insisted she was your true bride, false daughter that she is!"

'I assure you, I was most astonished – and frightened upon hearing her lies. I knew I would now have to try on the bloody slipper. And I knew my feet were larger than Christine's. I shuddered as I thought about what was to come.

'Again, Mother insisted we go into the house to fit the slipper on, and again the Prince granted permission. I followed Mother in fear and trembling, knowing the slipper would never fit, while Christine hobbled behind in dreadful pain.

'And, of course, it didn't fit. I couldn't even push my toes inside. And as I feared, as I dreaded with all my being, I heard my mother, "Cut off your toes! Then the slipper will fit. Go on! You will have no need to walk once you are Queen! Do as I say! Now! This minute!" And she handed me the knife, still stained with Christine's blood.

'So... so, I did.' Regarding her bandages sadly. 'I cut off my poor, poor toes and shoved my bleeding foot into the slipper, and somehow I managed to walk back to the Prince. Never have I known such pain. I was sure I would faint.'

She afforded herself a rueful smile.

'But fear of Mother pushed me on. We were only minutes down the road when I saw two pigeons – the two I know Cynthia is fond of feeding – flying along beside us. As we turned the first corner they swooped down and sat on the carriage roof. The Prince leaned out at once, as if this had happened before.' She regarded me carefully. 'Of course, I realise now it had. They began to sing loudly:

"Looky, look, look
"at the shoe that she took.
"There's blood all over, and the shoe's too small.
"She's not the bride you met at the ball."'

I marvelled at a world that contained talking birds. But then I remembered my recent visit from a talking mouse...

'When he heard their ditty, the Prince looked down at once at my foot and saw the blood on my stockings, the blood streaming from the slipper. I was so afraid! But he seemed more relieved than angry – I knew then he was not a cruel man, not like my mother. He simply ordered the coachman to turn back to the house.

'Of course, Mother was as angry with me as she had been with Christine. "Wilhelmina! You bring shame upon our house! How dare you!" And as the Prince drove off without a word, she pushed me towards the house. I wish I could not remember those moments. I stumbled and fell, again and again, as the pain and sickness overwhelmed me.'

She paused, looking spent. I had to comfort her, had to interrupt, whether it was 'correct' to do so or not.

'You poor, poor child! So that explains your... bandages. I am so very sorry!'

She looked up through sad tears. Simply, 'Thank you.'

We sat together quietly, until she spoke once more.

'Despite the pain – or perhaps the pain sharpened what I finally realised, who knows – I knew then that I could no longer live like this, in this household with this cruel selfish woman. I was so ashamed. I was ashamed of my mother's greed, but also of my own cowardice. I vowed to live no more like this, not one moment more.

'So when Mother ran out to chase the carriage...' A wry smile as she remembered the absurdity of it, 'While Mother was literally running after the departing carriage, I stood up, balancing as best I could, and I walked out, leaving poor Christine weeping in pain. I just walked away from that sorry existence, willing the pain to stop so I could make it to the woods, and then to come here. To you. Because I'd heard you can help. So please, help me find a new path. I cannot go back to... her, to that life, to such cruelty, ever again.'

Her courage and resolve, not to mention her tolerance for pain, were humbling. I had to help, though I wasn't at all sure how. I doubted women at that time had many options open to them. My first thought was a refuge of some sort, because surely everyone would agree she had been abused, and that she was no doubt still in danger. Did they have refuges, shelters, then? Probably not... but then I remembered...

They had convents.

Becoming a nun was seen as an honourable life for women at that time. And she would receive an education, an opportunity she'd no doubt seize. And she had such a generous nature, so much to give. To help others, to spend her life giving of herself... But I knew not to suggest anything. If a client is told what to do rather than coming up with their own solution, they're less likely to own that path, to remain motivated if the going gets tough, or even to feel proud if things manage to work out.

But I was worrying needlessly.

'I hope you're not thinking that no one would choose me as a bride? That's what Mother tells me, often, though I so wished someone would choose me. If I were to marry, I could escape my mother's tongue. But of course, she always insisted, no one would ever choose me.'

She regarded me carefully, then to my astonishment, she burst out laughing.

'Mother isn't always right, though she thinks she is. But in this one case, I think perhaps she is right. Mother says I am only fit for life in a convent.'

I had no idea what to say. I felt as if she'd read my thoughts.

'I suppose...The important thing here is not what your mother thinks, is it? The important thing is what you would like to do.'

'I know exactly what I would like to do. I realise now that what Mother suggests is right for me, although our reasoning differs. I would like to enter a convent, now that I feel free to choose for myself rather than forced to obey my mother. A life of service, a life of scriptures and learning. That would suit me perfectly.' A twinkly smile – how could she, given the pain she must be feeling? 'And I know they'll have me. The convent especially welcomes the... disabled.'

Glancing down at her poor foot, 'And the bonus? Mother will think I agreed with her.'

Wow! How she could laugh at her predicament was beyond me, let alone be so generous towards her mother! I felt the catch in my voice, tried to overcome it, 'May I say one thing about your decision?'

'Of course!'

'The nuns in the convent you enter will be incredibly lucky and blessed that you have chosen to be with them.'

She beamed. 'I expect you may be right. I think I might even dare to say you are right! I *am* worthy, and I *can* live a useful life.' She rose carefully, that generous smile again. 'Thank you.'

'No, Wilhelmina. I am the one who should say thank you.'

I watched as she walked gingerly towards the window, stood before it with outstretched arms, nodded once, then vanished deep into the night.

Rapunzel

She must have flown in. There could be no other explanation.

I regarded the old woman sitting across from me nervously. Only a minute ago Emma had switched off the lights in reception and shut the door behind her, and only seconds ago that chair had been empty.

She adjusted her dirty lace shawl with long crooked fingers. Her straggly grey hair was still settling back around her shoulders. She was enveloped in a thick black dress of some coarse material. She smelled of rotting herbs.

I longed to reach down and gather the papers scattered by the sudden gust of wind that had marked her entry, but to look away felt somehow rude. Without a word she was demanding my full attention, and without a word I felt compelled to give it.

'You will tell me how to get my daughter back.'

It was not a question, not a polite request. It was a command. Not a good start – she clearly expected to take total charge of this encounter. I needed a few moments to figure out how to rebalance our relationship.

'Would you mind if I fetched myself a glass of water? I'm feeling quite thirsty.' That was true – I must have been staring at her open-mouthed.

'Or for Hecate's sake, get on with it! I haven't all night!'

'Thank you.' I bent down and picked up the papers with careful deliberation. Placed my pen on them, and as I did so I glanced back at the window that opens onto the old forest. It was firmly shut. More disquiet.

As I stood up, she picked up the gnarled staff she'd leaned against the chair, placed it across her lap, and began stroking it. Could she have flown in on that, or with its help at least?

I willed myself to walk slowly, to appear as nonchalant as I could manage as I crossed the room to my little basin. Slowly I picked up the water glass perched on the side of the basin, filled it with cold water, returned to my chair. Swallowed a long refreshing mouthful. Better.

Still stroking the staff, 'You've had your time. Now tell me how to get my daughter back.'

That staff was making me nervous. Was it magic? If so, probably not the kind of magic I would welcome.

'My staff will indeed do my bidding. But I have not asked anything of it... yet.'

I was unable to suppress a cold shiver. How did she guess my thoughts? Must be a coincidence. Please let it be a coincidence.

She was regarding me intently now with her tiny pale blue eyes, almost more like bright pebbles than eyes. Little hole for a mouth. Long beaked nose. She has a daughter? I wondered uncharitably how she managed to find anyone willing to impregnate her.

She laughed harshly. 'All right. She is my adopted daughter. Is that better?' My jaw must have dropped in astonishment, evoking another cackle. 'You are surprised I can read your thoughts. Yet you seem unable to read mine. Haven't progressed much in two hundred years, have we?'

More harsh laughter.

I was really nervous now, but I also knew that if we were to work together, I absolutely had to rebalance this encounter. Therapy involves collaboration with mutual exploration, rather than one participant acceding to the demands of the other. Buck up, Helen. Deep breath.

'You have sought my help. If you want it, then you will respect me as I will... respect you.' Somehow I managed to hold her gaze as I waited while she summed me up anew.

Then she smiled. Nice smile, despite the teeth.

'I see you are a strong woman. Good. Then how shall we proceed?' Keep your advantage, Helen. 'I need you to start... at the beginning. You can decide what marks the beginning.'

Only fair – after all, she'd given quite a lot of ground just now.

Pause. Reflection. This was feeling better.

'I suppose... the beginning was the night when her father, clumsy old fool, climbed into my garden.'

How harshly she judges others! I filed that observation, but let it pass for the moment. 'Climbed?'

'Yes. I like to keep myself to myself, so I...' glancing fondly at her staff, 'I arranged for a high wall to surround my cottage and garden. No one had dared even to come near my garden, let alone enter it.' She smiled conspiratorially. 'I have a very bad reputation, you see.'

I ignored the invitation to allow her to embellish on that reputation. I needed the narrative.

'Go on. He climbed into your garden, you say?'

'I knew what he wanted. I'd seen his wife pining, sensed her longing for my salad greens.'

'How could you see into a neighbouring cottage? I thought you said high walls surround your property?'

'Don't be deliberately obtuse! Of course, I can see through walls if I wish!' Softening. 'But I am in a dell and their cottage is on the hill without.'

'Thank you. I understand now. Do go on.'

Again I noted her first reaction, her quickness to dominate. I wondered if this extended to her role as a mother. Might need that later.

'She was pregnant, you see. After many years, she was pregnant.' She paused, the arrogance fading. 'I've heard you can crave odd things when you are pregnant.'

Suddenly she was real, and I felt for her. She would have loved to have become pregnant and given birth. It was obvious. I stared hard, willing myself to focus my full attention on the details of her face, to keep me from thinking about Alex and the four long years of fertility treatment I needed before I was able to conceive my only child.

To distract myself further, 'You are so right. Women can suddenly desire the most surprising foods during pregnancy.'

'Yes, well… I decided on this occasion to let him steal the salad she so desired.' Looking at me sadly, 'I would have exchanged places with her.'

Wasn't sure what to say, but I could tell she wanted a response. 'I hope you felt richly rewarded for your… generosity.'

'I did not!' She spat out the words in her fury. 'My reward? Some fine reward. He returned next evening… for more! Can you believe it?'

I shook my head as if I shared her disbelief.

'I approached him as he bent over to cut the greens, just waited for him to stand up, his hands full of… his thievery.' Defiant. 'You can probably imagine his surprise! And his fear. And I was glad! Oh, he grovelled, and he begged. I enjoyed that. But when he used the excuse that it was because his wife was pregnant…' Bent her head. 'I suppose I rather lost control.'

No need to comment. We both knew why.

'I told him he could take all the salad he wished, but the condition – for that, and for me to spare his life – was that they would give me the child when his wife gave birth.' Her eyes, those bright pebbles, sparkled. 'Of course, he agreed. What choice did he have?' She laughed long and loud at this. 'And I… at last, I would have a child. And a daughter no less! I knew it was a girl.

'I watched him when he returned home, laden with *my* salad.' She looked at me in mock astonishment. 'He never told his wife of our encounter! I am sure he thought that if he did not speak of it, nothing untoward would happen. What an utter simpleton!'

Another wicked laugh. 'Oh, and I enchanted that salad, so his wife would be satisfied and crave it no more… and…' Huge smile.

'So, the child would grow up to be the most beautiful creature the world had ever seen. And she is.'

She sighed.

'But is that still true now? Even with my skills, I cannot know. That is why I have sought your help, to bring her back to me, back to where she belongs.' She must have noted my look of confusion – or else she was reading my thoughts yet again. 'Oh, but I am getting ahead of myself. You cannot yet know what happened.'

'I watched that woman every day as she carried my child. I looked into the cottage and observed her as she grew rounder and rounder. On the very same day when at last she gave birth, I appeared before her and demanded the baby – as my right of course.' A very unpleasant chuckle. 'You cannot imagine her astonishment upon seeing me when I confronted her – remember, her husband had told her nothing of our encounter. She stared uncomprehending, frozen with shock. I simply removed the babe she cradled in her arms, plucked it right away. She didn't react, didn't move. Just stared at me.

'As I left with my precious bundle, I passed her dicky of a husband coming into their bedchamber. Hah! He had much to explain to his wife.'

She grinned at me. I did not find this at all amusing, but neither did I wish to appear critical. I didn't want her to start questioning whether I was really willing to help. And after all, I'd been asked to help her find her daughter, not to pass judgment on her or feel sorry for the child's birth parents.

'Do go on.'

'My magic had been strong. Cassandra grew to become the most beautiful child under the sun. Sapphire eyes, the tiniest blush in her cheek. And her hair! It was as fine as spun gold, and it grew so abundantly that soon it fell nearly to the floor. For twelve blissful years she delighted in my company each and every day. We had such wonderful times! I never knew such perfect joy.'

She fell silent, remembering, wistful. But then her expression hardened.

'But not long after Cassandra's twelfth birthday, she began

to ask questions. Unnecessary questions. What was life like beyond the grounds of our cottage? Could she meet with others of her years? Why these questions? Why could she not simply continue to enjoy all that I offered? I could not understand.'

I could. Sounded like she'd hit adolescence.

'It came to a point... I feared she might try to leave the cottage. So, it became necessary to protect her. I had to!' She looked at me beseechingly, willing me to justify her actions. I nodded but said nothing. 'We created a high tower,' glancing at her staff. 'It had no doors or stairs, only a window at the top.'

She must have noted my astonishment, though I had tried hard to keep my concerned and caring mask in place, that well-practiced 'I understand you' look. But too late. She'd become defensive.

'Oh, but the tower was richly furnished within, and filled with all her favourite amusements. And the gowns we created!' Another caress of her staff. 'The gowns were exquisite. And I would bring with me the most delicious meals each evening when I came to see her. She wanted for nothing, I assure you.'

Nothing except a normal social life. I felt for the poor caged child, and thought how liberal most 'helicopter mothers' today suddenly seemed in comparison. But once again I reminded myself that this woman hadn't asked me to sympathise with her child or to compare her to other mothers, but rather to restore her child to her. My opinions and comparisons wouldn't help, nor were they relevant to the task at hand. Leave it, Helen, and focus on what my client is asking.

'But how did you get into the tower to be with her each evening if there were no doors or stairs?'

Big grin. 'Ah, that was our secret! Each evening I would approach the tower and call out:

'"Cassandra, Cassandra!"
'"Let down your hair!"

'And she would unpin her plaits, wind them round a hook I had fashioned at the window – I would never want to hurt her by pulling – and she would drop those golden tresses from the window ledge. They were so long by that time, they reached my outstretched hands. That was how I ascended, climbing her golden tresses, laden with wonderful things for her.'

The image of Rapunzel admitting the witch came from a fairytale that had affected me so powerfully as a child that, for the first time since the characters had begun visiting, the relevant story forced its way into my conscious thought. I'd managed always before to keep any recognition at bay, so I could focus my full attention on the client in front of me, without pre-judgement. I buried the association immediately, although not without effort.

'I see. Most ingenious.' Neutral enough I hoped. But what to say next? 'And...did she enjoy your visits, and the...gifts you brought her?'

'Oh yes. Most especially her gowns. How she loved to dress up!' But now an ugly scowl, eyes glittering in a way I had already come to dislike. 'But the gowns were her downfall. The gowns betrayed her, showed her faithlessness.'

Betrayed her? Showed her faithlessness? Those were strong words. 'She lied to you?'

'Worse! Far, far worse. She withheld from me. She had her own secret.'

A secret. Gowns that revealed what she didn't tell. In her effort to find something in her life she could control but that she felt compelled to hide, had Cassandra become anorexic? Was that the problem?

'Did the gowns...no longer fit her?'

She regarded me with a glimmer of respect. 'Ah, you're perhaps not as untutored as I was beginning to think! You're right. They no longer fitted. Perhaps I would not have noticed for a while longer had Cassandra not given herself away.

'I was pinning the stomacher to her new gown – peacock blue with diamonds it was – when she remarked, "Tell me, Mother, why is it my skirts are becoming so tight, and no longer falling evenly to the floor but rising at the front?"

'Then I did regard her, and... how had I not seen this? She

was with child! *With child!'*

She spat the words, disbelief mixed with anger – and, I suspect, envy. She was staring hard at me. I had to think of a way to distract her, to shield my thoughts, to stop her peering into my mind again.

'But this is astonishing! I thought you said there was no way a suitor' – I noted the look of warning – 'an *intruder* could get into the tower, nor she escape from it?'

Relief as she responded to my words rather than my inner thoughts.

'Oh, you can be sure I made her tell me all. Oh yes. It seems a foreigner, a *prince* she called him,' venom in her speech, 'a beard splitter I warrant, had come riding by one day when Cassandra was standing at the window singing a favourite ditty. She said he told her – that lying lobcock – that he fell in love with her at once and could not stop staring at the window. There he remained, rooted to the spot – or so he told her – until he heard me approaching the tower, whereupon he hid himself and his horse a way off. He watched me call to her, and when I had departed he approached the tower and called out to her, using my words exactly. Jackanape! Beard splitter!'

She was shouting now, standing up and sitting down repeatedly. A moment more of this, then she must have realised she was out of control. She stopped her chair dance abruptly. Deep breaths, hands unclenching, shoulders dropping.

'She said she was surprised to hear me, surprised I had returned to her so soon, but because they were our secret words she was sure it was I. She said she was afraid when she first saw him, when he climbed in the window. But...' She grimaced, finding it hard to go on, 'she said he was so *kind,* so merry and amusing... hah!' More deep breathing. 'She said that she began to be glad of his daily visits.'

Long pause, during which I fought to keep my mind clear, my focus steady, and not burst into a triumphant cheer for Cassandra.

'Well, I am sure I do not need to tell you what happened. Do I?'

I reassured her that she did not have to explain. But now I had to wait. She was fidgeting with her staff, forcing herself to stay seated, and making every effort to adjust her position so as to look tall and proud. It was clear that whatever she was about to tell me was even more difficult for her than what I'd just heard.

'I am afraid that when she confessed this... betrayal... after all I had given her, all I had done for her... I am afraid I... I lost control.' Her head bowed, 'I cut off her lovely plaits and took them from her. Even as she wept, I cast a spell upon her. I banished her to a desolate land, a land I know well, a place from which she could return only when she made a solemn vow to love me with all her heart and soul.

'I was certain she would come round, see her need for me... her *love* for me, particularly after she lost the child.'

I hated to ask, but had to. 'Then you cast a spell on the baby as well?'

'I knew there would be no need. Few can survive long in that land, let alone while carrying a child. Losing the child would bring her to her senses, I knew it would. Then she would have... only me. Then she would love *me,* and only me, once more.'

This was such a ludicrous definition of love! This was possession, not love. I hardly knew where to begin. Yet challenging her would only anger her.

'And the... intruder?'

That ugly, ugly laugh, eyes glittering in 'that way' again. 'Oh, I took care of him, I did! I tied Cassandra's tresses to the hook and I waited. Sure enough, just after I would normally have left, I heard the young bull calf ride up to the tower, bold as bold. When he called – hateful it was to hear – I dropped the tresses. Imagine his surprise upon seeing me!'

I hated to think. Poor guy.

'Such a jackanapes. Gollumpus! Fool!'

She had quite a vocabulary.

'I didn't even have to push him. He was so astonished he fell back and out the window, plunging to the foot of the tower where the briars grow. I heard him screaming, "I cannot see! My eyes, oh my eyes are pierced!"'

She regarded me defiantly. I didn't even try to hide my horror – she'd spot it anyway.

'I didn't need to kill him, did I? Better the wild animals devoured him as he wandered sightless and bleeding through the undergrowth!'

Now I was the one who had to breathe back some sense of calm, as I felt a wave of nausea at this image. Playing for time, 'When did this all take place?'

She bowed her head, stroking her staff sadly.

'That is why I have come. It has been near four months. She must have... lost the child long ago. Why has she not chosen to love me? Why has she not returned?'

Was she actually crying? After a moment or two, she looked up. Tear stains on wrinkled cheeks.

'She only needs to remember me, all that I can give her, and surely she will love me again.' Beseechingly, 'I chose you because I have seen so many mothers in your time who do as I have done. Who give their children everything, so they will love them and wish to stay with them always. I knew you would understand, because you see mothers like me around you! I knew you would understand and help me.'

I understood all right. Did I dare tell her that such behaviour is in large part why so many young adults are unhappy nowadays? That they crave independence? That they wish their parents would praise their efforts to forge a life for themselves instead of making their lives so easy – but so pointless – that they feel unable to break free? No. She needed to figure that one out herself.

But first, I'd thought of something that might help explain Cassandra's continued absence. It was a long shot – only a hunch – but I needed to try.

'Can we go back again to the spell you cast on your daughter? Did you say she could not return until... what exactly does she have to do?'

'She must love with all her heart and soul! Did you not hear me?'

Ignoring the insult, 'When you cast your spell, did you say *whom* she must love?'

She did not like to be challenged. 'There was no need! There is only me to love!'

But the fidgeting betrayed her. She might have made a mistake, and the thought terrified her. I better help.

'If she had been able, by some miracle, to give birth... or if the... intruder... somehow managed to find her...'

'No! No!' All too clearly she now saw the flaw in her spell. 'Those things cannot be! No!' Her voice had risen to a scream. I pressed on, regardless.

'But did you not tell me that the place where you sent her is too harsh to sustain her for long? You believe she is alive, I know you do, or you would not have sought my help. Therefore, she must have escaped. And you say there was only one way she could do that.'

We sat silently as she tried to reconcile these contradictions and try to come to terms with the unpalatable idea that she'd cast a spell that left room for unintended consequences. After all this time, if her daughter was still alive as she clearly believed she was, she must have chosen to love someone. Someone *else*. Not herself. At last, she looked up and met my waiting gaze. She was ready.

'Did your mother raise you?'

Surprise. 'No of course not! I was raised by the coven.'

'Okay, the coven. Did they demand you stay with them forever?'

'Of course they did no such thing! They taught me... our arts. They shared with me all they knew. Then it was for me to find my own place and time to practice my craft.'

'Your own way?'

'My own way of course. To thrive on my own was proof that I was worthy.'

I knew I needed say no more. What she needed now was time for reflection. I was happy for her to have it.

At long last, tears glittering in those eyes, 'If... if... she of course knows where I am. Do you think she might ever... ever wish to see me again? Ever, ever forgive me?' She was pleading now, and I felt for her, despite what she'd done. 'I would be oh, so, different! I would welcome her freedom. I would be glad for her. Truly I would!'

'I am certain you would. And I wish so much I could answer your question. But I cannot. No one can answer that question. You can only wait. And hope.' It was such a small crumb. 'And rejoice that she is alive, that you can sense she is alive.'

She looked up, resigned but accepting. 'I will keep hope alive then.' She rose as if to go, but paused and looked at me with a penetrating stare. 'Please, please tell other mothers, before it is too late for them.'

And with that she lifted her staff, and in a flash she was gone.

The Ugly Duckling

A sudden gust of wind, the momentary glimpse of a dark shape flying past me. Surely the witch hadn't come back for another session?

Thank heavens not. Sitting across from me – if sitting is something birds do – was a large white bird. It was hard to know what kind of bird because he was so hunched up. Wings tucked hard into his body, head bowed, and beak almost touching his chest. Total misery, dejection, and despondency emanated from every feather. He lifted his head slightly, just enough to meet my gaze. Beautiful dark eyes, equally beautiful melodious voice.

'I need you to help me end it all. I can't go on anymore.'

Good grief. I had not expected that opener. Then I remembered what we'd been taught about clients who seem utterly despondent. When they volunteer suicidal thoughts there's still a chance they're holding onto a modicum of hope. There's still some part of them somewhere that wants to believe it might be worth going on living after all. Sometimes – not always, but sometimes – they're making a last-ditch appeal for help to rediscover reasons for living. But I also remembered that the therapist must begin by accepting their request to talk about death, never, ever, disregarding it simply because the idea of suicide makes therapists just as uncomfortable as it does everyone else.

'Some really bad things must have happened to make you feel that way. I am so sorry.'

He sighed. 'Too many bad things. More than I can tolerate any longer – more than anyone could tolerate I expect. I've had enough.'

'Did you... make this decision recently?'

'Oh no. I've already tried to die, three times now. Failed every time. I even managed to fail at that.' A large tear gathered, dropping onto the desk. 'Just like everything else I try, I even failed at that.'

My heart sank as I remembered again; previous suicidal gestures increase the likelihood of future attempts. But still, he was here, and he did want to talk. I so hoped I could help. There was something so likeable about him.

'I'm really sorry. It sounds like you've been suffering for a very long time. Maybe if you tell me a bit about what's... what happened that has caused you to feel so... hopeless?'

'Hopeless *and* incompetent. Don't forget the incompetent part. It should be so easy to end it all, yet I've completely failed three times.

'First a wolf refused to finish me off because I was too hideous even to look at. Then I set myself up to freeze to death, and wouldn't you know it, someone rescued me.' I clocked that. Not everyone has been cruel to him. 'Then I lay down by the pond to try freezing again – and wouldn't you know, spring came along and everything warmed up.' He looked at me steadily with those beautiful dark eyes. 'So I've come here. You must have worked with those who... were successful. How did they manage?'

Was that last comment intended as a compliment? It really didn't sound like one. But this wasn't about me, I reminded myself sternly. Stop looking for applause and see if you can shift him away from the subject of death. Helen, you need to try to help him discover some reasons to embrace living – but without disabusing him of the idea that you are listening in acceptance, trying to see his point of view.

'Before we think about... endings... it would help me to understand you a bit better, to know why you've come to... think this way.' I saw he was beginning to doubt me. I needed to do some repair work quickly. 'What I mean is, if I can understand exactly what went wrong before, we can think of ways... to avoid those mistakes in future.'

That was pretty weak, but it seemed to restore his confidence. Thank heavens.

'Yes, you're right. That's important. Do you want... the *whole* story?'

'I really would. It would mean the suggestions I can come up with would be... more likely to work.' That was true. It was best he didn't know how differently we might interpret that statement.

'Very well. I shall start at the beginning.' He settled into the chair, looked comfortable for the first time. Clearly, he was delighted to have an interested audience. Poor lonely thing.

'I have six siblings, four sisters and two brothers. Mother told me they hatched first, long before me. She told me she had to wait many more days before I finally hatched.' He paused, reflecting. 'I couldn't even get *that* right. Couldn't even hatch without causing my poor mother extra effort.' Another large tear forming as he huddled back down on himself miserably.

Oh dear. Back to his place of safety as a hopeless case. I decided to take a chance.

'Your mother told you how much trouble you were, then?'

It worked. 'Oh no! She told me I was well worth waiting for! She said I must have been last for a reason.' Then, as if suddenly remembering, 'She said... I was the most handsome.'

A long-buried memory, a positive one. I let it settle.

'The day after I hatched, Mother said now we were all present, she'd like to take us to the duck pond, to make sure we could all swim well.'

'And did you – all swim well?'

His reply slipped out before he could stop himself. 'Yes, we all swam well, but Mother said I swam the most beautifully! She said I was the best swimmer of all!'

Not everyone had denigrated him then. I let this realisation sink in. Remarking on it might feel pushy. After a moment, 'What did you all do once you... passed your swimming test?'

He laughed at that. Glorious to hear him laugh. What a beautiful voice!

'Mother said she'd like to introduce us to everyone in the duck yard, because she was so proud of her new brood.'

He was smiling now and sitting up taller. He really was beautiful.

'And what happened in the duck yard?'

The smile faded abruptly. 'That's when things started to go... very badly for me. Mother introduced us to the oldest duck. When she saw me, she told Mother she should hatch me over again because I'd turned out so badly. And then a young duck from another family came up and bit me on the back of my neck.'

What had they seen? What was so wrong with him? Okay, he didn't look like a normal duck – but better in many respects. More elegant, more regal. 'That was completely unwarranted! You didn't deserve such treatment!'

'No! And Mother knew it. She flew to my defence. She chased away the drake who bit me, and she told the old duck I'd be handsome when I grew up – and that I could swim better than anyone.' He was glowing with pride, and I hadn't even had to prompt these positive memories. There *was* hope. 'Sounds like your mother really loved you.'

'Oh, she did. She did.'

Hold your tongue, Helen. Give him time.

He was sort of smiling now, lost in memories. But then his face darkened again. 'But even though the rest of that day was uneventful, things got worse over the next few days. It seemed like every time someone bit me or shoved me, it encouraged the others to do even more of it. Even my brothers and sisters turned against me. But... but... it was when my mother said she wished I was far away. That's when it was too awful to bear.'

I thought about his poor mother, how she must now regret

that throw-away remark! She probably didn't even mean it. Probably it just came out when she was overwhelmed with the effort of trying to protect her son. But my job was not to help his mother, or to excuse her

'I am just so sorry to hear this. What did you do when... when it became... when it started to feel like it was all too much?'

'I just ran away. I ran to the edge of the duck yard. Faced with a high hedge I took wing and flew over, away from the taunts. I kept going until nearly nightfall, when I reached a great marsh. There were so many reeds to hide in there! I fell asleep at once, not caring what would become of me.

'In the morning I woke to find there were a number of wild ducks living there. I feared they, too, would laugh at me and hurt me. But they did not.'

More friends then. But keep quiet, Helen. He's beginning to notice these moments himself, to adjust his picture of his past. Don't step in and rob him of the pleasure of noticing the positive moments himself.

As if to reinforce my observation, 'They were actually kind, accepting, those birds. And for two days no one challenged me at all. Not once. Two lovely days!

'Then some other birds flew in to visit the marsh. Judging from what I remembered in the duck yard, I think they were geese. Young males, like me. They began to tease me, but...'

Here he regarded me with dawning respect. 'Why? I didn't deserve it.' He was rethinking his history entirely by himself. I was only a listener. He was turning away from despair already. It was so heartening.

'Their teasing was gentle, not unkind. And they invited me to join them when they decided to go, for they were planning to meet some young lady geese. They said surely, I would be a success with the ladies.

'How I wish that had happened! Perhaps one of the ladies would have... would have found me acceptable. But it was not to be. They told me they would lead, fly first up out of the marshes, and then signal for me to follow.

'But no sooner had they signalled, even before I could run far enough to lift into the air, I heard something I can only describe as a thunderclap. Loud and sharp. One, then another. And my new friends dropped at once out of the sky. Fell into the water. They didn't move, and their blood… it was everywhere in that water.

'I stayed where I was in the reeds, frozen with fear. That's when the wolves, or dogs, or whatever they were, arrived. Howling, they jumped into the water and picked up those poor dead creatures, their jaws slavering. It was just too horrible!

'Except one of them. One of those creatures must have smelled me, for he turned away from the water's edge and ran into the reeds. Found me, and stood directly in front of me, jaws dripping in his eagerness for raw meat, still alive.'

He was shivering with the memory, poor creature. I needed to try to soften that memory, take his mind off the slavering mouth. 'Did you say you thought they were wolves? What did they look like?'

'Brown and white. Long ears. Short hair. Fearsome teeth. Glittering eyes.'

These were hounds, not wolves. But it didn't matter for our purposes. I leaned forward. 'Then what happened?'

'I decided in that instant that I no longer cared to live. If life was this cruel, what reason could there be to exist for even one moment longer? So, I simply bowed my head and waited for his teeth to crush my neck. 'But then… he turned suddenly and ran back to his companions.' Copious tears now. 'You see, surely you understand now! I am so hideous that even a hungry wolf does not see fit to eat me.'

I doubted that. I was sure now the creature sitting opposite wasn't a duck or a goose. The dog had recognised that as well, and knew he wasn't meant to bring this bird – whatever it was – back to his masters. What on earth is he? But he was continuing his sorry tale, and I needed to listen.

'I lay there all night, well into the morning, until I was sure the dogs and the thunder were gone. Then I began to run, run away, faster and faster, running and flying in turns, until I came upon an abandoned farm. The door was half open, the top hinge gone. I ran inside.

'I found I was wrong. It wasn't abandoned. Inside there were three very old creatures, a human, a hen and a cat. I recognised their sort from my time in the duck yard.'

'And were they... surprised to see you?'

'I am not sure. I do not think so. The old woman could not see well, I don't think. She was... she seemed delighted I was there.'

Another kindly encounter. 'What a stroke of good fortune! What happened next? I am so pleased to hear about this, after all you had endured.'

'Yes. Yes, you are right. I was lucky.' He wasn't sure whether to allow himself to admit to this. 'Yes. The woman said she was so glad to see me, because surely I would lay some lovely duck eggs. She could not see my gender to be sure!' For the second time, that lovely laugh. 'And the cat purred. And the hen... spoke, encouraging me to lay eggs for the old woman.

'But of course, I did not. I could not. What an idea!'

We sat in silence for a few moments. I knew he needed time, both to let go of the bloody scene in the marsh, and to accept the idea that someone – several creatures in fact – had been kind to him.

'I stayed with them for some weeks. The old woman kept asking for eggs, but she fed me even though I gave her nothing in return. 'But then, slowly, but every day more so, I began to long for water, to swim again.' He'd been looking far into the distance, but now turned his gaze on me. 'Do you know how lovely, how perfect, is the feeling of gliding through the water? There is no feeling so wonderful, I can assure you.'

I found it easy to agree. I used to love swimming, and realised at that moment how much I missed it.

'I tried to explain how I needed to feel the water beneath me, but they – the cat especially – did not understand. Why was I not grateful for shelter and good food? They kept asking, was that not enough?

'At last the longing became so strong that I had to leave.'

'Even though they were so kind?' I had to remind him gently about this, yet another instance of goodness in his life.

'Even despite their kindness. Yes, that is true. But I had to find water, I had to. So I left. I flew away from the cottage, but I did not wish to return to the marsh.' A shiver. 'I could never return there.'

'Of course not. No one would blame you for that!'

'At last, I came upon a lake. Remote, beautiful.'

This was great. He was picking out the positives in his narrative much more often now.

'I decided to make it my home. For many days I swam and ate and slept as I liked. 'Then one day, as autumn was coming to a close, a flock of the most beautiful birds I had ever seen came to share the water.' His eyes sparkled and he smiled. He was so, so beautiful. 'They were dazzling white, with long supple necks, and they uttered the most wondrous sounds. I felt I was dreaming, that I was enjoying the best dream I could ever have.'

'They didn't chase you away?'

'No, no, not at all. They invited me to join them, and we swam together as if... as if... we belonged together.' He snapped his attention back to me. 'But of course, that would be impossible! They were so beautiful! And me? Well, just take a look.'

Tears again as he continued. 'I was in a happy daze all that day, all that night. The happiest I have ever been.

'But the next morning, without a word, with but a nod of their beautiful heads, they rose as one and flew away. I was alone again.' Beseechingly. 'But more alone, oh so much more alone, than ever before! It was much worse then, to know the best and watch it disappear.

'And that was when I decided. Decided there was no point living any longer, not if I had to live without those... those perfectly formed creatures. It would be better to die. At least I would know I had seen perfection before I died. 'So I resolved to stay in the water as winter overtook me. That way I would freeze. There in the water, where we had spent time together. It took such a long time. Each day as the ice grew and thickened across the lake, the circle where I could still swim became smaller. And I grew wearier. Until at long last, blessedly, I suppose I just fell asleep, the ice encircling my feet.'

Oh boy. He did mean it that time.

'But you survived.'

'Yes, but not by choice. One day, I can only think the farmer spotted my body in the lake and took me home with him, because I woke up in a warm cottage. This time there were no old creatures. Just the farmer, his wife, and two young children. His wife must have warmed me slowly, carefully, and offered me grain and milk, before I could remember, for when I woke I was feeling strong and restored.'

'What kind people!' I wanted to reinforce their goodness and his luck.

'Yes, to be sure. But then, as usual... I ruined everything.' I remained silent, so he continued.

'I suppose I was startled when first I woke. I can't remember now. But my instinct was to fly away. My wings were far bigger than I had remembered – how I must have grown.' I noted with delight that he did not call himself 'clumsy' – or anything else negative for that matter. Just more mature. Another small victory.

'As a result, I misjudged my flight. I knocked over their milk churn, upended the butter trough and the flour barrel. I made a thorough mess in their tidy cottage. So ashamed, so horrified was I that I flew directly out of the cottage – by then I could gauge my wingspan – and determined to fly as far away as possible, so as to trouble them no more.

'I flew – it was so much easier to fly now. I was so much stronger somehow. I flew until I spied another lake, and slowly circled, then settled down beside it. I had determined to freeze, but this time I would remain undiscovered.

'But there was no ice. Spring had arrived. I was too late.'

'And so, you came here?' But I had been too hasty.

'Oh no. There is one more event to tell you. One more... was it a failure? I'm not sure now.'

Excellent! He was questioning himself.

'I was thinking how to find another way to die when I heard...' he paused, transfixed by the memory. 'When I heard those wondrous calls once more, the sounds those perfect birds made when we met at the lake.

'I was sure I must be in a dream, that I had died already. But no. Three of those... perfect creatures such as I had seen last autumn had come into the grounds, as if this place belonged to them. I realised then it must be their home, and that I was an intruder.

'I thought – I remember exactly – I so wanted them to kill me, for I had invaded their tranquil home. Oh, to be pecked to death by such glorious, royal creatures! It would be an end better than I deserved!'

I was leaning so far forward that once again I'd nearly fallen off my chair. Definitely not the cool, objective therapist I was supposed to be. I moved back as unobtrusively as I could. 'And then what happened?'

'They appeared to accept me! To welcome me! An ugly, worthless creature such as I! In their graciousness and majesty, they chose to accept me!'

I was lost. 'But that sounds perfect! Did you not stay? They invited you, didn't they?'

'Stay? I? An abomination such as I? How dare I, all fuzz and no feathers, grey, with short stumpy wings... how could I accept their generosity? I would but detract from their... exquisite beauty! That's why I've come to you. Save them from me, please!'

My first reaction was utter astonishment. Grey? Fuzzy? Who was he talking about? I couldn't see much of him, but what I saw was definitely neither grey nor fuzzy. Had he never looked at himself?

'Please, could you excuse me for a moment? I need to get something from the other room.'

He nodded, no doubt assuming I was planning to gather the items that would help him end his life.

I hurried into the loo, and in my tremendous excitement I quite literally ripped the face mirror above the basin right off its hinges, leaving an ugly hole in the wall. Later I would marvel at this show of strength. But just then I couldn't get back to him fast enough. 'Here!' thrusting the mirror in front of him. He glanced at me quizzically. How was this an instrument of death?

Impatiently, eagerly, not remotely professionally, 'This is a looking glass. You have looking glasses in... in your world, I know you do.' I was sure about that – I'd remembered the huntsman telling me how the Queen had carried her looking glass with her wherever she went. But then I realised my absurdity. How ridiculous to think a bird would know about looking glasses!

'This, this is called a looking glass, because you can look into it and see... yourself. It's just like looking at the surface of the water on a sunny day, when everything is reflected and repeated in its surface.'

He regarded me sadly. 'That was something I never dared to do, not after that first time I looked in the water, when I saw how very hideous I am. I vowed then I would never again look at myself.'

'Oh, but please! *Please!* Look now! Just one glance! Please!'

He sighed heavily. 'You are cruel. I thought you would be kind. You wish that, just before I die, I should reflect on my hideous visage?'

'Please just *look!'* This was so out of line. But I was too excited, too eager to watch him discover himself. Professional conduct had gone out through that magic window behind me.

Another tear slid down his beak as he regarded me sadly. A big sigh. Then he picked up the mirror and held it to his face.

Silence. For how long I don't know. Then tentatively he lifted one wing. How huge it was, how white the feathers! He moved it experimentally in the glass, watched the image faithfully repeat his actions. Beginning to believe. Next, the other wing. Then slowly he lifted his head. How had I overlooked that long, oh so elegant neck?

He looked up, joy dawning. Standing, shaking his magnificent wings back and forth. 'I am... I am just like them!'

'You, too, are a swan. And you are... incredible!'

He nodded agreement.

'I must go.'

'To join your friends.'

'My friends. Yes. I must go now, to join my friends. Farewell, and thank you.'

He rose up, and how he managed to fit through that window I'll never know. But he did. Gone, without a whisper of a sound, gliding proudly into the night.

The Emperor's New Clothes

For once I forgot it was Tuesday. I was deeply engrossed in an article extolling a new treatment to help patients suffering from delusions when a shape sailed past, sending my papers flying. The creature, whatever it was, seemed to be entirely uniform in colour, a very pale brown. It landed – a man, I could see now – with a thump just short of the basin on the far wall. He stood up, gesturing or moving his arms about in the oddest way, rather as if adjusting a cape or loose jacket.

But he wore neither cape nor jacket. He wore, to be exact, absolutely nothing. He was entirely naked except for a crown sitting askew atop his curly brown locks. Was this some sort of deranged king? Or a deranged person who thinks he's a king?

After another moment of adjusting the air around him he raised his chin proudly, and asked with incongruous decorum where he might sit down. I pointed to the client chair opposite. 'Just there would be perfect.'

Oh boy was this going to be interesting! I reminded myself rather regretfully, however, that psychotherapy was futile when someone was fully psychotic. Medication was necessary first to tame the hallucinations and/ or delusions – just as I'd been reading moments before. Watching him adjusting what I can only assume he – and he alone – believed were articles of clothing left me in no doubt. He had to be delusional.

'I've come to ask you how I can bring my son back to his senses.'

Ah, projection. He was placing the mantle of madness on his son. Interesting.

'He... he's seeing what is not. Oh, and it is so terrible!' And he began to sob. I handed him a tissue, my automatic reaction. He accepted it gratefully and wiped his streaming eyes and nose. I felt ashamed of myself for my cold and disinterested speculations. He was deeply distressed.

'It is indeed terrible. I am truly sorry for your son... is he a young child?' He had to be. The man couldn't be more than thirty.

'He is soon to celebrate his sixth birthday.' More sobs. 'He is my only child, you see.'

Poor guy. If he was indeed a king – and I couldn't believe anything about this man yet – his son would be important in all sorts of ways, his only child, his only son, and therefore the heir to the throne.

I wanted him to ask him all sorts of questions to determine the nature and extent of his delusion. But I remembered my training; when seeing a new client, it's imperative to start with whatever they consider the problem to be. Never mind what you might think. If you don't, they may not engage fully with you, because they won't believe you're really prepared to listen to them nonjudgmentally, not willing to see the world from their point of view. So instead, I decided on a question that might allow me to offer him some reassurance.

'Did your son's problem come about... suddenly? Or did it start small and you only realised gradually that he has a real problem?' Given the child's age and his father's high anxiety, I figured the problem must have come on suddenly – and if so, the odds for recovery were in the child's favour, relying on the psychological truism that in most cases, the more dramatic and immediate the onset of a mental health problem, the greater is the chance of recovery. That is, if it was the child who had the problem.

'Oh suddenly. Most suddenly. Until this morning he has been perfectly well.' He paused, considering fondly. 'In fact, until this morning he has shown himself to be without doubt the cleverest child in my Kingdom.' Touching fatherly pride.

'You and your Queen must be so proud of him.'

Wrong comment. A fresh torrent of sobs wracked his naked chest. 'My wife died when giving birth.' Looked up, 'That is why he is my only child. I could never love another now.'

Was I dealing with an abnormal grief reaction here? Did the death of his wife catapult him into madness? I'd not heard of such a reaction. And besides, her death occurred over five years ago. Surely by now he would have begun to recover.... Still, it was touching – and unusual, I guessed – that he had remained true to his wife. Surely, as King, he could so easily have remarried!

'You poor man! You have truly suffered. Has there been anyone you could turn to for comfort? Are your parents still alive?'

He shook his head vehemently, and issued forth another torrent of tears. Yet another blunder on my part, that question. I really was not doing very well tonight. After a few moments during which he gradually brought his sobs under control, 'My mother died when I was but fifteen years old.'

'And your father?'

He screwed up his face unpleasantly. 'I do not wish to speak of my father. He went away not long after Mother... died. He knew the rumours and feared the repercussions.'

Good heavens this was complicated. Both important women in his life dead, an absconding father, a disturbed child – if the last was true; I still wasn't sure. In those circumstances, a mental breakdown wasn't so surprising. But I was getting lost in speculation, and such thinking was premature anyway. I needed some sort of timeline, a sense of order to this tale of woe.

'Perhaps, if you can bear it, perhaps you might tell me a bit about your mother, about... what happened to her.' I saw a look of doubt cross his face. He hadn't come here to talk about his mother. I hurried on. 'I mean, if I can understand a bit more about what you've had to endure... even before this... tragedy with your son... then it might help me when we think together about... about how to help him.'

Luckily that appeared to do the trick. He relaxed, began to lean back into the chair – but then as if reminding himself of something, sat back up abruptly, untied what he must have decided was his 'cloak' from around his shoulders and did something with it – I think he tried to drape it over the back of the chair. Satisfied, eyeing me surreptitiously – looking for approval I think – he settled back into the chair and began his tale.

'My mother loved me so much.' Pause, deep breath to push back fresh tears. 'She had given birth to five girls – five *Princesses* – before I came along, much, much later. I am told my father and she were utterly delighted. At last, they had an heir to the throne.' He reflected for a moment. 'I was given everything. Everything I could ever wish for, and more.' Looking directly at me, 'Most important of all to my mother's way of thinking, I was clothed in the most magnificent apparel. Every day, sometimes twice in one day, a servant would come to me with a new garment to try on. He was always instructed to tell my mother what I thought of it, whether I thought it suited me – and if so, I was invited to show her. If not, she ordered the garment to be burned.'

He was far away, remembering. 'I possessed such magnificent clothing. Mother did likewise, and whenever she was pleased with a garment, I was the first to be allowed to see her wearing it. Everyone said the royal household was without compare, that we were the best dressed family in all kingdoms. No one, everyone agreed, could rival our... perfect appearance.'

That must have touched a nerve. I waited as he quelled this new bout of tears. Poor, poor man!

'By the time I was fourteen, all my sisters were married, Princesses and Queens in other lands. I lived in the castle alone with my mother and father. At first, it was wonderful to enjoy their full attention, and to receive so many new outfits and other gifts. Something new and wonderful every day. But after a while I began to sense that things were not right between Mother and my father.

There was growing tension between them that I could not understand. But I could feel it, feel it whenever I was in their presence.' Thinking, choosing his words carefully, 'When I was with Mother, I felt only joy. When both were together I felt like... running away.

'As the months passed, Mother began to spend more time engaged in her toilette – sometimes she would spend the entire morning dressing. And she began more and more often to request my presence. I would watch as her maids dressed her in the most fabulous gowns of silk and satin. So many petticoats! And her stays, she demanded such tight lacings – sometimes she would grow faint and I would fear for her health. But beauty, she would remind me, was everything. One must appear perfect.'

Was this appropriate? I wondered. For a teenage boy to sit in attendance as his mother was dressed?

'And her paint took nearly an hour, the white, the rouge, reddening her lips with vinegar... and of course at least one mouche...'

Sounded like torture to me, but he clearly didn't think so. It was obvious by his dreamy expression these mornings were pure joy. Not for me to judge... at least not at this point.

'And finally, every morning, her hair. Glorious! The maid piled her hair high over the toque, added feathers, ribbons and pearls – Mother demanded more and more jewels and ribbons with each passing day. And more paint, tighter stays...'

Abruptly leaving his reverie to address me, 'But I began to see that despite all these... outer decorations, she was not happy. It became obvious that no amount of jewels or silks could satisfy her, that nothing could stop her doubting her appearance. Many times, so many times each morning, she would ask me if I thought she was beautiful. Did I detect even the tiniest flaw, even one hair misplaced? I must be truthful, she would say, and if I noticed anything that was not perfect, I was to tell her at once.'

It was easy now to conclude he had an obsession with appearance.

'Then one day, after I was at last dressed to her satisfaction, and she was at last satisfied with her own appearance and had given me leave to amuse myself elsewhere, I decided to take a long walk to stretch my legs. On my return I wandered through the palace gardens, and as I passed beneath my father's chamber window, I heard him laughing.' He glowered. 'It was not pleasant laughter, and for some reason I felt compelled to stop and listen. Then I heard Mother. She was crying, even as he laughed. "You are old, my dear. Old! Your preparations are all in vain! Anyone can see the lines on your face. Paint cannot hide your age, nor your growing imperfections! And your figure! How sad you no longer have pleasing curves!" And he kept laughing. I hurried past, unable to bear anything more.'

I suddenly realised I had completely forgotten that the man sitting across from me was naked, nor did I any longer think him mad. Just desperately, desperately unhappy. I felt so sorry for him. I waited while he prepared himself to continue. Clearly, worse was to come.

'The next morning I knocked on Mother's bedchamber door – she always requested that I wake her each morning. But no matter how loudly I knocked, she did not answer. When I could knock no louder, when even my greetings went unanswered, I... I pushed wide the door.'

How I felt for him! This was clearly a terrible memory. Why had I asked him to tell me this story?

'Mother was in her bed, lying on her back, her eyes wide open. Pale, oh so pale...' He looked up at me, as if pleading for me to erase this memory. How I wished I could! 'I found the vial of poison, on the floor where she must have dropped it. The glass on her table was empty. I'm afraid... I'm afraid I was overcome. I ran from the chamber, to my own quarters, to be alone. I had to be alone.'

There was nothing I could possibly say, so we sat in silence, for how long I'm not sure. At last he looked up again, 'The servant who found the vial reported it to the marshal at once because he, like everyone after him who heard the news, could not believe Mother would have administered the poison herself. It must have been murder, everyone said.'

Again he appealed to me silently to reassure him. What could I say that could help? 'But I knew. I knew.' His face hardened again. 'Word was round before Father heard it. And because it was well known, I learned later, that Father had a new mistress, and that everyone knew he openly despised Mother, well... Father feared suspicion would be cast on him. He declared an urgent need to travel – "a business affair," he said.'

I couldn't help myself. 'He never returned?'

He was relieved I had guessed what he was about to tell me, so he didn't have to say anything more about his father. Nod.

'After the funeral I was made Regent, and after three months I was crowned King.'

'How old were you?'

'Seventeen years and two months.'

He was silent now. Waiting for me to direct him? I was hesitant to say anything more, because without intending to, I had caused him so much pain already. I didn't want to risk more suffering.

'You were incredibly strong, and brave, to answer my question about your mother so fully and so honestly. Thank you for your courage.'

He looked grateful. And definitely not deranged. Just weary.

'I think it is more than your turn to choose what to tell me next, what you think will help me understand best your... your son's problem. It is more than fitting you choose what we talk about next.'

He looked across the desk, still overwhelmed with sadness. 'You have drawn much that matters to me from my past.' He looked up, appealing to me to approve his reply. He really did rely on others for reassurance and direction. As if reading my thoughts, 'Surely now you understand me better? Why I value perfection, why I so wish to please others with my appearance? It's because of Mother. Because I wish always to honour my mother.'

I nodded. I did understand that much. What really baffled me, more than ever now, was why he was sitting across from me stark naked.

'Jean's mother – my boy is called Jean – was a kind, quiet woman, the daughter of a nobleman. A fitting Queen. She was with child soon after we married. But she was not strong.'

We shared the silence as he drew himself together. Then, 'She died on giving birth to Jean.' Tears as he remembered, but less of them. I sensed he felt this loss far less than that of his mother. 'Oh, but she did see her son before she died. And the nurse told me she smiled upon seeing him.

'But Jean... Jean never knew his mother.' Reflecting on his own childhood, 'I cannot imagine such a tragedy, not to know one's mother. But Jean has been well looked after, always given the best. He was nursed by a wet nurse, and the servant maids – all of them had loved my gentle Queen – they all care for him well. I, too, spend time with my son every day.' He paused, reflecting. 'He has grown quickly and is strong and beautiful.' Again, that silent appeal for my approval. 'And he is all I have.

'When he was four I thought it time to commence his education. I found him the best governess in the Kingdom. He loves his lessons. He is curious about everything. Everyone remarks how clever he is.' Shook his head, bowed it. 'That is why I cannot understand... cannot believe... what he said this morning.'

'Go on, please. What did he say?'

'He said...' He paused. Was he unsure whether to go on? Afraid to repeat his son's words? I couldn't guess what was holding him back, so I just waited.

'He said... when I showed him my new garments, that he couldn't see them!' He waved his hands around and picked at his arms and neck as if holding up something. He laughed. Actually *laughed* at me! At his own father! He told me he could not see these... these most magnificent garments!'

I don't think I've ever had to work harder to keep a straight face. Here we were at last. He *was* delusional after all.

But evidently I didn't manage to hide my reaction completely. I caught his look – horror? Relief? Suspicion? I couldn't tell.

'*Surely* you can appreciate these rich robes? Oh please! Do not tell me you cannot!' He was like a child himself now, begging for reassurance. I was beginning to wonder if I was right about the delusions. Could it be he didn't believe them himself?

Carefully, 'Each person sees things differently. Neither your son nor I will see... what you see... exactly as you do.'

'Oh but you *must!* You *must!* If you do not, I will know you are either unfit for your position, or inexcusably stupid!' He was bouncing in the chair in his desperate insistence. He really did look ridiculous. But because what he'd just said was so preposterous, I didn't even take offence.

'Whoever told you that?'

'Charles and Albert of course!'

'Whoa! Can you hold on just a minute, and please explain to me who are Charles and Albert?'

Astonished, 'You have not heard of Charles and Albert?' He took a deep breath, then, 'Oh, of course! How could you know them? You do not dwell in our time. Let me explain. Charles and Albert are the finest weavers in my Kingdom, probably the finest weavers who have ever lived. I am a most fortunate man, for they sought me out. They told me they had heard I have incomparably good taste. They offered to weave a magical garment, the most exquisite garment ever woven, just for me.' Pleading for reassurance again, 'They had heard of my reputation, you see, of my love of the most beautiful clothing, and they sought me out.'

I'll bet they did. They'd also probably heard of his gullibility. Sounded like a couple of swindlers to me. 'And when did they... find you?'

'Early this season. Seven weeks and two days past they arrived at my gates.'

He was calmer now, thank heavens.

'And they offered...?'

'To weave the loveliest cloth imaginable for me. They informed me that if I paid them enough, not only would the colours and patterns be extraordinarily beautiful, but the garments would possess a magical quality. They said it would be invisible to any person who is unfit for his position, or inexcusably stupid.'

I couldn't help admiring these guys. This was brilliant. No one would dare admit they couldn't see the cloth – s unless they really had nothing at all to lose, or only if they valued truth above everything else. Not many like that around.

'Of course I was delighted. Clothing that was not only beautiful, but that had magical properties as well! I paid them what they asked... it was a lot... and they set to work.' There was that appeal again, for me to approve of his decision. I nodded encouragingly.

'How fascinating! I've never heard of magical garments. Do go on.'

'I had hoped the garments would be ready for our great procession, a festival we hold every year. But as the days wore on, I began to wonder if the garments would be ready on time. In my impatience, I sent my most trusted minister to observe their progress.'

'Very wise. And what did he report?'

'He said the cloth was most charming. And he described the patterns and colours to me in detail.' Plea for reassurance. 'He is a clever man indeed.

'But Charles and Albert continued to demand more silk and gold for the weaving. I always paid, but the cost was becoming so high... and we were then only a week away from the great procession. So, I sent another of my trusted officials to observe their progress, and ask if the garments would be ready for me to wear on this most important day. My official returned to tell me of their progress, extolling the wonders of the patterns and colours on the loom.'

He paused here, doubting something, unsure. But the need to justify his actions won out. He continued, 'He also told me Charles and Albert demanded yet more gold. I could not imagine how costly, how grand their garments must be. I gave my official the sum they had demanded, and in return I requested that they guarantee the garments would be ready for our procession.'

'And when is the great procession?'

'Tomorrow.'

'I see. And... do you think the garments will be ready in time?'

Cautiously, 'They are. I was awakened this morning by an official with the welcome news that the garments were ready for me, and that I was to come along at once for a fitting.'

He seemed surprisingly subdued now, not brimming with excitement as I would have imagined. 'So of course, you went to them straight away?'

'Oh yes. Of course. Without even taking time for my breakfast. I asked that Jean be brought to the dressing rooms as well once I was... fully dressed.' I noticed he glanced down at himself nervously. He seemed confused, even a bit frightened.

'Charles and Albert informed me they had stayed up all night, to ensure every stitch was woven perfectly. They said they were more than pleased with the results, but that my opinion was more important to them than anything.

'They invited me into their workroom, and pointed to the... the garments... which they said were draped across the loom.'

'They *said* they were there? Did you not see them?'

Mistake. That was too strong.

'Of course I saw them! Do you consider me to be unfit for my position or inexcusably stupid?'

'I am so sorry! Please, accept my apologies! Of course you are not stupid. It was just... an unusual way of telling me... what you found in the weaving room.'

He relaxed, but only slightly. 'After I had admired their... exquisite work, they asked me to take off my clothes, and to stand in front of their mirror. Then they handed me each piece of clothing, article by glorious article, allowing me time to put each one on and to admire it in front of the glass.

'They were delighted with how well everything fitted me. They assured me the colours suited my skin perfectly. They were especially proud of the weight of the garments – a special touch, they said they'd worked hard to perfect. The garments, they explained, were so light I would almost feel as though I was wearing nothing at all.'

Geniuses.

'Then my chief chamberlain reminded me, as was my custom, that the time had come to excuse everyone and call in Jean to inspect my new garments.'

How uneasy he looked! 'And that's when it happened. As Jean came in, I bowed low – another little game we play – and asked if he thought the garments were suitable for the great procession tomorrow.

'And that's when the worst happened. He burst into merry laughter. "Father, you aren't wearing anything at all! Not a stitch! Surely you will not lead the procession tomorrow wearing nothing at all!" And he laughed and laughed.

'I did not know what to say, so I bowed again and asked that Jean return to his governess. Then I... oh it was so terrible!'

What was so terrible? What he'd realised about his son – or more likely, about himself? 'And that's when you came here, to see me?'

'Yes, I fled here immediately! What could I conclude from his reaction? This must mean my dear son is either unfit to be heir or inexcusably stupid – and that simply cannot be.' He was shaking his head in disbelief. 'He cannot be unfit...'

I couldn't help myself. 'He cannot be unfit to be what he is? A child?' Then more gently, 'Children tell the truth, do they not? Especially to those they love and wish to keep safe.'

He looked down again at his lap, then slowly stretched out his bare arms and observed them. For a long time. Then he sighed, shook his head, and smiled ruefully. 'Do you perhaps have a piece of cloth or an old garment with which I might... cover myself?'

'Of course. Just one moment.' I was so delighted to see the change in him that I literally ran to the little storage room behind our reception area. I knew Emma kept some spare towels back there, in case we needed them for the guests' toilet. Sure enough, there they were. I grabbed the largest one and hurried back to my office.

It was empty. He was gone.

I returned to my desk, not sure what to think. There on top of my notepad I found a hastily scribbled note:

'Thank you. I can dress once I reach the palace. It is most important that I return to my *clever* son. He has much to teach me.'

Beauty and the Beast

Bending over my notes, I felt the familiar gust of wind, sensed someone walking past me to take a seat in the client's chair opposite. I looked up in happy anticipation. The sight was horrific. So horrific I felt a sudden wave of nausea. What sort of creature was seated across from me?

I swallowed hard, drew in a slow breath through my nose to control the nausea while staring back down at my notes. Writing nothing much, to make it look like I needed to finish what I was doing, to buy some time. Another slow breath, in through the nose, just like I teach it. Hold. Slow exhalation, then look up again.

It was definitely human. Male. He was strongly built, the hands folded on the desk were gnarled, the skin coarse. Tufts of thick hair sprouted about the knuckles. I raised my eyes to meet his, for I could sense he was staring at me intently. 'Take your time. I know my visage must shock and appall you.'

A kindly voice, unsuited to the body. Now that I felt able, I met his gaze. His eyes were small, pale blue, emanating suffering and resignation, but also great wisdom. It wasn't easy to find his eyes – they were set deep into thick nobbly – or was it scaly? – skin. His face was covered with some sort of growths I guessed were warts, with tufts of ungainly hair similar to those on his hands, scattered randomly across his cheeks and chin. His nose was huge. And he drooled, although he tried to control the mess by dabbing the corners of his mouth constantly with a large linen cloth. I had to look away, compose myself again before I dared look back.

On second observation I noted how clean and well-kempt he was. His hair, though coarse and of many dull shades of brown flecked with grey, was well combed and powdered, a black satin bow carefully tied around the wig tail. I could smell lavender. His fingernails, though mottled brown and yellow, were neatly trimmed.

His clothing spoke of great wealth. The outer coat, a dull gold silk with rich embroidery, fitted beautifully across his broad chest. He wore it open, revealing a waistcoat in the same colour and style, the top buttons undone to show off the ruffles around the neckline of his fine linen shirt. The generous shirt sleeves ended in ruffles as well.

'May I remove my coat?' Such a lovely voice.

'Of course. And if you like, you can hang it on one of the hooks on the wall just behind you.'

He nodded politely and stood up, removing the coat with care. As he adjusted it on the hook, I noted the breeches matched the rest of his suit. A ditto suit. His black leather shoes were polished to glowing. He really must be wealthy. With his back to me, it was easier to admire this glorious ensemble and to notice – even admire – the strong well-built body it housed. He'd certainly done his best with... what he had been given. Poor guy. I must try to hold this version of him in my mind, although now as he turned round to return to his chair, he kept his head bowed, as if sparing me the sight of his face.

'Thank you for... bearing to see me, for even just daring to look at me.'

'Of course.' I had no idea what else to say. The silence that followed was comfortable, companionable – as long as I didn't look at his face. I wasn't sure, but I guessed he was trying to work out how to frame what he was about to say. Not just intelligent – thoughtful and reflective as well.

At last, 'I cannot make a decision about... something very important.'

I hoped this was not another contemplated suicide. The duck had really drained me. Try something neutral, Helen. 'It's often the case that the more important a decision, the harder it is to decide how to communicate it clearly.'

He nodded, approving. 'It's about... whether or not... to let her go.'

Was he planning to fire an employee? I didn't know they hired and fired people in those days. I thought you 'served'. 'Has she... done something that's offended you?'

'Oh no! Oh, not at all! That's why it's so difficult. If I let her go back home, as she wishes, I so fear she will never wish to return. And that would be... unbearable.'

I was having real difficulty trying to understand the situation. 'Has she... always lived with you? Or did she just come for a visit? And perhaps you might let me know who 'she' is?'

At this he laughed, at first hesitantly, then when he saw I didn't seem to mind, with more abandon. It was a low, pleasant laugh, but unfortunately it caused him to spew slobber everywhere. He stopped abruptly and started mopping furiously. 'Oh, I am so sorry!'

'Don't worry. But let me get you a... towel.' I crossed the room to my basin and handed him the towel on the ring beside it. He accepted it gratefully – his own cloth was fairly sodden.

"Bella came to my palace of her own free will. That was the condition I laid upon her father. But now she wishes to visit him.' He shook his head sorrowfully. 'If I let her go, why would she wish to come back to me?' Looking down, 'To this?' Then, as if chastising himself silently for showing self-pity, 'They are, you see, the only two visitors I have had in over one hundred years.'

'What? In a hundred years? How can...? But you don't look that old!' Now I really was lost.

Such sadness in his eyes. 'Ah, that is part of the curse. I was not granted the privilege of growing old so I might gain release by dying.'

'You know what? I think we need to back up. To back up

quite a long way. It really would help me... help us work together, if I can be privy to the whole picture. You say you've been cursed.' That might explain his appearance. 'By whom? Why?' Then catching myself, quelling my eagerness. 'I mean, would the curse be a good place for us to start?'

He was thinking, considering possibilities, weighing up. Such a deliberate, thoughtful way of approaching things! His manner made him so likeable...if I could just block out the outer appearance. He started to look up to reply, but then thought better of it. Keeping his head bowed, 'I will start before the curse. You need to understand... why it came about.'

'Okay. I'm here, and I'm listening.' I settled back. Why did I feel so comfortable with this creature?

'My parents were the Count and Countess of Henneberg, Augustus and Sophia. I was their only child, Heinrich. 'We enjoyed great wealth. A beautiful castle. Generous grounds, immaculate gardens, stables. And... we were beautiful. We possessed... a terrible beauty.'

'That's an unusual way to describe beauty. Can you explain why you chose that particular word?' He was too careful. It couldn't have been an accident.

He forgot his appearance for a moment and looked up gratefully, acknowledging an equal. I felt absurdly flattered. Watch it, Helen. Stay objective and keep your own needs out of this.

'Terrible because we abused our... power, and our privilege. I've come to see that over these years of... living alone. Whatever we wanted we took, whether it be treasures, human freedom, or...' He lowered his head still further, 'human dignity. Father sent his armies to kill, to plunder. At home, I watched my parents beat the servants – or inflict even worse punishments – regularly, if they made even the slightest mistake.'

Forgetting again, looking up with eyes so full of sorrow and regret, 'And I? I was perhaps the cruellest. When I wanted a wench, I took her. Watched her cower, submit... then enjoyed – actually enjoyed – casting her away, bleeding and bruised.' He had to stop for the tears and the slobber. Then reflecting again, 'I have thought back so often to those times. I regarded myself so highly. But now I see I wasn't happy, merely consumed... consumed by a desire to dominate, to inspire fear, a desire that only increased whenever I tried to satisfy it.'

So far I couldn't imagine what I was going to be able to offer. He'd figured out so many things already.

'So, you will not be surprised when you hear about the peddler.'

Wrong. I was surprised. I waited.

'One day – a cloudless summer day it was – an old peddler entered our courtyard, just at the moment when Mother, Father and I were berating the Lord Chamberlain about some small failing.'

Looking up, gratified to see I was so engrossed in his tale I did not flinch, 'I think now it was a matter of no coincidence. The peddler wished to see our cruelty directly. He knew when to arrive.'

What an odd remark.

'After Father took his time to... kick the Lord Chamberlain to his knees, he turned to the peddler. Demanded he show us his wares... adding they had better please him or... and he nodded, sneering, towards the fallen servant.

'The peddler bowed low, opened his knapsack, and... oh such beautiful cloth Such lovely silver! We were dazzled!

'But Father...' Shaking his head. 'Father snatched the skein of cloth the peddler held up and handed it to me. "I'll thank you for that!" he said haughtily. Then nodding towards the wretched Lord Chamberlain again, "Now go! Unless you wish to invite me to turn my anger on you."'

He closed his eyes, took a deep breath. 'I remember so well the next moment. The peddler nodded and turned away, began to walk back towards the gate. But then, he stopped. Turned back.

'Even the birds stopped singing in that moment. When he turned round... he was no longer a peddler. A sorcerer in carmine robes, white hair and beard caught in the breeze, his staff now a wand full of light as if on fire.

'"Ah, Count, such a mistake you have made!"'

'That was all he said. I remember him raising his wand. Then... darkness.

'I awoke because the birds had begun to sing again. I saw the servants, crowded together, a frightened distance away, staring, staring. I tried to stand, but my legs... I could but limp, my legs, my arms, so misshapen, so twisted.'

But he didn't limp now. And his arms as well as his legs were powerful, strong. How he must have worked so hard to overcome any aspect of his deformity he could change.

'Mother and Father... I would never had recognised them except for their clothing. They had become... monsters.' Tears, drool, lowering his eyes. 'And I knew then, as had I.

'I heard the sorcerer laughing, far away. "You shall appear now and forever as you truly are. Farewell, beasts!"'

I couldn't help myself. 'I am so truly sorry.'

He ignored me, shaking his head. 'We well deserved the curse. I know that now.

'Mother and Father? What became of them I would never know, for in my shameful condition I only wished escape. So I walked away – no, I crawled away. It took me many days to learn to walk again in my... new form. But I was determined to get away. I crept, steadily growing stronger, deep into the forest. I ate berries, roots. They were easy to find and gather, for all creatures fled before me as soon as they saw my face.

'Then one day, how long after the curse I cannot say, I chanced upon a clearing with a wide path leading down a gentle slope. I knew... somehow I knew... it was intended that I should follow that path. At its end I found an abandoned cottage, and I knew again – although I cannot say how – that this was to be my home.'

'You sound as if you were learning to listen... more deeply. To ignore greed and power... to listen from where perhaps your purpose lies?' It was a wild guess, but he was describing a most profound inner change.

Those eyes again, regarding me with humility and respect. Be grateful that you guessed well, but not flattered, Helen. You're here for him, not to score points.

'I thank you. But it was not by myself alone. I had help.' He watched me carefully. Did he dare go on? Would I abandon my high opinion and think him mad? 'Although I have not seen him in my waking life since the cursed, the peddler – the sorcerer – has visited often in my dreams. And each time he does so, I wake to... another change.' Still watching me warily, 'I believe he took... an interest in me when I left my parents. I have come to believe he helps me whenever he sees me trying... to make amends. To learn to live differently.'

'That makes sense to me. Wouldn't you do the same for someone else, if you could?'

He made an odd noise in response. A sob? A moan?

'Thank you. You believe me.'

We sat quietly, comfortably. Then, 'Tell me about the changes the sorcerer has made for you.'

A lovely smile. And I was getting used to the drool. It no longer bothered me now – well, not much. 'If I made a simple chair, I would wake to find it intricately carved, the seat and back covered in damask or clothed in silk. Everything I planted in the garden flourished. And... rare plants would appear alongside the ones I'd planted. New rooms were sometimes added to the cottage. Now, I live in the most wonderful manse, with gardens filled with rare and fragrant plants and trees, where birds sing and something new blossoms every day.

'I need no longer prepare meals, for they appear, most beautifully presented, elegant viands, every day as if by... by magic. With no need for cleaning or cooking, my time is my own. I spend it caring for my beloved plants – especially my roses, which I love above all – and feeding the many birds who have chosen my garden as their home.' He paused, scrutinised me. 'I should be happy, should I not?'

Stop. Think. What is he asking really?

'Of the many lessons you have learned in your... time alone... which speaks most loudly to you?'

No hesitation. 'That joy is found by looking to others first. That by encouraging others to flourish – be they plants, beasts or humans – by discovering what brings them health and the chance to thrive... that's what brings true happiness.'

'Well spoken. But how did you discover this if you were... alone?'

He was so animated now! 'The creatures in my garden

taught me! No, the plants were my first teachers. Tending the plants, watching my roses bloom, unfurl, drink the rain and seek the light. And the birds. Especially the birds. Caring for the birds, who thanked me with their song. Sometimes... I forgot how lonely it was there.' He was far away now, reliving the moment he was about to share.

'Then one cold winter night – one hundred years since I had stumbled upon that small abandoned cottage – I heard someone approaching along the path I had taken so long ago.' Clarifying for my sake, 'The path is now a wide road, lit by many lamps and lined with tall beech trees. I can see anyone who tries to approach, although no one ever does. Until this man came along. In one hundred years he was the first.

'He was an old man, a merchant I guessed by the trunk he dragged behind him. Weary and oh so cold he was, plodding in the snow, his horse equally spent, trudging down the path, drawn as if in a trance to the lights of my home. Upon seeing the manor house he dismounted and fell to his knees in gratitude, for he was in sore need of shelter.' He smiled and regarded me. 'But he was afraid, unlike his sensible steed. As soon as he had dismounted, the horse turned and fled to my barn, where warm mash, water and soft straw awaited.

'But though I had opened the door, the merchant hesitated to enter. He waited the longest time – hoping I think to encounter the owner of the manse, or one of the servants. But of course no one came.' The reminder of his appearance brought him back to the room with me, self-conscious and ashamed. 'As I looked down at him, I decided I could not frighten him with my appearance.

'After some time, hunger and the cold overwhelmed him, and at last he stepped inside.

'I had imagined food and wine, a table laid for one, and of course as usual it had appeared. And a clean nightdress, and a soft bed. At first cautiously, then with increasing joy and vigour as the life flowed back to him, he ate, drank, then finally he slept.

'He did not awake until near midday. Laid out on the chair beside his bed he spied a handsome new suit of clothes. I cannot begin to convey my delight, watching him in his new raiment as he enjoyed the breakfast I had laid out! He was like a small child, peering through the window into my... beautiful garden.'

But now a dark look had come over him, bringing his ugliness back into focus. 'But did he repay my favours?' He was roaring now. No more the lovely voice. It was dreadful to see this side of him. 'No, he did not! He chose instead to steal what is most precious to me! He plucked one of my roses. Broke its stem!' More of those moaning sounds, so very discordant, horrible to hear. I waited as he calmed himself, cleaned himself up again.

'He did not deserve my kindness! I did not care if my appearance might distress him. In fact, I welcomed the thought.' He was in full flow. I'd better step in.

'Sounds like you became your old self again then?'

Shocked. Then quiet, head bent, dabbing the spit with the sodden towel. 'Alas, I fear you are right. I called him terrible things, threatened to kill him at once.' Regarding me. 'Yes, you are right. And I was ashamed, for he fell to his knees and begged me to spare him. He said he was so grateful for all he had been given, that he had not meant to offend. That he had thought no one would mind if he took away with him just one rose. That one of his daughters had asked him to bring back a rose.

'When he told me he had daughters, I seized upon this as a chance to escape my loneliness.' As if apologising to me, 'And besides, I was still so very angry.'

'But you spared him?' I realised that once again I was leaning almost over my desk to drink in this tale. Eagerly, unprofessionally, 'You did spare him?'

He nodded, glad I had offered him the chance to show his merciful side. 'I did spare him. I told him he could return to his daughters, tell them all that had passed. That he could even take the rose with him. That he could stay for three full months, until spring had truly arrived.

'But then... I told him he must return, and that he must then stay with me forever, and allow me to do with him as I wished. But I tried to be merciful – although truly I must add, in doing so I proffered a bargain that I could only have dreamed of before his arrival. I said that if one of his daughters would come with him, all well and good. She must come willingly, however, willing to stay with me in his stead. I gave him leave to go, reminding him that at the end of three months, he, or he and one daughter, must return – or I would use my powers to come and fetch them.'

'A touch of the old you again, threatening force?' He bowed his head.

'Again you speak true. But I was so lonely! So very lonely! And here was a chance for companionship! Can you blame me? Truly, can you blame me?' He was pleading with me. Please forgive him, he begged wordlessly.

'My place is not to judge you.' How devastated he looked! I couldn't leave it there. Too uncaring. 'Perhaps when we face such... profoundly sad feelings, then... temporarily... we forget all we have learned.'

Relieved to think he could be forgiven, he continued. 'Those three months passed more slowly than had the hundred years before them. But true to his word, on the very day that closed the third month, I saw the old man riding slowly down my path.' A tear, a happy tear this time, found its way down his deformed face. He still could not believe his good fortune. 'And he was not alone. Riding with him was... Bella. Bella. The most beautiful young woman ever to grace this earth. As beautiful as I am... hideous. 'I thought the old man must have tricked her, must have lied to her about what she would find. For no one would willingly come to... this.' Glancing down. 'I did not wish to frighten her, so I hid as I had done when her father first found his way to my home. I wished for them a delicious meal and a night's rest.' He looked to me as if for approval.

I nodded encouragement. 'Do go on.'

'Next morning after they had eaten, I came in to them. The old man, bowed and tearful; Bella, afraid and of course... horrified. But she smiled! Can you imagine! She smiled at me!'

Wiping away the slobber that accompanied this outburst, 'I asked her if she had come of her own accord.' Looking out from his memory back towards me, 'You will recall that was the condition I had demanded.'

'I remember.'

Defensively, 'I would never... have a chance like this again. But if I were to have a true companion, that person must choose to live with me, is that not true?'

I hadn't meant to appear judgemental. 'Of course you were right. And you have learned a great deal. She had to want to be with you. You knew from your past deeds that forcing someone to submit to your will brings neither of you joy.'

Relieved again, 'She told me it was she who had requested the rose, and that she was happy to exchange her life for that of her father, that she had insisted despite his protests. And I could see from the expression on his face that this was true.

'The old man left after many sorrowful embraces, but not until he was out of sight did Bella begin to weep. But not in fear of me. No, not in fear of me. She wept for the love of her father.

'She is a most perfect woman.'

'So Bella is the 'she' of whom you spoke?'

'Bella has graced my home for nigh onto six months now. At first, I stayed away, to spare her my... presence. Instead, I took my delight watching her from afar. I did my best to ensure she had everything – she needed only think of something she desired and the next day I would see that it was provided. A library, musical instruments, sweetmeats, beautiful gowns. Anything. Everything. For it was so joyful to observe her enjoying herself.

'After some weeks, I decided to take a chance. Late one afternoon I appeared before her, and asked if I might have leave to watch her sup. She replied that I must do as I please, for I was lord of this manor.'

He looked back from the memory at me once more. 'It was not the answer I might hope for, but it was enough. Enough. 'At first I would come in only as she finished her meal, so as not to... ruin her appetite. After but two weeks, she asked if we might enjoy our evening meal together. Enjoy?' He beamed. 'She said that. Truly she did. And I have joined her every evening since. 'We have had the most wonderful conversations. Sometimes we even laugh together! Each morning I wake and simply wait all day for the evening to arrive.

And Bella… she told me one night that she, too, looks forward to our evenings together. Oh, I felt so fortunate!'

He met my eyes again, his own now brimming with fresh tears. 'But now what I am about to say will no doubt displease you. It displeases me. I began to fear my good fortune would not last. I began… each evening, just before the sad moment when I knew I must take leave of her, I would ask her if she would promise always to stay and be happy here with me. I know it made her uncomfortable, that there was something she wanted to say but dared not. Instead, she always replied with the same words, "I came willingly. I am here now. And we have just enjoyed our meal together, have we not?"'

Pleading for reassurance, 'But that's not an answer to my question, is it?'

I could only shake my head. It wasn't.

He took a deep breath. 'One afternoon, last week it was, I came upon her unexpectedly in the garden. She was standing beside the rose plant, the one her father had chosen to plunder, to take a sweet rose home to her. She was weeping.

'"Bella, Bella. Whatever is it? I shall make it right, whatever it is! Tell me now!" She looked at me with such sadness. Looked at me and said she… she was missing her father. That she wanted to see him one more time. Just once more. That she wanted him to be reassured she was well and had been… spared.

'Oh, what pain her admission caused me! All I had given had not been enough! Despite all I had done, she still wished to leave me!'

'Wait a minute. She didn't say she wanted to leave you, if you're remembering what passed between you accurately. She said she wanted to see her father again. She didn't say anything about staying with him, did she?'

'But I want her to love *me!*'

'Love is not a limited resource. She can love you both.'

He wiped his tears and his slobber. Took a deep breath.

'I wanted things to be as they were. Not for her to wish for something… else.'

'Is this the decision you can't make? Whether to let her go?'

He nodded, still cleaning his face.

'And you wish her to be happy… but you fear if she goes, she won't come back?'

'Look at me! Would you come back… to this?'

'This isn't about what I would do. This is about Bella. And about you.' Carefully, 'Do you accept that Bella has truly enjoyed herself in your company lately?' Nod. 'Sometimes, awakening joy reminds us of other sources of joy in our past. Those memories and wishes do not detract from what she feels for… you.'

He wanted so badly to believe me.

'When you… had… your wenches, were they happy to be with you?'

'Of course not. I forced them. I told you that.'

'So, forcing someone to be with you didn't… awaken or nurture joy, or make that person happy?'

He was silent, not sure he liked hearing this.

'Let's turn to the birds you care for so well in your garden.' He looked totally surprised. 'Okay, I know they're not human. But they have hearts, and… I'm no expert on birds, I bet they have feelings.'

It was nice to see him smile again. 'Oh yes. I am sure they have feelings.'

'Well, do they ever leave you?'

'Of course! Every winter they fly to warmer climes.'

'And do they return in the spring?'

He was beginning to understand.

'But if when you sensed they were ready to leave… what if you stopped them, imprisoned them in a cage? Then if they managed to escape – and no doubt they would try – would they then fly back to you in the spring?'

'Ah. I see.'

'Love can never be forced or caged. You know that really. You learned that lesson well – just look at how you treat the birds. You only forgot… for a little moment.'

We were nearly there.

'And consider the old man. You – mercifully, and quite rightly

– allowed him to return home for a time. Did he come back to you?' Nod. 'Did you have to force him?'

'No, I did not. He came back... freely.'

I smiled. 'She comes from pretty reliable stock, wouldn't you say?'

It was good to see that smile again.

'Of course, I must let her go. No – I must *encourage* her to visit her father.'

'I'm sure that's right. You can hope she returns – and I believe the chances are high – but no, you can't be sure of it. But you can be sure she will be happy, because you... showed her you respect her, showed her you want her to have what she wants, even when it might not suit you.'

Did I dare go on?

'And in my opinion, she's lucky to be loved like that.'

Oh dear. Lots and lots and lots of slobber. And tears. And to my astonishment, a big wet hug. And with that he was gone, out through the window, leaving only the sodden towel.

The Frog Prince

Just one more push and I'll be up the hill. Last one I have to endure this morning.

I really am tired. Last night was sheer torture, a series of bad dreams that woke me repeatedly. In every one of them I was about to enjoy something – a good meal, my favourite film – and then Freya would come in to wherever I was, flashing her obnoxious fake smile, and take it away. And every time, there was nothing I could do.

Of course! Why hadn't I realised? Just because I'm a therapist doesn't make me immune to what everyone else must at times endure. Of course. I was having an anniversary reaction. It was exactly one year ago today when Theo announced he was leaving me, and when he told me it was because of Freya. He was sorry, he'd said; he didn't want to hurt me.

They all say that.

Well, I'd certainly just clarified the meaning of those dreams. Being robbed of everything I'd enjoyed, feeling utterly helpless while it happened. I remember, after the initial shock wore off, when I looked up Freya Matthews on Facebook. Young. Pretty. Very pretty.

Pretty in a way I could never be, a slender delicate blonde.

Everyone says that when you think it happened out of the blue you're mistaken, that if you look back you'll see the signs. But to this day, I don't remember any warning signs. It really had come out of the blue for me.

I dearly hoped my case list would challenge me sufficiently, keep me alert and focused so I could get through the day. Then I could go home, and go straight to bed.

Except I'd forgotten it was Tuesday.

The now familiar gust of wind hit me as I was shoving my notes into my backpack and preparing a hasty exit. The lightest of feet landing on the floor behind me, followed by a delicate clearing of the throat. 'Do you have a looking glass? I must arrange my curls. Oh – and don't look up until I have done so.'

How bossy and demanding! So why was it, then, that I found myself pandering to this individual? There I was, bent over my backpack with head down and eyes firmly on the floor, directing her with a wave over my head to the basin across from my desk.

I waited. And waited. Finally, beginning to feel dizzy from bending over for so long, I glanced up furtively.

She was a young woman, very young – possibly an adolescent. Petite, delicate. She was richly dressed, her cornflower blue silk gown somewhat windblown, but fitting exactly to her exquisite curves. White lace petticoats underneath, how many I could not begin to imagine. Generous sleeves with what I guessed were lace cuffs capturing her wrists. A dainty linen day cap.

The curls that needed arranging were long, blonde and looked already perfect to me – but evidently not to her. She was wrapping each tendril – every single one of them – around her finger one at a time, and holding, waiting until she considered it ready to spring into place exactly as she wished it. Before moving to the next, she would scrutinise it and all previous curls in detail. This could take a while, and I was feeling distinctly light-headed, because I'd maintained my bent position over my rucksack so as not to look at her as she'd requested. I asked myself again why I was taking orders from this... self-obsessed teenager?

'I'm going to sit down in my chair now.'

'Very well. But mind you, no looking until I am quite ready.'

Such a tyrant, and thus far, definitely lacking in empathy. I was already beginning to speculate on a diagnosis. Narcissistic personality disorder?

Five minutes more primping, then she turned around. 'You may look at me now.'

Okay, I'll admit it. She was stunning. Rich full lips curved in a self-appreciating smile, set above a perfectly sized retroussé nose. Above, huge light blue eyes rimmed up and under with thick black lashes.

'No doubt you find me beautiful? Everyone does, you know. Father says the sun itself is astonished whenever it shines upon my perfect face.'

Add adoring father to her case description.

But at the mention of her father, the perfect face changed abruptly. Gone was the (if you ask me, fake) smile. Enter the storm cloud. 'It's Father I came to talk about. You need to tell me how to make him change his mind.'

'About what?'

She looked surprised. Why wouldn't I know? Another mental note: she was completely, not just partially, self-centred. What else but narcissistic personality disorder?

'About... him!' No longer the storm cloud. She'd moved on to disgust. The thought of 'him', whoever he was, clearly appalled her. 'He says I must allow *him* to sleep in my bed with me!'

Oh my God. Incest. 'Your own *father* wants to sleep with you?'

To my surprise she laughed. She really could change moods quickly. 'Oh no, not Father! Father says *he* must be allowed to share my bed.'

At least she hadn't been shocked at my mistaken suggestion. She probably thinks it unsurprising that even her own father would find her irresistible. Her diagnosis really was crystal clear.

'He meant the visitor... the odious creature who demanded entry to our castle yesterday.'

Good heavens what a progressive household! The day after

a guest arrives they're given permission to bed one of the children? I was finding it hard to keep up, let alone make sense of her story.

'Your father is encouraging a visitor, someone you've all just met, to sleep in your bed with you? Is that what you're telling me?'

She lowered her head, trying to look bashful, but not succeeding very well. 'Well, actually we haven't all just met. He and I first met in the forest three days past.'

Ah, now we're getting somewhere. Perhaps this guy had already had his way with her, and her father figured there was nothing more to lose. 'Why don't you tell me about that... first encounter.'

'Will it help you if I do? Will it mean you can tell me how to make Father change his mind? Because if it won't, then that's just a waste of my time. In that case I see no reason to tell you.'

Okay, that nails it. Narcissistic personality disorder, no question about it. She'd already demonstrated eight of the nine possible indicators, when I only needed five to confirm the diagnosis.

Now that I knew where we were coming from, I felt better able to focus on what she thinks the problem is, and speculate on whether I can help. I know one thing for certain already; she won't concede there's anything wrong with her. But I'll see what I can do about that later. For now, I know how to frame my approach. Everything needs to be about her, and for her.

'I always find that if I hear the whole story, then what I can suggest is usually more... appropriate for the person who's asked for help.'

That seemed to satisfy her. 'Very well. It's because of my golden ball.' She noted my quizzical look. Good, finally beginning to notice that I might not already know everything she knows.

'You don't have a golden ball? I'm so sorry. It's my favourite plaything. It's beautiful and perfect, just as I am.'

I nodded, trying my best to show warmth and understanding. Failing, I'm sure – not that she'd notice.

'And I'll tell you a secret. On very warm days, I take my golden ball and walk deep into the forest close behind our castle. There's a well under an old tree in the middle of a clearing that I know. It's cool there, and the water is oh so deep – you can't see the bottom, it's that deep. I love to sit on the edge of the well and throw my golden ball high up in the air and catch it, over and over. I have such fun!'

I was beginning to wonder whether she was rather simple. Maybe just still very young. 'That sounds lovely! Do go on.'

'Well, three days past, I went into the forest just as I always do. I sat down by the well and threw my ball high as high. But when I reached out to catch it, instead of falling into my hands my silly ball hit the ground, and then it rolled straight into the water.'

Her narcissism was breath taking. She even managed to blame the ball rather than herself when she failed to catch it.

'I'm sure you can imagine how upset I was. My favourite toy! My best plaything! Deep at the bottom of the well. I wept, at first only a little, but then more and more. I didn't think I could ever stop. But then, I heard a voice.' She made a nasty face as she attempted to recreate the voice she'd heard. 'An ugly, croaky voice. "Oh lovely Princess! What ails thee? Why do you weep so?"' She paused, proud of her effort. I waited, not commenting.

'Well, I'll have to tell you because you'll never guess who was there. It was a frog. A *frog!* A slimy, cold, green frog. He must have come up out of the well when my ball disturbed the water. I told him I was weeping for my golden ball, because it had sunk to the bottom of the well.' Coquettish smile. Fake, I think. 'You can probably imagine just how taken he was when he saw me!'

This was getting tiresome. 'No doubt.'

'...and of course he wanted to help me, seeing such a beautiful princess so distressed. "Do not weep, Princess! I can help you." But then the old croaker got greedy. "But what will you give me if I fetch your plaything?" You would think my smile would be reward enough, wouldn't you? But no. So I told him he could have anything of mine he wished – my pearls, my jewels, anything. Even my golden crown!' A little dramatic pause while I was evidently meant to appreciate her generosity. 'Well, can you believe his answer? No, you won't believe it. I'm going to have to tell you. He said he didn't want my pearls or jewels, not even my golden crown! He said he wanted to be my companion and playfellow, to sit with me at table when I took my meals, and... and he said he wanted to sleep with me in my royal bed! If I promised him that, he said, he would dive deep down into the well and fetch my golden ball.'

'And you did? You promised him all that?'

'Of course I did! How else was I supposed to get my ball back?' She clearly thought me stupid. But then, seeing my undisguised incredulity, she became defensive. 'He is only a simple frog after all. And frogs have to live in the water. Doesn't everybody know that? – although clearly *he* forgot, the simpleton. Frogs don't live in castles. I didn't have to mean what I said, because what he asked for was clearly impossible!' She laughed, enjoying herself, thinking back on how clever she was.

By now I was feeling irritated. Visions of Freya kept flitting through my mind. I was imagining her just as self-satisfied as this child sitting before me. Helen! This will never do. How can I possibly help this kid – and she really is only a kid – if I allow personal associations and my own emotions to cloud my thinking? Step back. Listen mindfully. No judging. Imagine the world from her point of view. I was slipping probably because I was tired. I took a deep steady breath, then composed a sympathetic, understanding face. 'Do go on. What happened next? I'd love to know.' And now I really would.

'He dived down. He was gone such a long time! But then there he was, in the middle of the well, holding my beautiful golden ball in his... slimy mouth.' Look of disgust. 'At least he threw it on the grass so I didn't have to touch him.'

'How courteous of him. And then?'

'You can understand I'm sure that I didn't feel like playing there any longer that day! So I picked up my lovely ball and hurried back to the castle.'

'And the frog?'

She looked surprised. He'd done her bidding. Why did it matter what became of him after that? 'I suppose he... dived back into the well.'

She pulled at one of those perfect curls, agitated now. 'Well, not for long I guess, because the next day... that's when things went all wrong.'

'All wrong?'

'Yes. All wrong. I was taking lunch with Father and all the courtiers,' I wondered if her mother was still alive. But I couldn't see how it was relevant to know about her mother – I was just curious. I decided not to interrupt her. 'There was this... sort of wet sound... splashy sound, on the staircase. Then a knock at the door, and someone calling for me. Father said I should answer the door, so I did. And when I opened the great door, there sat that horrible frog! Can you believe it? How did he ever manage to find me?' An anguished look – this might even be genuine. 'Of course I slammed the door and hurried back to my chair. I tried to look like it was nothing. But Father could tell I was upset. He asked me what had so frightened me. Was there a giant at the door who wanted to carry me away? he asked. I told him it was a frog. He said I must explain.' She refocused her gaze on me.

'Father can be very strict, you see. I explained what had passed between myself and the frog the previous day. I was certain Father would understand, that he would send the silly creature away.' Tears welled. She was genuinely distressed now, and I almost felt sorry for her. 'Instead, Father said if I'd made a promise, I had to keep it. He told me to leave the table again, and this time to let the frog come in.'

I saw a chance. 'Does your father always make you keep your promises?'

'Oh yes always. He says we must always honour others by keeping our word.'

'And does he? Does your father always honour others and keep his word?'

'Oh, always. Whenever we go out for a ride in our carriage, the people always throw flowers and shout to us, "A salute to honest King George, who always keeps his promises to us!"'

This couldn't be better. 'So, in your Kingdom, if you're someone who always keeps a promise, everyone loves you?'

What a revelation! Those lovely blues eyes widened. 'Well, yes, I suppose that's true.'

I still had her attention. Seize the moment, Helen. 'That is truly wonderful! Because whatever age you are, whoever you are, you can still keep promises, and that means you can always be loved.'

'Why do you say 'always be loved'?'

Careful, Helen. Go slowly. 'Well, some of the reasons why other people love us can last forever, whatever our age or however we look. We can even get better at things like keeping our word as the years go by. But other things... things like how beautiful we are,' I saw those eyes narrow now, in what was either distrust or dislike. Perhaps both.

'Other things... things like beauty... can't last.'

'*My* beauty will last forever!' A little too forceful, that. The seeds of doubt had been planted. Good.

'Is your father handsome?'

'Of course not! Not now! Once he was handsome, so I am told, with golden curls...' she patted hers lovingly, 'just like mine. But he's not beautiful now. Of course not! Because he's old.'

I waited for that to sink in. Enough for now. I could see that if I pushed my point further I'd lose her. 'How wonderful that you and your father are so very much loved, you for beauty, and he for his *constant* truth-telling and promise keeping. What a wonderful father to have!' She wasn't so sure whether she dared agree with me now, whether I might trick her. Nonetheless, she was willing to accept my praise. 'But that's enough about your father's good qualities. I want to know about you! What happened next?'

She relaxed, glad to escape these challenges to her world view and get back to her story. 'I did as Father bade. I left the table, crossed the dining hall and opened the door to that... thing. Then I hurried back to my place at the table.

'But...' A shiver. 'But he followed me. He hopped right up beside my chair, all slimy and green and croaky. And then he said, so loudly everyone heard, "Lift me up beside you, Princess, just as you promised."'

She looked at me beseechingly, a genuine tear sliding down her cheek. 'When he asked to be lifted up beside me, to eat with me... from my golden plate...' She closed her eyes and shook her head vehemently. 'It was just too dreadful!'

'But like a true daughter of your father, you did pick him up and place him where he could share your meal, didn't you?'

Was this act praiseworthy? Did I mean to compliment her? She wasn't quite sure how to respond. 'Yes of course I did. Father said I must, because... because I promised. 'But of course I could not touch another morsel. Not when *he* was taking his fill from my plate!

'When at last the meal was over, I told Father I was very tired, and please could I go to my bedchamber. But then...' Now she was crying freely. 'Then, that *thing* said he, too, was tired, and that now I must carry him with me to my bed chamber, and allow him to lie with me on my silken bed.'

'And did you?'

'I promised, didn't I?' Head bowed as she wept harder.

'What an honest, trustworthy young woman you are! Your father must be very proud of you.'

She looked up, those periwinkle eyes filled with free-flowing tears. 'No. I do not deserve his good will. I... I have to tell you the rest. I was so ungracious. I picked up the slim... the little frog with two fingers only, not gently, and I carried him with me, up to my bedchamber. He stayed very still. But then I dropped him roughly in the farthest, coldest, darkest corner in my room, and ignored his pleas while I settled myself into my bed.' She looked far away, remembering, reworking the memory. 'How cruel I was, when he wanted only what I had promised him.'

There are moments like these in therapy – too few, but so delicious when they happen – when it's all I can do not to jump up and hug my client. This was such a huge admission from her!

She looked back from that time to regard me now, full of shame. 'It gets worse, I'm afraid. He hopped over to my bedside, and he asked me to lift him up so he could lie beside me. He said he was tired, too.'

Tears stopped her narrative. I waited, then felt a need to prompt. 'And did you lift him up?'

She shook her head, still sobbing. 'Oh, I picked him up. But I didn't place him beside me as he asked. Oh no! I... I... I threw him as far as I could across the room! I threw him! As if he were a stone, not a living creature!' She was crying so hard now that her shoulders were shaking. 'And I... was so... surprised at what I had done! I didn't dare look at what I'd done. I just ran, ran directly out of my chamber and down the staircase, then outside, still running, until I arrived... here.'

No wonder her curls were all askew when she'd come through the window. But she didn't care now about those curls, or about her tear-stained face either for that matter.

'Do you think I killed him?' Then answering her own question, 'No. I know I didn't. I heard him still pleading... although his voice seemed changed... but I did hear him! I am sure of it! He is still alive! I can still make amends! I can still keep my word!' Turning to me one more time, with not a question but a vow, 'And that is what I must do!'

And with that she leapt from her chair, ran to the window, and vanished – curls, gown, cap, all in disarray. But no matter. A kinder person she was now, and far more beautiful than on her arrival.

The Story of the Three Bears

OMG! He – or maybe it's a she – is huge! I can't begin to imagine how whatever it is got through the window. I glance behind me. The frame and both panes of glass are still intact, the window is tightly shut. No sign at all of a disturbance.

The vast creature wasn't moving. Balanced evenly on four enormous paws, it appeared to be taking in its surroundings, moving its head slowly from side to side. I noticed with some trepidation the long claws on its front feet and the massive hump of muscles rippled across its shoulders. Small ears, a long snout ending in a sizeable black nose. Little eyes, inky and seemingly unfocused. The only oddity was some sort of pink plastic container – a child's purse? – on a matching pink strap hanging from the left shoulder.

The creature was completely covered in fur, deep brown and uniform in length – except across the top of the head. There, it looked like someone had hacked the hair short, rubbed in some sort of grease, and forced the stubble to stand upright. Perched in the centre, rather askew, was a pink satin bow. Despite this extraordinary 'crown', the face – in contrast to the hugely powerful body – didn't appear menacing. Benignly inquisitive was a better description. I exhaled and took in a welcome gulp of air – for the first time, I realised, since the creature's appearance.

Mistake. I might as well have fired a cannon. The creature stood up at once – taller than I am, I could see now, much, much heavier, and oh so much stronger – and moved its head side to side. 'Where are you? I beg your pardon, but I can't see very well.'

Good heavens! The last thing I expected to hear was a sweetly musical feminine voice. 'I'm here, just across the room from where you're... standing.' Take the tremor out of your voice, Helen. 'I'm sitting in a... black chair, and I'll turn it around now if that's okay, so you can see me.' I definitely wasn't going to do anything, even breathe again, if the creature objected.

'Oh, I think I see you! Wait...' She fumbled for the little pink purse, opened the latch and pulled out a pair of black rimmed spectacles and pushed them in place atop her long snout. 'Ah yes! There you are! May I sit down somewhere, if there's a chair that's just right for me?'

Odd phrasing. 'The chair opposite me carries... accommodates most... visitors.' I pointed to the intended chair with a dramatic flourish, just in case the spectacles weren't up to the job.

'Thanks.' She dropped back down and padded flat-footed but sure, over to the chair, negotiated her bulk into the seat carefully, then looked up with what I swear was a smile. 'I'm so grateful you didn't run away. Most humans do, and that makes me frightened, and then I think I need to chase them.'

I was extremely glad I hadn't run away as well. She might be bulky, but she looked really fast. I waited.

'I suppose you must be wondering what brings me here.'

A statement, not an invitation to reply. I waited some more.

'Well, I need you to help me. I'm feeling less and less happy every day. I don't have any idea what to do with my life, and we'll be saying goodbye to one another soon, so I need a purpose. And everyone always overlooks me. It's... it's like I'm invisible, like I don't count.' A tear slid down her snout, which she wiped away absently with one huge front paw.

All I could think was that she must live with titans. Who could overlook her? And besides a lack of purpose, what sort of parting is she facing at this time? Have she and her partner decided to end their relationship, and would doing so entail a move as well? A great deal to cope with simultaneously. Poor thing. 'Sounds like you have a lot on your plate.'

She looked surprised. 'My plate? You mean my bowl? No, food is not a problem. I'm the best cook in our family, at least that's what Mama always says.'

Wait a minute. Despite the size, I'm beginning to realise this creature must be a mere child! Maybe she's at some critical age when the young of her species leave their mother? She certainly seemed wistful when she referred to her mother.

'Sorry, I wasn't very clear there. What I meant is that it sounds like we have a number of issues here. Whenever that's the case...' I noticed her look of alarm, as if she'd said the wrong thing. Mental note; very sensitive to what others say, and anxious not to cause offence. '...whenever that happens – and it happens really, really often...' She relaxed. Good. '...then it's always best to start by deciding together what the problems are, and then put them in order so we can deal with them one by one.'

'In order?'

'Yes, that's right. Once we've agreed on the problems, I will want to know which one is most important to you. And that's where we'll start.'

Her eyes brimmed with more tears, this time tears of gratitude. 'You mean what I want matters most in here?'

'Absolutely.'

'Golly gosh! Thank you!' Poor thing! She was so pathetically grateful. She has definitely been overlooked.

'Oh, and I forgot to say that the problems are usually interconnected, so solving one or two may mean we don't then even have to solve any of the others. They might just go away on their own.'

She was utterly beaming now. 'I'm so glad I came now! I wasn't sure whether I should, because it was such a long journey.'

I couldn't imagine. 'It sounds to me like you want to get

straight to work.' She nodded eagerly. 'Okay, let me see if I have the problems you want to work on clear. It might take me a few minutes to gather what you've said together and make a list.' Looking up, 'And while I do that, can I get you anything to drink after your... journey? A glass of water, perhaps?'

She considered carefully. 'A jar of honey would be nice.'

This was a first-time request for sure. But then I remembered that Emma has a sweet tooth. 'I'm not sure we have any honey, but give me a moment and I'll look in our cupboard in the kitchen.' She nodded happily, thoroughly enjoying the attention.

Thank you, Emma! In the kitchen cupboard I found a jar of honey, about half full. I made a mental note to bring in some in a matching jar, also half full, tomorrow, to replace it – hopefully before Emma noticed. Coming up with an explanation for eating half a jar of honey after work was too challenging. I loosened the lid – I wasn't sure how she could manage such a manoeuvre with those massive paws –and carried it carefully back into my office.

'Oh goodie, goodie! Thank you!' She removed the lid deftly – I'd misjudged there – but before tasting, brought the jar close to her face. Turned it round several times, tipping the contents this way and that, scrutinising carefully. Then sniffed it. Quite the gourmet, this girl. She met my expectant gaze. 'Not a flower I recognise. But lovely and sweet. Thank you.' Dipped a claw delicately into the jar and sucked the sticky result. 'Oh lovely! I love new tastes!'

'Good! You enjoy that while I make some notes.'

Now what did she say exactly? A parting – that's right, having to say goodbye soon... 'to one another'. More than one parting? Anyway, number one is about having to part. Number two, feeling overlooked – 'invisible' she'd said. I believe that, given her overwhelmingly grateful response for my small attentions to her requests already. And three, lacking a purpose or sense of direction. I glanced over the list thoughtfully. The problems she'd told me about, especially feeling overlooked and lacking a clear purpose or goal, in addition to her unusual appearance suggested she was a middle-born. I remembered from my training that dressing outrageously, wearing odd makeup and/ or sporting unusual hairstyles are all classic middle child behaviours, attempts to gain notice because of feeling overlooked compared to one's siblings. I made a mental note, in case the observation became relevant. 'I think I'm ready now, if you are.'

'Oh yes, of course! Ready.' She put down the nearly empty jar with great reluctance. 'How do we do this?'

'Let's start by seeing if I've covered everything. You feel left out and overlooked?'

A nod and a sticky 'um hum', although she didn't seem to be feeling that way quite so much right now. 'You have a painful parting coming up?'

'Painful partings! Not just one goodbye. Mama *and* my sisters.' I made a note.

'And you're not sure about your purpose?'

'When we say goodbye, I'll be alone. We all will. I want to do my best. I want to know how to fill my days... properly.' There it was again, that need to please, to appear acceptable.

'Okay, that's clear. Did I miss anything?' Shake of the head. 'So, where would you like to start?'

She was loving this. 'I'll choose... saying goodbye please. Because that happens tomorrow.'

'Okay. Why don't you start by explaining to me why you all have to say goodbye to each other tomorrow?'

She seemed surprised. Why didn't I know? 'Mama says it's time for her to make new babies. Whenever that happens, she says goodbye to the ones she has already.' Pause, reflecting. 'Mama has done her work so well! She's taught us everything. How to gather grubs, how to find honey, how to mark trees. Everything.'

The sweet snack must have taken the edge off her distress, because she seemed less upset now. Almost philosophically, 'It is time, really. Mama has been telling us it would come soon. But... I will miss everyone so much!'

'Why does everyone have to say goodbye all at once?'

'Oh, we don't exactly. Mama says we sisters can stay together until the nights come in early. But then... when I say goodbye to my sisters, then what will I do?' She was working up to a good cry. Maybe it would be better to divert her – we'd spent enough time already eating snacks and making lists, and I wasn't sure how long I might hold her attention, and as ever with the fairytale characters I knew I had only one session with each one.

'Why don't you tell me a bit about your sisters.'

Easily diverted. Good. 'Ursula One is my big sister. *Really* big! She is so big and strong! Mama is really proud, because being big is the best thing we bears can ever be.

'Ursula Three is just a darling. Everyone loves her right away. She's so cuddly. Everyone wants to take care of her. Mama says she's just right.'

There was that odd phrase again. 'And you... are you Ursula Two?' Thought I'd take a chance with my middle child theory.

'How did you know?'

'It was just a lucky guess. May I ask why you're all called Ursula?'

She didn't wish to offend, but clearly thought me really quite stupid. 'We're not! I'm Ursula Two, and my sisters are Ursula...'

'Sorry, yes. I get that. But why do your names all start with Ursula?'

'Because girls always do! Aren't you Ursula?' I shook my head. 'That's very strange. Mama says she's so much happier when her babies are girls, because she doesn't like the boys' name.'

'Which is?'

'Ursus One, Ursus Two, Ursus...'

'Okay, okay. I understand about names now. Thanks.' I shouldn't have let my curiosity take us off course, although at least she was no longer about to burst into tears every time I asked another question. 'Thanks for explaining. If your Mama has taught you everything, then won't you be okay when you and your sisters... set off on your own?'

She hadn't thought of that. 'Well, that might be true. I suppose so. I will be all right. You're right, I guess. But I will miss them. I like it now because everyone else decides what we do, and that's how I know what to do. And I get to cook for them.'

'So now we've moved straight onto one of your other problems, haven't we? The one about not having a purpose, not knowing what to do with your days when you're... independent. Why don't we wait on the goodbyes and think about how you might find a sense of purpose.' She nodded her agreement. 'What do you love doing most?'

No hesitation there. 'Eating! And making meals! That's the one thing Mama says I do well. Except sometimes Mama says I'm too fussy.'

What? 'I don't quite follow. Sometimes you're too fussy when you make meals? Could you explain please?'

'If I'd just served the porridge plain, then that horrid girl would never have come into our cottage yesterday. That's when everything went wrong. That's when it became clear to me that I'm not really good at anything, or special for anything.' A big tear appeared and slid down her snout.

Her narrative didn't seem very well joined up – or at least I had trouble making sense of it. 'Did the horrid girl tell you you're too fussy as well?

Still deep in self-pity, 'She didn't have to. Mama had already pointed that out. But if I hadn't insisted we find some berries to garnish the porridge, that girl would never have come in to our cottage, because we would have all been there.'

I was lost. 'I think it's really important that you tell me what happened yesterday, from the beginning.'

'Yes, all right.

'We got up as usual yesterday, and I got our breakfast ready. I wanted to make it special, because it was our last whole day with Mama. So, after I put the porridge in our bowls I said we should all go out and find some berries, to make the porridge really tasty.' She was far away now, deep in the events of yesterday. 'So, we all set out with our baskets. And we found lots of berries. Lots!' She smiled proudly. 'I know when it's the best time of year for all our foods, and yesterday was a berries day.'

She really was a natural gourmet. I nodded encouragingly. 'Go on, please.'

'But then, when we arrived back home... that's when the trouble started. The door was open. Just standing wide open. We were so surprised! There was no wind, and no one ever visits our cave. It is well hidden.' Another little swell of pride. 'Mama went in first – she said she would protect us if there was anyone in there. But there was no one inside! Maybe, Mama said, it was just a gust of wind, or that we'd left the door open when we went out. She said, "never mind, girls. Nothing to worry about."' She paused for dramatic effect, well into her story.

'But then, when we sat down to put our berries on the porridge… well everything was all wrong! My big sister's spoon was standing in her porridge bowl and the porridge was all stirred up. And poor Ursula Three – her porridge was all gone! She started crying. Mama tried to comfort her.' She looked up at me sadly. No one noticed me, no one cared, that my porridge had been spilled all over my lovely, lovely chair. No one noticed that my spoon was on the floor! No one.

'While Mama was comforting our little sister, I cleaned all our bowls…. and my chair…' Self-pitying again. 'And I made fresh porridge. At first Ursula One said hers was too hot, but I stirred it for her and put in some extra berries from my basket, and she told us that then, it was just right.'

'You really are clever with food.'

I was rewarded with a bearish smile. 'Thank you.

'When we finished, Mama said we should all go upstairs and take a rest. So up we went. But then… you'll never guess what we found in our bedroom!' I had a pretty good idea – I'd guessed this story, another childhood favourite – but didn't want to spoil her dramatic moment. I shook my head.

'Go on!'

'When we went into the bedroom, my big sister found her bedclothes all crumpled up. Oh, she was so angry!' A moment of sad reflection. 'And my bedclothes were worse. They'd all been thrown on the floor!

'But then when we looked in my little sister's bed… there she was! A horrid, horrid little girl. Fast asleep in little Ursula Three's bed! And her mouth was sticky all over with porridge! She was a thief, that girl!

'Ursula One – big Ursula – roared because she was really, *really* angry, and that woke up the horrid girl. When she saw us, she screamed and screamed, and then she jumped out of my sister's bed. But Mama was standing in the doorway so she couldn't run down the stairs. So, guess what she did? She was so scared she ran to the window and jumped straight out – and ran away fast as fast.'

'And I suppose no one helped you sort out your bedclothes?'

She shook her head sadly. 'No one. Ursula One made her bed up easily, because it wasn't really very messy. Then she and Mama helped my little sister.' Reflecting, rethinking. 'And maybe that was right. I was straightening my own bedclothes, and really, poor little Ursula Three's bed was a terrible mess, all sticky with porridge. She couldn't fix that by herself, could she?'

Gently, 'So sometimes, when you thought you were being ignored or overlooked, that wasn't what was really happening. Maybe what your Mama and your big sister thought was they had to help little Ursula Three instead of you, because they knew you *could* cope, but that she really can't because she's the baby?'

This was a new way to look at things. She was staring hard into her lap with the effort required, rethinking past events carefully. A thoughtful creature, and open-minded. Then slowly, steadily, I could see the rethink working, her mood lifting. She raised her head, a huge grin on her face.

'I get it. Well, I *think* I get it! Mama doesn't overlook me because she doesn't think I matter. No! She knows I can solve problems myself, that I am ready to be on my own. *That's* why she doesn't help me. She knows she doesn't have to! Oh, this is wonderful! Mama might even be proud of me!'

'I'm sure she is. And your big sister probably thinks the same about you, that you're really capable.'

'I didn't know you could see the same thing differently, that... that the same thing might not be... the same thing?'

'That's right. You *are* quite clever, you know. We can all look at what happens to us in many different ways. What happens stays the same of course, but the way we feel about it can change.'

'Of course!' She was so proud of her insight.

'Our feelings can change depending on how we look at what happens. And that looking, the way we decide to think about whatever happens, is our own choice. It's entirely in our own power *how* we think about things.'

'Oh, this is so clever!' She clapped her huge paws in delight. 'Now everything can be all right... I mean, whatever happens, I can decide how to look at it, which means I can feel good even if what happens seems... bad at first?'

'That's right. And even if something happens *is* bad – I mean, having porridge spilled all over your chair, and finding your bedclothes in a mess, those weren't good things. But even those bad things gave you the chance to show that you know how to take care of yourself. You're much more capable than your little sister. That's something your Mama already knows, and it's why she...'

'...She doesn't really overlook me! She just helps when... someone needs help.' Sitting up taller in her chair, 'So not me very often. I can take good care of myself.' More reflection, bigger smile. 'I can be on my own, you know. I am ready to live on my own.' Looking at me proudly, 'It will be easier now to say goodbye to the family. I can do it with a smile, because I know it's time.'

I waited quietly, allowing her to bask in well-deserved pride

'Do you remember that I said solving one problem can sometimes solve the others? Well, that's happened for you. You started by feeling overlooked, but now you know that's not the only way – probably not even the right way – to think about your Mama's attitude to you. Perhaps she doesn't overlook you so much as she assumes you know what to do, and how to take care of yourself?

'And as a bonus, perhaps your new way of thinking also means you can choose not to about saying goodbye to everyone tomorrow?'

She nodded enthusiastically. How easy it had been to help her.

'Thank you, thank you! I can go back home now.'

'Hey, hang on there! Slow down a minute! Of course, we can stop now if you want to. But...' Making a show of glancing at my list, 'We still haven't talked about finding you a sense of purpose, have we?'

She regarded me pityingly, and I realised immediately I'd been unfair, taken charge instead of encouraging her to lead the discussion.

'Why do you have to ask me about my purpose? My purpose is clear now. Do you not see it?'

Now I felt like the one who needed a bit of help. I really didn't understand what she meant. 'I... I'm not sure. Do you mean your purpose is that you know how to take care of yourself really well?'

This made her laugh. How simple-minded she must have thought me! Even so, she replied kindly. 'But that is *everyone's* goal, everyone's purpose, isn't it? That's not special.

'What I see now is that I am...' She stopped herself, realised she was getting carried away by her new-found insight, and might be in danger of hurting my feelings. She really was a compassionate creature.

'What I mean is, this time with you has made me realise what I'm especially good at. When it comes to making delicious food, I am the very best. Mama has often told me that. Why did I not hear her – well, why didn't I hear her, or at least believe her?' She smiled at me. 'But it doesn't matter now. 'This is my purpose. When I have babies, they will have the best food any bear can have! And I will teach them how to have their own best food when it's time for them to be on their own. I'll show them how to tell when the berries are ripe, when the nuts are ready, and when the grubs are tastiest...'

She noticed my look of disgust at the mention of grubs. However, instead of trying to make amends, instead of worrying whether she'd upset me, she simply grinned mischievously in her new-found confidence.

'And if ever I decide to take my children out to look for garnishes before breakfast, I will fill our porridge bowls full of grubs before we go. That should take care of any thieving humans, wouldn't you say?'

And before I could reply, with one more parting 'thank you,' she stood up abruptly... leaned towards the window, held out her arms, and disappeared.

The Nightingale

The window burst open with such force I was sure the hinges wouldn't survive. Whoever I will be seeing tonight must be quite powerful. I hoped it wasn't another bear. Looking behind me cautiously, I was surprised to see a bent figure leaning against the wall, one thin, wrinkled hand gripping the open window frame to steady himself. It was an old man. Very, very old. I couldn't see his face yet, for his head was slightly bowed.

But his clothing… oh how splendid! He wore a richly textured robe, made of what must be heavy silk. The material had been dyed a vibrant yellow-gold and richly embroidered with birds, trees and dragons. The garment was full-length, extending to the floor in a wide skirt; loose sleeves captured above the wrists by deep blue cuffs. Over it he wore a cape, fastened at the neck by a gold clasp, the collar of the cape extending wide of his shoulders almost like wings. It, too, was fashioned of deep yellow-gold silk with fine stitching, lined with rich black fur. His slippers were cerulean blue and silken, turning up at the toes. A long string of dull red stones – pearls perhaps? – hung round his neck. A two-layered cap of cerulean blue and black fur – or maybe velvet – encircled his head. Some intricately carved ornament, a sort of thin golden tower, rose up from the top of the cap. Slowly, wearily, he raised his head and regarded me keenly.

His skin was olive, the face long, thin and lined. Dark glittering eyes, thin lips. An elegant moustache dropped from either side of his nose. The moustache and his well-defined upturning eyebrows were black, but the long wispy beard was flecked with grey. He met my gaze squarely, taking me in, measuring me up. 'May I sit down? It's been a long and wearying journey, and I am not well.'

'Oh yes, please do.' I gestured towards the client chair across the desk from me, wondering if he could make it.

He did. Slowly and steadily, he edged to the chair, centred himself carefully, then sat down with a heavy sigh. 'I hope this will have been worthwhile.'

'So do I.' The challenge slipped out before I could stop myself. I knew better than to rise to that sort of remark, and wished I'd caught myself and kept quiet. I must be tired.

But to my surprise, he liked my volley. 'You are strong, then, and you know your worth. Good.'

I nodded, but said nothing, waiting for him to begin where he chose. Already I sensed that he wanted to work with me as an equal, so gentle questioning – which might be construed as condescending – was out.

He took his time, head bowed again so I couldn't match his gaze. He studied his hands, choosing his words with care. 'I have lived long, and I fear the end may come soon. But there is one medication, one elixir, that could revive my... weary soul. I had her once, but she flew away. I want her back.' He looked up beseechingly. 'Can you help me? Please.' Dignified and respectful, but there was great power behind the voice. A man accustomed to having what he wants, and – perhaps for the first time? – finding himself unable to do so.

And who was this 'she'? His wife? A daughter? A mistress? Did she run away? Is she in hiding, and if so, why? Oh, so many questions! 'Perhaps you would let me know who 'she' is?'

'Perfection.' He was staring hard at me, 'She is perfection. But to the eye, a plain little thing. It is when she sings... that is heaven.' A tear trickled down his cheek. He wiped it away, chiding himself, 'Emperors do not cry.' Then as if reminding himself, 'I never cry!'

I didn't want to appear as lost as I felt, but I had no choice. At least I could try out a few guesses. 'Was she a singer at your court then? And is her voice so beautiful it makes you weep? But she has... now gone away?'

He laughed, despite the tears. 'You must think I am speaking in riddles. She is a little bird. A little brown and grey bird. Very ordinary, no special markings. Not beautiful to look at. But when she chooses to sing... her song can melt even the stoniest of hearts. Or as with me, it can cause the Emperor to weep.'

'But now... she is gone?'

He nodded sadly. 'She is gone. I tried to keep her. I gave her everything, a golden perch, a gilded cage, silk ribbons. None of these offerings seemed to please her.' His face darkened. He couldn't understand why she hadn't felt indebted.

He went on, 'She sang whenever I commanded, but after a time, I was given something I thought was better – at the time. It was a most wondrous gift. It was a sensation in court. Everyone loved it. And it was so... predictable. I suppose that is when I forgot to care for the little bird.'

I figured that was as close as he'd get to an apology or an excuse.

'It must have been when we forgot to tie the ribbon on her leg that she escaped. Oh, how careless we were!'

'I am sorry, but to me you are still speaking in riddles. Why don't you start by explaining to me how you first encountered the little bird, and then... perhaps describe the gift that you thought was better and how you came by it?'

'Of course. A story. Every life, a story. You must hear my story, and I must begin at the beginning.' He settled back. 'I was raised with every privilege, all the education and pretty things anyone could have. The son of an Emperor, now an Emperor myself. My palace is the most magnificent in our world. It is, I must tell you, made entirely of fine porcelain. In my gardens you will find the most wondrous flowers, and tied to the most splendid of them are silver bells that sing with heavenly music when the wind blows. My gardens are the loveliest in all of China. Travellers come from all over the world to admire my city and my palace and everything that is mine. Before she came, I thought I was happy, because I believed I had the best of everything.

'But one evening, six years ago now, one late autumn evening when the darkness falls early, I encountered something so much more beautiful, so much more precious, than I had ever known. I had just laid down in my imperial bed when I heard...it.' He paused, more tears. 'The most enchanting, the most perfect song. I wept, though the Emperor never weeps. I wept, as I am weeping now.

'Then the song ceased, and the silence was too awful to bear. I rose at once from my trance, and hurried to the window to find what I expected would be a most exquisite creature, waiting to sing to me again. But the windowsill was bare. Empty. There was nothing there.' He looked up out his memory. 'You cannot imagine, I suppose, what it was like for me to encounter something so perfect, then for it to stop without my permission.'

So, he thinks he can own beauty. I made a mental note.

'Early the next morning – it is my custom to rise early – I called for my Lord Chamberlain. I told him what had happened, told him he must find the creature who sang to me, that I might offer her a place at court to sing at my command.' He shook his head sadly. 'I still don't know why she left, why she had not wished to stay with me. To be allowed the privilege to sing to an Emperor, how could any creature wish to leave that?'

He assumed, I noticed, that everyone would consider his wishes far more attractive than any alternative; that in fact any other alternative was not even worth considering. Interesting. I would need to approach our work carefully, working with an ego like this. I doubt he would take well to being challenged.

'We do not all share the same values. Do you think it might be that the little bird was happy with her life as it was already?'

Mistake. He reddened, eyebrows furrowed, shook his head irritably. 'No one can be happier than when they are allowed to serve the Emperor! You are wrong! I demand you do not speak further until I have finished the whole story!'

I nodded my agreement, secretly pleased with the vehemence with which he rejected my suggestion. Angry, defensive denial suggests doubt. Good.

He lowered his voice. 'I am sorry. But you must hear me out, or you will not know the best way to help.' I nodded again, not risking a comment.

'My Lord Chamberlain was gone two days and two nights. On his return, he told me he had at last found someone who could lead us to the little bird. Of course, the first people he consulted were all the learned men, but no one knew of this creature. It was only when, quite by accident, he came upon a serving girl from our kitchen. A serving girl! Can you imagine this? A girl, and someone without education, a simple thing. But she knew about the bird. She said it was called a nightingale, and she said she could take him to where the creature lives.'

Okay, note that, too. Unless you have outward credentials he deems respectable, you cannot be considered wise.

'So of course, I demanded to see the kitchen maid at once. I told her that if she led my Lord Chamberlain to this bird, she would be given a permanent post in the royal kitchen. That she might even be allowed to watch the Emperor when he eats his meals.' He gave me a self-satisfied look at the mention of this act of generosity. What an ego!

'The maid set out straight away, my courtiers following her. She took them to a tree where the little bird likes to sit and sing. It was lucky she pointed to the little bird, because my Lord Chamberlain would not have believed such a plain little creature would be capable of producing divine music.' He paused for dramatic effect. 'He commanded the little creature to sing, and so she did.' A reverent pause. 'And as she sang, he and all the courtiers began to weep, just as I had done, so he knew she must be the creature I sought. He informed her that the Emperor himself wished her to sing for him at his court, that he had ordered a royal celebration to fete her that very evening. He told me she was reluctant to accompany him back to court – can you imagine? She told the Lord Chamberlain her song sounded best out in Nature! But, she said, if that was what the Emperor wished, then she would accompany the Lord Chamberlain back to the royal palace.'

'Meanwhile I had ordered everything to be cleaned and polished in preparation for her arrival. I commanded a thousand gold lamps to be lit to welcome her, and the feasting tables were to be adorned with the finest flowers from my gardens, the plates piled high with the finest delicacies our chef could create. 'I also ordered the creation of a golden perch. I had it placed just beside me, where the lucky creature might sit when she sang. 'When at last she arrived, she sat on the imperial perch and sang, just as I ordered her. So wondrous was her music... ' His voice trailed away. Then addressing me gravely, 'Her song goes straight to one's heart, you know.

'I showered her with gifts. I even offered her my golden slipper to wear round her neck. But although she thanked me, she said my tears were gift enough for her, that she needed nothing more because she had seen the Emperor weep.' He looked at me as if astonished, even now. 'She did not accept my gifts! Can you imagine this?'

I shook my head to appear as if I couldn't imagine it. There was no need to speak just yet. Let him stir up the self-doubt on his own.

'I began to fear she might fly away, for if she refused to accept my gifts she would not be in my debt. So, I ordered a silk ribbon be tied to her leg to allow my courtiers hold her lest she try to leave.'

He appeared to think this a clever idea. I found it repugnant, but tried not to show it.

'I had a golden cage built especially for her.' Despite my attempt to produce a neutral expression, he must have caught my look of pity this time, for I felt for the poor imprisoned creature. 'Oh, she had everything. I gave her so much privilege! I commanded that she was to be promenaded twice every day and once at night, preceded by my courtiers who held the ribbon on her leg, so she could enjoy freedom and exercise.'

Privilege? Freedom? Poor bird. But I knew now was not yet the time to challenge him.

'Then one day I received a large package from the Emperor of Japan. It was a work of art, a true work of art.' He paused to remember, and smiled greedily. 'It was a mechanical bird. It could sing several tunes when you wound it up, tunes like those of my nightingale. But this creature... this creature was exquisite! It was encrusted with diamonds, rubies and sapphires, and when it sang its tail moved up and down, glittering with silver and gold. I thought the mechanical creature far superior to the plain little bird from the forest.

'Even so, I wished to give the real bird the chance to combine her voice with that of the beautiful one.'

Hmm. Beauty and worth could only be judged by external evidence according to this man. No wonder he's not happy. But he still had more to tell.

'So I commanded our nightingale to sing a duet with my wondrous new creature. But it didn't sound right because the little bird insisted on singing in her own way, not consistently, predictably, like the mechanical bird. I thought I would punish her for this, so I took her off her golden perch and placed the mechanical bird on it instead. But even then, she continued to sing in her own manner. We all turned from her cacophony to listen to the jewelled wonder, whose songs we were beginning to know ourselves. We forgot about the little nightingale, forgot to hold onto her satin ribbon. That was when she just... flew away, out the window and back into the forest.

'At first I did not care; in fact, I thought her ungrateful, and I was glad to be rid of her. Now... now I am not so sure.'

Thank heavens! A seed of doubt at last. But even now, I sensed it was not yet time to challenge him.

'In those first days after she left, I told myself it didn't matter. I had the more beautiful bird, after all. And she would sing whenever I wanted – I had only to wind her up. I didn't even have to ask her. And soon, everyone in my Kingdom knew her songs.

'But then one evening when the mechanical bird was singing its best and I was lying in bed listening to the familiar songs, suddenly we heard an odd sound, It came from inside the bird. Something had broken. Its gears spun round and round, and the singing stopped. Of course I called at once for the royal watchmaker. After much discussion and a great deal of study, he managed to get the bird singing again, fairly well. But he said we must now be careful, that the bird must be wound up only once a year lest the cylinder pegs, which were irreplaceable, wore out. It was a terrible shame!'

He looked up pleading for my sympathy, very much an old man now. I nodded understanding as best I could, but failed to muster sympathy.

'After five unhappy years had passed, I'm afraid I began to ignore the royal watchmaker's advice. I was growing weak, even sick from lack of the heavenly sounds, so I wound up the mechanical bird even though a year had not yet passed since it last sang.' He sighed. 'It sang. It sang one song. One song I knew already. And then... it stopped. 'I'm afraid to say I lost my composure. Sick as I was, I raged at that... mechanical object.'

Interesting change of name. It was no longer a bird now, I noticed. A mere object.

'"Music!" I screamed at it. "Music! Sing now, sing!" I reminded it of the gold and precious things I'd given it, and of my golden slipper that I'd placed around its neck with my own royal hands! Yet it remained... silent. Broken.'

'As you must have felt.'

'Yes. As I felt. Broken. My gold, my jewels, all my precious things, how little they seemed to matter. It was heavenly music I was craving.' He looked up, so sad. 'That is when I began to miss the real bird.'

Those two new labels. Mechanical object. Real bird. It was time at last for us to do some work. 'But I thought you said the mechanical bird did sing one song. Did that not revive you?' Of course it hadn't. But he needed to admit it.

He studied his hands for a long time. Mistakes are hard to admit when you're an Emperor.

'It was... a song I already knew.'

'But...wasn't that nice? I mean, it was familiar.'

Still not wishing to look up and face me, 'When you know something already, when a repertoire is predictable... that can be comforting. But it is soon not beautiful.' Deep breath, and at last he was ready to meet my gaze. 'I was wrong. The really beautiful songs are the ones I... I do not command. They are the ones I do not already know, offered freely rather than at my command.'

'So now you think beauty fades with repetition? That maybe part of the reason we judge something to be beautiful is that it seems new each time we experience it?' He nodded, happier now. It was time to push things a little. 'And perhaps... just maybe, beauty is not something we can always detect by outward appearance?'

A light of understanding in his eyes. 'So that is why my jewels, my gold...' He glanced down at his magnificent cape and robe, 'all my material goods no longer seem as beautiful, as...' He didn't want to have to finish.

'Not as beautiful as something that may be outwardly plain, but that surprises you? Do you think that's part of what made the nightingale's songs so exquisite, that you couldn't command them, 'pay' for them with a gold slipper or enjoy them by winding up a mechanical object? That you had to wait for the plain little creature to choose her moment? Isn't that part of the reason why it was so joyful when she did sing?'

He was crying now, and he didn't try to stop himself, no longer caring what emperors are supposed to do or not do. 'I want her back! I want her back so much!'

Unbidden, unwanted, tears sprang to my own eyes as I saw an image of Alex as a toddler, laughing and singing in his bedroom as he did when he woke every morning. I wanted him back so much. I knew how this man was feeling. Stop it, Helen. Focus on *this* person. This is not about you. I took a deep breath, spoke the words that had always comforted me, hoping they would help him as well, 'And ever has it been that love knows not its own depth until the hour of separation.'

'How wonderfully you explain my feelings!'

Thankfully that did it. The image of Alex vanished. 'Thank you for your praise, but I can't take credit. Those words were written by someone... far more gifted than I.'

'A scholar I presume?'

'No, he was a poet.'

He nodded sagely. 'Of course. A poet. I should have known. And did he live before my time, that on my return I may access all of his works?'

'I'm afraid neither of us can meet him. He lived before my time, and after yours. We both lose out there.'

He smiled. He was becoming more animated. In fact, he seemed to grow younger and stronger with every moment. It never ceases to amaze me how people are transformed when they start to feel hope again.

'I am seeing life so much more clearly now!' Reflecting, 'I suppose I was happy before I heard her song that first time. But once I heard it, my understanding of what is valuable, what really matters, should have changed. Instead, I fought that understanding, clung to my old beliefs...'

I had to interrupt. He'd eaten enough humble pie for the moment. 'But you'd had a lifetime of accepting one particular set of values. How could you expect yourself to change it all in a moment?'

'But now... is it too late to do so now?'

'Are you still breathing?'

That caught him off guard. 'What?'

'If you're still breathing, there's still time to change, still time to choose a different way of living.'

He was loving this.

'I must go back at once. I shall take away those silly trinkets, the gold and silver ornaments I set out beside my bed, because I thought it would entice her back. Entice her with gold trinkets? Hah! What a silly fool!' But then, as suddenly as it had infused him, his new-found sparkle vanished. 'But...if my gold, my jewels, all that I have is of no value to that precious bird, then what is? How can I ever hope to see her again? How would she ever believe I would not try to imprison her again, make her sing on command? Oh, this is terrible! I will never hear her songs again, will I? There is nothing I can do to bring her back. Oh, such loss!'

'Of course, there is something you can do, and you know

what it is already, because she told you. Think back to the time she first sang to you at court.'

He was thinking hard, studying his hands intently, his way of bringing his memories to life. Finally, despairing, defeated, he shook his head sadly. 'I do not remember.'

I was determined not to tell him, determined he should rediscover it himself. It would be so much sweeter for him that way. 'When you offered her your golden slipper, did she accept it?'

'Of course, she did not! I told you already! Did you not listen? I told you, nothing I offered seemed to interest her.'

'Nothing at all?'

Suddenly, there it was. That moment of discovery, the reward for doing my job, the real reward.

'She told me that my tears... my tears were gift enough for her. She said she needed nothing more than my tears!' He hurried on eagerly, almost falling over his discovery, 'I need only return to my palace. Get rid of those ridiculous... trinkets. Then I shall lie back in my bed and recall her song... and let it do its magic, allow my tears to flow.' He grinned at me like a naughty child. 'The tears that an Emperor must never show. Ha!'

His eyes literally sparkled as he stood up, tall and strong now. Oh how different than when he arrived!

'Farewell... for now!' He strode powerfully towards the window, paused, turned back to address me once more, 'We will, you know, meet again.'

And with that he spread his arms in a gesture of royal command, and vanished.

Little Red Gap

I woke this morning thinking about Alex again, plagued by self-recriminations. Surely, I could have done something differently. Surely, he'd still be alive, if only I hadn't allowed him to go out unsupervised with his friends? Had it really been such a good idea to encourage him to be so independent? I don't know how many times the police told me it was a freak accident, that it was no one's fault. There were no charges against the driver. But still… the guilt.

All day, whenever a client mentioned their child or spoke of a loss, I sensed that self-blame pushing against my therapeutic boundaries. By evening I was thoroughly exhausted, glad when the last client hour came to a close. I should write up my notes, I kept telling myself, even as I continued to sit at my desk amid scattered scribbles, pen in hand, staring vacantly into space.

The gust of cold wind made me sit up straight. I'd forgotten, but hooray! It's Tuesday! 'Real' or not, magic was on the way. I waited expectantly as someone behind me brushed themselves off – sounded like whoever I was about to meet was wearing a skirt, so probably a female – and picked up something heavy they'd dropped when they landed inside my office. I sat up attentively at the sound of a delicate feminine voice, but didn't turn around lest I intruded on her preparations.

'Is there somewhere for me to sit down? If I'm not troubling you too much. I would so very much like to speak to you, if you would be so kind.'

What a polite child! Because child she must be, by the sound of her gentle high-pitched voice. 'Of course you can speak to me. I'd really like that. You can sit down over here,' I gestured, 'across from me, so we can see each other.'

She came round with a light step, youthful, dainty. Must be quite young. But as she came into view, I was no longer so sure. She was at least as tall as I am. Nonetheless, she was wearing a child's frock, white linen patterned stitching, lacy cuffs finishing full loose sleeves, and a generous skirt of thick moss-coloured cloth. I could see her cotton pantalets easily because the skirt finished at her knees. That length, I seemed to recall from school history lessons, meant the wearer was a young child. Yet I could see the swell of her breasts above the tightly laced bodice, the curve of hips below her waist. Over the frock she wore a velvet cape of rich crimson clasped at the neck, and a matching crimson cap that was perched slightly askew on her golden head of curls. She carried a large wicker basket – that must have been what she'd dropped. How incongruous the childish apparel and the young woman within!

She walked lightly past me, unclasped her cape and arranged it carefully over the back of the chair before sitting down. 'Thank you so much. I just knew I had to get some help before I go home. I've been... bad.' She wiped clumsily at her lovely blue eyes, missing the tear that continued freely down her cheek, pulled nervously on one of the golden ringlets encircling her doll-like face, then looked up at me remorsefully. 'You see I've done a... bad thing. A very bad thing.'

Interesting. There was ambivalence in that statement. Remorse, yes. But also, a frisson of excitement. I waited for more, nodding encouragement.

'I can't tell Mama and Papa about Lucas. And... well, Lucas keeps on asking me to show him where she lives and I don't know why but I don't think I should tell him.'

She began to cry freely now. Maybe I'd been too judgemental. She really was distressed.

'Why can't you tell Mama and Papa about Lucas? And who is this she, and why is where she lives a secret?'

'She is Grandmama, and where she lives isn't a secret, not really. It's just that I don't think I should tell Lucas where she lives. But he keeps on about it, he keeps asking me and asking me.' She was crying hard now, big sobs, grabbing for deep breaths.

Where to start? 'Why is it so bad if this person Lucas knows where Grandmama lives?'

Between sobs, 'I don't know! I don't know. But it feels like it is... I... I don't think it's a good idea.'

Still lost, trying to think of a question that might enlighten me, make some sense of her garbled story, 'Maybe you can help me with something else. Perhaps you can explain to me why can't you tell Mama and Papa about Lucas? Do you think they'd be angry if they knew about him?'

She nodded. 'I could never tell them! I promised them I wouldn't talk to strangers, and now I have.' Deep breaths, trying to recover herself. 'That's why I've come here. I can't go home yet. I could never tell them that I've been so bad, but I just don't know what to do.'

'Wait a minute. Hold on. I'm guessing here, but it sounds like your Mama and Papa are worried because there are some bad people around, and they don't want you to put yourself in danger? Is that right?'

'They always tell me that all strangers are bad. And they don't know about Lucas. They would be so angry if they knew about him! Oh, why was I such a bad girl?'

I handed her the box of tissues, pulling out the top one and using it to dab my cheek to make sure she knew what to do with them. I remained silent, giving her time to calm down rather than haranguing her with yet more questions. She wouldn't be able to talk to me coherently right now anyway. And it might help me to spend some time constructing a few hypotheses, so my questions would appear less random.

My first thought was that this Lucas, whoever he is, had tried to seduce her and either moved too fast and scared her, or achieved his aim and scared her. Or maybe Grandmama is fabulously wealthy and Lucas is a conman who wants to get hold of her money. But why is Grandmama in hiding? Most concerning of all, given the possibility that Lucas has had his way with her, how old is this person sitting across from me? Is she old enough to consent to sex if that was Lucas' intention? And should the family need such assistance, I wondered if they have social services where she comes from. Boy, what a mess!

Then I caught myself. Shame on me! My job is to help my patient with what *she* feels is most important, not delve around in what interests me most.

'Sweetie – I'm sorry, but I don't know your name...'

'Ruby.'

Like the hat and the cape.

'Ruby, what's done is done. We can't go back and change the past – and it doesn't help referring to the things that have already happened as 'good' or 'bad' and upsetting yourself. They're just things that happened, okay?' Tearful nod. 'What matters now is to figure out the best thing to do now that we are... where we are. So why don't you start with when you began... not to feel... right. Tell me about that.'

She took a deep breath, glad to be given a clear instruction. 'I think it's when I started talking to Lucas. Mama said when I go to Grandmama's I mustn't talk to anyone on the way, because other people are dangerous.'

'Yes, you said that. Does your mother think everyone is dangerous?'

Vigorous nod. 'Well, not Grandmama, or herself or Papa.' She permitted herself a little smile.

'But *everyone* else?'

She wasn't sure. 'Well, I don't know anyone else.'

This was remarkable. 'No one? You don't know anyone else? Don't you have any brothers or sisters? Don't you go to school?'

She shook her head. 'Mama says I am her miracle baby. She

said she and Papa didn't believe they would ever have a child. Mama said she waited fifteen years, waiting and wishing, but then she stopped dreaming about having any children. She said that's when I was born. Every day Mama says I am her miracle, her little miracle girl.'

And Mama and Papa definitely wanted her to remain their little miracle girl forever, by the look of her childish clothing. Judging by her curves I didn't think she could possibly be younger than fourteen.

'So it's just you, Mama and Papa at home. Okay. Do you ever have visitors?'

She shook her head. 'No visitors, only the gamekeeper when he brings us meat and we give him goat's milk and eggs. But he never says a word. He just comes to the gate with some game and an empty jug, and waits for Papa to fill the jug and give him the eggs. Then he leaves.' She thought some more.

'Our cottage is all by itself in the woods. There's no other cottage around except the gamekeeper's, and Papa says he lives alone.'

'But your Grandmama visits?'

Again she shook her head. 'Grandmama is really old, and she can't do anything now. She can't even walk. Mama and Papa and I used to go together to her cottage. It's a long way away, on the other side of the woods, but that was when Mama could still see.'

'Your Mama is blind?'

'Almost blind, yes. That's why I wear my red cap.' She was still wearing it – I hadn't even noticed. 'I always keep my cap on, because Mama says she can always see me that way.' She smiled engagingly.

'How long has your Mama had trouble with her eyes?'

'Oh, a long time. Two winters at least, since I was twelve, I think. At first we could still go to Grandmama's because Papa could lead Mama there. But one morning last season, Papa fell in the garden when he was seeing to the goats, and since then he can't walk far at all. So they ask me to visit, so Grandmama won't feel too lonely.'

'I see. And how often do you go there?'

'Mama likes me to go every day, because Grandmama is so unwell now. She can't even cook for herself or anything. She just lies in bed and waits for me to visit. Mama makes her sandwiches and cake and I take it to her every day.' She smiled fondly. 'We have a lovely time. I sit beside Grandmama on her bed and we share the cake and she tells me stories. Wonderful stories. Then I go home.'

'Wow! Your Grandmama is lucky to have such a devoted granddaughter!'

She nodded, but then she began to cry again. 'But now Lucas wants to visit her! She will be so frightened! She's only used to me visiting her!'

Ah yes. Lucas. I'd forgotten about Lucas. Probably a defence mechanism, to keep what I was sure would be bad news at bay. I tried to keep my tone even, as if I were asking about just an ordinary detail. 'And when did you and Lucas first meet?'

A sheepish look, crimson blush. 'I met Lucas just four days ago.'

Allowing the pause, then, 'Why don't you tell me about that first meeting.'

Another crimson blush, although I also spotted some agitation. She clearly had mixed feelings about this Lucas character.

'Last week I decided I would take a different path to Grandmama's house. You see, I kept hearing laughing, people laughing, every day on my walk, and it made me curious. Who were these happy people? I had noticed there was another path going in the same direction as the one I usually take. So I decided to try it, hoping maybe I would see the happy people. And I was right.' She beamed with pride. 'It turns out the path runs alongside a row of cottages where...' she was faraway, dreamy-eyed, '...there are children. Oh, so many children, in the gardens of those cottages. Children of all ages. They were laughing and playing together. It looks like such fun!' She trailed off again, remembering. Poor overprotected, isolated kid!

'At the end of the row of cottages the path forks right. I knew where I was then, and that I was about to join my usual path. But just there, just after the last cottage, I saw... something... on the path ahead of me. I was very frightened, because it looked like a large hairy animal. It was crouching on all four legs, staring and staring at the children. 'As soon as it...as soon as he...saw me, he stood up.' She looked up to make sure I understood how clever she was to recognise this creature. 'I was wrong you see! It wasn't a beast at all. It was a man. A very dark man with lots and lots of hair. He has such big shining eyes and very big teeth, and he's very hairy!'

That infatuated look again, yet once again I noticed something else as well. Fear? Anxiety?

'At first I was very frightened because he was a stranger, so I started to run away. But he called out, in such a kind and gentle voice, "Don't run away, sweet child! I will not harm you! Please, please stay. I'm so lonely, and you are so lovely."' She looked at me to see if I disapproved. I kept my encouraging non-judgemental therapist smile firmly in place and nodded encouragingly.

'Do go on.'

'Well, his voice was so kind and gentle, I couldn't see the harm if we just walked on the path together.' She studied me carefully, to make sure I hadn't changed my expression. Smile encouragingly, Helen.

'We talked and talked. It was lovely! I told him about Grandmama and that I take her cake every day,' I wish you hadn't, darling. 'And he said what a good granddaughter I am. When we reached the top of the hill where I go down to Grandmama's house I said it was time to say goodbye, because I always visit Grandmama alone. The first day he was lovely about that.'

But such politeness wasn't going to last. I could feel it.

'The next day, there he was again. He said he had been waiting for me, because he enjoyed my company so much.' Another blush and a shy smile. She was smitten, that was clear, but at the same time, I felt something more. Sexual excitement? Or fear? I still couldn't read her clearly.

'That day he asked if he could hold my hand,' She glanced down to her left hand, lifted it, scrutinised it carefully. 'It was so lovely to hold his hand.

'Yesterday he was there on the path again of course, and at first I was so glad. We held hands again, and that part was still lovely. But then he started asking if he might go to Grandmama's house with me. He said her bed sounded so comfortable and cosy...'

Oh no. My worst fear. I noticed she was hunching her shoulders now, and that she'd begun clasping and unclasping her hands. She looked up at me, desperate for approval.

'I told him Grandmama wasn't well, and that the only visitor she likes is me. So then he started asking if I might just describe the way to her cottage. He said it might be a good plan if he visited her first himself, so he could show her by his kind voice that he was a friend. Then next time, we could visit her together.'

She was wringing her hands now, and shivering slightly.

'I said no, I couldn't do that, I hadn't asked Grandmama.' She looked up. 'And if I asked her, I was afraid that she, too, would disapprove of me talking to a stranger. So I asked Lucas if it was okay if we just kept meeting on the walk?' Pause, little shiver, eyes downcast again. 'I don't think Lucas liked that very much. But he agreed and he went away, at the top of the hill where we always say goodbye.' She looked up anxiously. 'But that was yesterday. Then today....' She began crying again.

'Ruby, you are such a brave girl! You're telling me your story so well and so clearly. Let me fetch you a glass of water and some more tissues,' I noticed she'd pulled out the entire contents of the box I'd given her, and there were crumpled tissues strewn all over the desk. 'Then you can finish your story and we can make a proper plan to help Grandmama and you.'

She nodded dumbly, the tears still flowing.

I hurried across the room and out the door, leaving it wide open so she could hear me and not feel abandoned. I spoke to myself loudly to reassure her. 'Now where are those extra tissues? Ah yes, here they are. And here's a perfect Ruby-sized glass for some lovely cool water.' Back in the room, I filled the glass at my basin and offered it to her, placed the new box of tissues beside the empty one, avoiding the crumpled messes as best I could.

'Thank you. You are very kind.' I wasn't sure I wanted to receive the same accolade as she'd bestowed upon Lucas, even if she did mean well. She took a long draught of the water, dabbed her eyes with a few more tissues, dumped them on the desk along with the others, and smiled wanly.

'Ready to finish? You're nearly at the end of the story, aren't you?' She nodded and took a deep breath.

'Today he was waiting again. I took the other path today, the path that doesn't go near the happy children. But he was still there, still waiting. 'That's when I had the bad feeling. He said he hadn't stopped thinking about Grandmama all night, how lonely she must be. He said he really wanted to call on her. He... he was rather forceful.'

That alarmed me. 'Did he do anything to you? I mean, did he hurt you in any way, or touch you in ways you didn't like?'

She seemed surprised. 'Hurt me? Oh no. We just held hands.' She glanced down at her hand again, recalling the pleasurable sensation. Poor naïve, confused young woman! It can be so difficult to disentangle sexual excitement from fear.

'It was just that... well... I think... he watched me when I went down the hill. I think he followed me... and now I think he knows where Grandmama lives.' More tears. 'I didn't stay very long with her today, because I kept thinking, what if he comes to her cottage after I leave? What if he frightens her? I knew I had to do something to protect dear Grandmama, but I didn't know what I could do. That's when I decided to come here.'

I wish the worst thing I could imagine was that when Lucas called on the poor old woman he'd merely startle her. More likely she was already history, and that after dispatching her remains, Lucas might even now be trying out her bed, imagining what he'd do to poor Ruby when she arrived the next day. I had to convince her of the danger she faced without frightening her too much, and get her to ask for help so someone could capture this monster. Her instincts were good, but she really was vulnerable.

'Ruby, you must listen carefully. You really, really have to tell someone about Lucas.'

This produced such alarm that she knocked over her glass of water, although luckily it was nearly empty. 'Oh no! I can't tell Mama or Papa! They would be so angry with me for talking to a stranger! For four days now! I've been so bad for four days!' Sobs welled up again.

I realised she was right, although her parents' anger was not the only reason to bypass them. In truth, they'd be unable to do anything constructive. A blind woman and an old man who can hardly walk? I needed someone strong and decisive. Then I remembered the gamekeeper.

'Ruby! Ruby, listen to me, please.'

I told myself sternly to lower my voice and slow down, while I waited for her to lift up from her sobbing. Shouting hadn't helped convince the mouse to change its plans; and my pleas, if that's all I offered, were unlikely to help Ruby, either.

'You don't have to tell Mama and Papa about Lucas.' I saw her relief. 'You need someone...who can walk over to Grandmama's cottage and make sure she's not... upset or worried.' Then as if the idea just occurred to me, 'I know! How about going straight from here to the gamekeeper's cottage?'

At first she brightened – probably, I suspected, because I hadn't insisted she confess her recent exploits to Mama and Papa. But then she shook her head.

'But I don't really know him. He's another stranger. That will just make Mama and Papa even more angry with me!'

'Ruby, the gamekeeper feels like a stranger to you I know. But he's not a stranger to Mama and Papa. So, he's not a stranger to any of you, not really, and furthermore Mama and Papa believe he's a nice person. I'm sure they would be glad you tried to protect...' Oops. I saw the alarm on her face. 'I'm sure they'd be glad you tried to help Grandmama, that you tried so hard to make sure everything is just the way she likes it to be.'

She relaxed a little and considered this idea carefully, allowing me a glimmer of hope. But then she started shaking her head again, unsure, and twisting her hands while she considered other possibilities. Suddenly she looked up, eyes shining.

'I know! I'll tell Grandmama myself! I know she will understand about Lucas. I'll tell her he has been so kind to me,' glancing at her hand fondly again. 'And I will explain how he only wants to make her happy, and make sure she doesn't feel so lonely. I know I can explain everything to her.' She was alight with her plan, while my own heart sank.

'I'll go home now – it's not even late, so Mama and Papa won't know I've been... here. They'll think everything is just fine. Then tomorrow I will leave early, before Lucas would be waiting for me, so I can go straight to Grandmama's first. I will tell her all about Lucas, and then I'll go and fetch him, because by then he will be waiting on the path.' She grabbed for her cape and picked up her basket, full of energy and purpose. 'I must go now, so I won't arrive home late, so Mama and Papa won't suspect anything is different. Oh, this is such a wonderful plan!'

'Ruby! Ruby!' I hated to hear my voice rising. The mouse's demise was forefront in my mind. 'Hang on, just for a minute! We need... we need time to go over your plan in every detail, to make sure you've not forgotten anything!' It was a desperate plea to get her to sit back down. But no luck.

'No, no, it's fine. This is a perfect plan! Thank you. I can fix everything now. Thank you so much for listening to my story, and for understanding!'

And with that she ran to the window, jumped up lightly, and disappeared.

I sat for some time before I could summon the energy to clear the mass of tissues and the water spill on the desk.

Oh, I understood all right.

Poor Ruby.

The Story of the Three Little Pigs

The creature crouching across from me must have once been proud and beautiful. His was a full coat of short dense fur – variegated white, tawny and charcoal. Two large paws with dangerously long black claws rested on the table, a bushy brown tail trailed off to one side of the chair. His long snout finished in a coal-black nose, ears angled towards me as he stared at me with unforgettable yellow eyes. I met those eyes evenly, though I felt extremely nervous.

He was huge – probably twice my weight and on two paws, probably taller than I am. Even so, he was far too thin, although what remained was still capable of wreaking destruction. His upper jaw suggested disconcertingly sharp canines.

However, despite the forbidding shape, he gave off an aura of despondency and self-neglect. Looking more closely, I noted the claws although long, were dull, jagged and chipped, and his coat was matted in places with flakes of dandruff and patches of scabby skin here and there where he must have rubbed it hard or picked at himself. His expression could only be described as pitiful as he searched my face, imploring me with those penetrating eyes. What was wrong?

It was a Tuesday evening, so I'd been expecting a visitor from fairyland. But this creature had come in through the window so silently I hadn't registered his presence until he was seated across from me, so I needed a moment to take him in. He waited, watching me carefully.

Finally, 'How nice to meet you, Mr...?'

'I am called Adolfo. I have no title.' A rich voice but weary. I could hear echoes of a proud commanding tone. He sighed long, then let out a doleful howl – just one – before carrying on. 'I seek your help because my adversary has defeated me.' He lowered his head, then raised it with effort. 'At least he believes he has defeated me.'

'And do you think he has?'

'For now, yes. But... but I have not yet lost all hope.' He looked down at his left paw, rubbed an irritated spot hard against the table surface, leaving a trail of red ooze. 'I no longer knew where to turn.' He looked at me again – perhaps I should say through me. I felt utterly naked in that gaze.

'But then I heard about you. The bears speak well of you, even a Princess and an Emperor have sung your praises. I thought... perhaps I might ask for your help as well.'

How unprofessional to blush with pride! But how do you stop a blush? 'Such kind words. I thank you.' He remained still, waiting for more, continuing to fix me with those eyes.

'I don't know as much as you do about wolves,' I wanted to try to boost his self-esteem while also playing for time so I could gather my thoughts. 'But what I do know makes me surprised that you would ever feel... defeated.' I'd always regarded wolves as proud, undaunted, and utterly fearless.

Another long sigh. 'Perhaps once I felt that way. But... no longer.' Another single howl, then he hung his head once more. Absurdly, I felt like rushing over and cuddling him, reassuring him he'd be okay.

'It's often best... before we talk about what's caused your

distress… for me to hear about how things were before you… lost your… your sense of mastery.' I was choosing my words carefully, trying to inject as many positive phrases as I could into my questions. I wanted him to remember that there are always positive ways to look at life, whatever happens or has happened.

'Ah, you are asking for my story. Of course you would. You are right. There was a time when I felt… masterful.' He was bringing a memory to light. I swear he smiled. 'I was one of six pups. Four of us males, two females. I was the largest and – she told me often – my mother's favourite. She taught us well, and we hunted together with other wolves. Those were indeed masterful times. But last winter was harsh. The deer, the boar, even the chamois – so many died in the cold, so few bred. We had to part as a pack and hunt singly, entering farmyards by moonlight to slaughter livestock for food. I knew it was risky, but what choice did I have?' Another long howl. Another penetrating stare.

'Spring began at last, the earth began to warm. One evening I overheard a sow in the farmyard I'd chosen to stalk and, when I could, to plunder. She was speaking to her three piglets. She told them there was not enough food left, and that her milk was gone. She explained that they would have to leave the farmyard, one each day just before daybreak so as not to be detected, to seek their fortune. If not, she told them bluntly, they would surely die there, as she knew was her fate.'

Did I detect pity for the old girl?

'At first light the smallest pig – hardly a mouthful he was – set off. I shadowed him silently. Very soon he met a man carrying a bundle of straw. He begged the man to give him some straw so he could build a house, and the man obliged.' Regarding me again, 'Silly little fool. A house made of straw! He took the straw and built a house in no time of course, because the structure was of no real substance.

'It was too easy. I didn't even have to touch the structure. I simply blew on it with one deep breath, and down it fell.' He reflected. 'A tasty morsel he was, even though he was tiny. Then I knew, if the other two were as stupid as this one, that I had two more meals ahead to savour. It was a thought to enjoy not just for the nourishment, but because our mother had always told us that pigs were the cleverest of all farmyard creatures. I would be proud to outsmart a creature she'd held in such high esteem. I slept off that pork meat contentedly.' He patted his now hollow stomach, remembering.

'Next morning early I set off again, back down the road leading to the farmhouse, hoping the second little pig was preparing to leave the farmyard. He was. I followed him of course, with high hopes. Soon the brainless creature met a man carrying a bundle of furze. He waddled straight up to the man, without any introduction at all – and asked him if he would part with his furze so he could use it to build a house. Can you imagine? A house of *furze?* Have you ever heard anything more foolish, more pointless, than trying to build yourself a house out of flowers!'

I wondered why he felt such a need to impress on me the stupidity of these piglets. Perhaps he sensed my discomfort and thought it was because I didn't believe he was telling me the whole story. In truth, it was because I'd given up eating meat years ago and had always thought piglets adorable, so all his talk of tasty meals of raw piglet meat brought extremely unpleasant images to mind. I inhaled deeply through my nose, held the breath, exhaled slowly. Always banishes nausea.

But if he was trying to big himself up, why did he choose their level of intelligence to justify his desire to eat the piglets? Why did intelligence matter so much to him? I wondered if it was a reflection of his mother's values. The only thing he'd mentioned about her teachings was that she'd impressed on her offspring that pigs are extremely clever, so she must have considered intelligence to be a valuable asset. Had he adopted her value system? Or was he still trying to gain her approval? He'd told me he was her favourite, so there was a lot of pressure to live up to her expectations. If I remembered rightly and the third pig had outwitted him, it would be a low blow indeed, and might account for his depression.

But I was running way ahead of his story. I reprimanded myself sternly. Avoid jumping to conclusions or expecting a particular story line. Otherwise you'll create a bias that might mean you miss a crucial detail. Or you might inadvertently snuff out the spark that will awaken the client's motivation to change. Let each one tell their story, their way. Only then is it time to draw conclusions – and only then, together. It was a fault of mine, pigeonholing clients early on and coming up with plans for them rather than with them. Nonetheless, the controlled breathing and my flight into speculation had helped, because the nausea had subsided. I shut down the inner dialogue and refocused my full attention on the wolf.

'Of course, it was more than easy to blow that flower house away. One big puff and that stupid creature was left without anywhere to hide. He made a meal that was bigger and tastier than the one his brother provided me. I enjoyed every bit of him.' He closed his eyes and patted his stomach again, remembering things I didn't want to think about. Breathe through your nose, Helen, and hold each in breath. Think of something neutral, a pastel colour or a type of cloud.

He continued, 'You can imagine, then, once I'd slept off that lovely meal, that I was eager to hurry back to the farmyard for more. It must be time, I thought, for the third pig, the biggest and tastiest of the three, to leave his mother. And I was right. He had just set off, and I followed. I couldn't imagine what he would settle for! Perhaps a few stalks of young wheat to build his house, or a few blades of grass?'

I tried to smile, but it was getting harder to like this heartless killer. Luckily, he didn't seem to notice.

'But no! Unfortunately, this pig chanced upon a man carrying a load of bricks. Just like his freeloading brothers, he approached the man and asked him for some of the bricks so he could build himself a house. The man obliged – he even helped him build the house.' Reflecting for a moment. 'Otherwise, I could have slaughtered him then and there, while he was on his own with the bricks. But the man was there, and I saw he wore a hunting knife. So, I had to wait.

'Finally, some while after sunset, the man departed. The pig was firmly ensconced inside the house by this time, and they'd built a door with a lock.' He paused, then added bitterly, 'I suppose he was a bit bright... well, a bit cleverer than his brothers. I tried blowing on that house, but it was extremely sturdy. I blew and blew, but finally

I had to resort to knocking on his door.' Pause for another single howl, a howl of shame this time. 'The pig came to the door but he wouldn't open it. Instead he peered through the small window they'd built into the centre of the door. I asked him to let me in – said I was a tired and hungry traveller...' He looked to me to share his little joke. I managed a wan smile.

'He said he was sorry but he didn't open his door to strangers. There was nothing I could think to do, so I had to leave.' I noticed he was rubbing his poor paw on the table again. His anxiety levels were incredibly high. 'A few hundred steps away I found shelter in an old tree. There I tried to sleep...'

More rubbing, shredding what was left of the skin on that poor paw. 'But my mind wouldn't allow it. So instead, I spent the night devising a clever plan. Next morning, I returned to the pig's house. He was planting something in his little garden, so I tried to sneak up and grab him. Alas, he spotted me and ran inside his house at once and locked the door. I had to humble myself and knock on his door again.' The memory made him furious – first another howl, then he rubbed both paws so rapidly against the table edge that both were now bleeding.

'When he came to the door and peered through that infernal opening, I told him I'd found a lovely field of turnips.' He paused to regard my expression, wondering what I knew about the habits of pigs. 'Pigs love turnips, you see. I told him if he would be ready the next morning at six o'clock, I would call for him and take him to the field so we could both pull some turnips for our dinner.' He grinned. 'He is so stupid, isn't he! He thought a wolf would want to eat turnips!'

I nodded, trying to show that I appreciated the joke.

'I appeared next morning, ready for a good breakfast. I knocked on the door and asked the pig if he was ready to gather turnips.' He stopped staring into space and fixed his gaze on me, yellow eyes glittering with anger. 'And what did he say? He told me he'd already been to the field and gathered enough turnips for his dinner! And he had the temerity to *laugh at me!'*

With that he banged his poor arm so hard on the table that I must have gasped in alarm.

'Oh, I do apologise! I didn't mean to startle you. But that pig was so rude!'

And pretty clever.

'I managed a fair job of looking pleased. I even congratulated the pig on his ability to rise so early. But inside I was furious, and I became even more determined. I vowed to try again.' Reflecting, needing to explain away the pig's trouncing of his scheme, 'No doubt it was mere chance he woke so early, so I thought I'd try something different, to entice him with something even more pig-delicious. I told him I knew of a nice apple tree, and that I would take him there tomorrow morning at five to gather apples for our dinners.'

I noticed his agitation had risen once again. He was bouncing on his chair and rubbing those poor bleeding arms against the table. They looked like raw meat.

'I had to pass the apple tree next morning on my way to call on the pig, and *what do you think I saw?*' He was shouting now. 'He was already up in the tree picking apples!' One good slam on the table with his clenched paw and a deep breath, blood flying everywhere. 'I absolutely refused to let him think he had the better of me! Instead, I smiled sweetly and asked if the apples were good ones.'

He looked to me for approval.

'He offered to throw me one so I could taste it for myself. But as I ran to pick it up, he hurried down from the tree and fled for home. I looked up to see his hateful little pink tail disappearing ahead of me. I gave chase of course, but by the time I reached his cottage he was inside, and he'd locked the door.

'I could not bear to humble myself yet again to this arrogant creature, so I walked right past his cottage as if I didn't even know who lived there. I could feel him peering at me as I passed by.

'I went back to my tree, and began to make a new plan. Mother always told us to take time to make a plan, so it can be really good. I thought and thought, and then I had an idea. If I were to tell him about the Shanklin Fair, if I could encourage him to attend and agree to meet him there rather than at his house, then once he was out in the open I could move in on him. I would grab him fast before he had a chance to get away, and take him with me unnoticed amid the noisy crowds.'

Another searching appeal for me to praise his superior intelligence.

'What a clever plan!' I said. He liked that.

'We'd agreed to meet at the fair at three – I'd promised to buy him the largest sack of corn we could find. But just as I began to climb the last hill before the fair, a great... *thing*... came rolling down the hill. It was huge! And it was heading directly for me.' Another appeal to my sensitivities, this time to appreciate the danger he'd faced. I tried to look horrified

'Do go on, please!'

'I had no choice of course. I had to whip around and run back to my tree to avoid being crushed to bits. I never got to the fair.

'The next morning I thought I would go to the pig's house and apologise for not turning up and meeting him as we'd planned. I explained it was because I'd been taken by surprise by a great round thing that came rolling down the hill heading directly for me.'

Here he stopped, let out a howl, and banged those poor arms on the table yet again, more blood flying. At least I was expecting these outbursts by now, so I managed to stay steady in my chair.

'He *laughed* at me! *Again!* That hateful, cruel, arrogant creature...' I noticed he didn't refer to him as stupid. 'He laughed at me. That was himself, he said, inside a butter churn he'd just bought. He'd seen me coming, jumped into the churn and rolled towards me, deliberately.' Now he really was shouting. 'He made a fool of me!

The pain he'd been repeatedly inflicting on himself must have finally registered. He looked down at his battered and bloody forearms. 'Excuse me. Do you have some cloth that I may stench the blood?'

'Of course! Let me fetch you some nice ones, soft and clean, for your poor arms.'

'This is all the pig's fault you know.'

'Of course it is.'

It was a relief to get up and leave the room. His fury was as loud as a shout, and I could smell the blood from his wounds. I needed a moment outside the intensity to steady the rising nausea.

Once in the office kitchen, I extracted two clean dish towels from under the basin and turned on the hot tap, hoping there was enough warm water to soak them.

I began to think about the best way to approach this wolf's *idée fixe.* He wasn't depressed as I'd thought at first – at least, that wasn't his primary problem. Sure, he'd lost weight, he wasn't sleeping, and he was showing signs of extreme agitation. But those symptoms weren't the result of a depressed mood or a loss of interest in everything, which are the main indicators that suggest depression. On the contrary, this creature was extremely interested in something – but it was in one thing only – whether he or the pig was the more intelligent. All he could think about was how to outsmart the creature, and the only relief he knew was while he was executing one of his plans to outwit the creature. He hadn't even mentioned the desire to eat him, which had been the original motivation for stalking the piglets. The wolf's mood was low, but only as a result of his continuing fixation on outsmarting the pig. His must be an obsessive compulsive disorder, not depression. How could I have thought it was anything else?

Given that was the diagnosis, I needed to change my approach. When someone has OCD, listening kindly only gives them permission to continue focusing on their obsession. I needed to get him to think about something completely different. But wait a minute! Who was the rigid thinker now? Why was I so convinced that if I managed to find a diagnosis for this poor wolf, I could help him? Sure, it would make life easier for me. As soon as a therapist decides a patient has, say, depression or OCD, they can stop listening carefully and simply suggest the depression or OCD treatment plan they've been trained to dole out. No. I needed to go back in there, put down my preconceptions and my standardised treatments, and listen. Listen open-mindedly so we can together formulate a treatment plan. I hoped I wasn't too late – we were far into the session already, and I knew I only had the one. With renewed purpose I hurried back to my consulting room, ready to be a better therapist.

I found him sitting quietly, no longer bouncing in agitation.

Instead, he was patting his sore forearms tenderly. He took the towels I offered him gratefully.

'I feel so much clearer now. Thank you.'

'I'm so glad you feel better. What is it that seems clearer now?'

'Oh, it's all so obvious. I've been thinking about this problem in completely the wrong way!'

I waited, hopeful.

'You see, I've been spending all my time trying to lure the pig outside, where he'd be easy to catch and kill. But if I go into his home... well, then he has nowhere to escape, does he? And he won't expect this new tactic. Since he won't open the door to me, I'll climb onto the roof and slide down his chimney! Ha! If he won't come to me, I shall go to him!'

He looked at me triumphantly. I wanted to argue, to try to persuade him to think differently, let go of this obsession with the pig and think about other activities – *anything* else. But I remembered my resolve. I needed to challenge, but not to direct. I hoped more than ever now that my change of tack hadn't come too late.

'What do you imagine you would you achieve if you catch the pig?'

'I will prove I'm the clever one! Ha! Cleverer than any pig!' He was truly gleeful now.

'It would prove you could outsmart that particular pig, true. But how would it prove that you're cleverer than all...' I saw those yellow eyes narrow dangerously. 'I mean, that would be impressive, but why are you so sure it would offer you lasting peace?'

'What a ridiculous question! Of course I'd be happy, peaceful – whatever you want to call it – if I outsmart that pig! And now that I've come up with this plan I need to carry it out. Immediately!' He stood up on his hind feet, towering over me and almost bouncing in his excitement.

'I just needed time to think, time to come up with the perfect plan. And now I've got it. I'll get him this time!' With that he ran to the window, let out an ear-splitting howl of triumph and leapt straight up and out, disappearing into the night.

Sadly, I gathered my notes from the day, put on my backpack

and locked the office door. All the way home I couldn't stop thinking about my complete failure to engage with this creature. My own obsession, rather than his, had been the real problem – my 'need' to diagnose him. If only I'd listened openly from the beginning, without wasting time first trying to pigeonhole my client.

Why are therapists taught that we must work from a diagnosis? It wasn't to help us respond to our patients' unique problems, I realised, but to allow us to feel 'safe', to believe we have a clear way forward. After all, a diagnosis suggests a set of standardised treatments, doesn't it? Okay, it overlooks individual uniqueness, but... at least the therapist feels safe and sure of their direction. How misguided this approach was beginning to look.

These strange Tuesday encounters were unsettling not only because they were so fantastical. Now they were beginning to challenge the very foundations of my training.

Snow White and Rose Red

The brisk November wind kept me cool as I toiled up the last hill before arriving at the clinic, although I hardly noticed. My mind was on last night's dream.

I was a child again – well, as much of a child as I ever was. I was in my first year of secondary school. It was evening, and I was preparing supper for my sister and brother and feeling sorry for myself. Why was life such a drudge? Why couldn't I just play around after school like all the other kids seemed to, instead of feeling compelled to take care of everyone else all the time?

On reflection I figured the image was more a memory than a dream, which probably meant I hadn't slept much yet again. It was no doubt triggered by the phone call from my brother announcing his departure for a six-month backpacking trip across South America. Lucky kid. But in truth I knew I'd never have the courage to embark on an adventure like that, even though I so wished I could. My childhood years, taking responsibility whether requested or not, created deep habits. Too cautious, overly solicitous, overly responsible Helen. No wonder I'd become a psychotherapist.

And now at home, I had no one to be responsible for. I locked my bike and entered reception feeling as grey and unhappy as the lowering sky.

Emma was, as usual, already at her desk, having tidied and cheered up the waiting room ready for today's clients. She'd also brewed a pot of her wonderful coffee. The aroma filled the room and, as always, lifted my spirits. She smiled her business smile and without a word handed me my list for today along with a steaming mug of brew. Thank heavens for Emma.

I had a full schedule, so it was easy to keep my mind off myself, bar one exception. My last patient was new, a paralegal in her early thirties who was having an affair with a married colleague and had begun to doubt whether he would ever leave his wife, despite repeated promises to her that he would. There were too many similarities with Freya, making it hard for me to consider her dilemma sympathetically and look at the problem from her point of view. But the hour ended at last. I heard Emma bid the woman good night as I reflected on our time together, hoping I'd done a reasonable job of batting away my desire to pass judgement rather than to listen non-judgementally. I heard Emma leave, and wearily began to write up my notes.

A blast of cold air sent the papers flying, and for the first time all day I felt fully awake. Hooray for Tuesday!

I turned around to see a young man picking himself up from his whirlwind entry, rearranging his knee-length battered brown leather coat. He appeared to be a woodsman or possibly a hunter – thick woollen vest over a white linen shirt, fitted silk breeches buttoned at the sides and full at the back to allow for horse riding. Plain black leather hunting boots almost to the knee. He wore a tricorne pulled down low over his ears, which looked odd; too tight a fit somehow. Despite the masculine gear, he was slender, almost delicate, his face shining clear with a youthful glow.

'May I sit down please? I'd like to talk to you if you can spare the time.'

'Of course! You're most welcome here.' I gestured to the chair opposite me. I was struck by the extraordinarily high-pitched voice – another incongruity – and his light almost dance-like step. He had an aura of playfulness, sauciness and boundless energy. I liked him at once.

After removing the heavy coat and dropping it behind him, he sat down lightly, with perfect grace. Then he looked up at me with a mischievous grin and removed the hat. Cascades of glorious chestnut hair tumbled onto her shoulders. No wonder the hat had looked odd! And now I looked more closely, the swell of breasts was unmistakable despite the tight-fitting vest.

'I'm Rose. And I have a problem.' A deep dimple in each cheek accompanied the huge impish grin. What a beautiful young... woman. I was still re-adjusting.

'Fooled you, didn't I? Oh I so love dressing up!'

I didn't want to speak – it was utterly delightful just to observe her. But she didn't come here to be stared at. Putting on my caring face, 'Yes, you took me by surprise, that's for sure. Is... is dressing as a man part of your problem?'

Merry laughter. 'No problem there! It's just so amusing to pretend, to be someone else for a little while.' Conspiratorially, 'And of course dressed like this, I knew no one would approach me as I journeyed through the forest.'

What a self-confident, fun-loving person! It was hard to imagine she could have a psychological problem so troubling it had caused her to journey here – or anywhere.

'It's nice to meet you, Rose. But you know, I think I'm going to have to ask you to explain your problem to me, because I can't imagine what it could be. Based on our time together so far, you seem really well adjusted.'

She liked that. 'Good! I've always considered myself happy-go-lucky. Mother always says I'm the fun-loving sister.' Silence, then a frown replacing that lovely smile. 'And I always *used* to get on so well with Lily. But now...' She looked up at me, 'It's just not fair! It's totally unfair! Queen Lily! I want to be the Queen! And I deserve it more than Lily! I don't even think I like her much anymore.' She looked away, glanced down at her attire, 'At least I forgot about how unfair it is for a little while. Pretending helps, you know.'

'You're so right. But we can't escape the real world all the time, can we?' I realised what an absurd remark that was, considering I was talking to a maiden who lived in some other world over two hundred years ago – if she ever lived at all. I hurried on. 'Why don't you fill me in on everything? Lily, your mum, and why Lily is now Queen.'

'Oh, she isn't. Not yet. But he chose her and not me. That's the unfair part. I mean, I did all the work to free him. She only made things more difficult.'

'Him?'

'The bear. Well, really he's a Prince. But he was bewitched, so when we met him he was a bear. But now he's a Prince. And that's more because of me than Lily.'

Okay. She's fallen out with her sister. This has something to do with the effort she put in to free a Prince from a magic spell. But then once he was freed, he chose to marry her sister. I marvelled at how this sort of scenario now seemed commonplace to me.

But back to Rose. No wonder she's upset, so what exactly is causing her distress? She hasn't said anything about loving this prince. It sounds more like she just wants recognition for her efforts on his behalf. Or maybe she wants to have a go at dressing up as a queen? Where on earth to start?

'I'm really looking forward to hearing how you managed to free the Prince. But first, I think it would help me understand you better if you would describe your relationship with Lily before the bear came along. Did you get on well before then?'

'Oh yes!' Eyes sparkling. 'We grew up together with our dear Mother in a cottage deep in the woods. We were always the best of friends. We did everything together, and we always got on so well. It made Mother so glad to see us like that, and every day she told us so. And... she would remind us every day that we must always share everything equally.'

'Except maybe not a husband?'

Despite the scowl she laughed. 'Yes. That's the problem.' I nodded.

'Tell me if I'm right here. You lived together, the three of you, and were getting on brilliantly until you met the bear?'

'That's right. He knocked on our cottage door one winter's evening seeking shelter from the snow and the cold. He said he could see the fire in our hearth, and asked if he could come in to warm himself. At first, Lily and I were afraid of him.'

'But your mother wasn't?' She shook her head.

'She never seems afraid of anything. She said she was sure the bear meant no harm, that in fact she could tell he meant well.' I wondered if she knew he was enchanted, whether their mother was a witch. 'I let him in. Lily was still hiding, still afraid. She's always the timid, careful good girl. But I am the brave one.' I nodded.

'That first night the bear just lay down by the fire. He said he was so glad to be warm! He asked if someone would please brush the snow out of his coat with a broom, so I did. Lily was still too afraid. Mother told him he could stay all night, even after we went to bed, and he did.

'But he must have gone away early the next morning, because he was gone when we awoke. Then he came back again that evening. And he did that again and again, every evening throughout the winter. After a long time, even Lily was no longer frightened of him, and we all began to look forward to his visits.

'Then one morning, when spring was well along, the bear told us he had to go away, and that he would be away for the whole summer. You can imagine how sad we were! We had grown so fond of him.' Her gaze was far away now. We begged him to stay, but he said he had to rescue the treasures he had hidden in the forest. He said there was a wicked dwarf who would be waking from his winter sleep, and that if he didn't gather his treasures, that greedy dwarf would soon find the riches and take them for himself.'

She tore herself away from her memory to address me. 'We were all so sad to see him go! But he promised us he would come back the next winter, so we had to make do with that.'

'Did you love him?'

She seemed surprised. 'Well, I don't really know... I suppose I did love him. But not as much as Lily did. She pined for him for weeks. She didn't even want to eat. Mother had to make her.'

So, Lily loved him. I wondered if the bear sensed it. And Rose? I didn't think so. Not as a lover anyway.

'By the time the summer was ending and the cooler weather beginning, we'd practically forgotten about the bear, and our life was much as before. Then one late afternoon, Mother sent us out to gather some firewood. Off we went, holding hands and merry as ever. After walking for some time we spied a big tree that had fallen to the ground. The wood would be perfect for making our fires, for it was quite dry and strong. As we began breaking off branches to take back to Mother, I spied something jumping back and forth on the other side of the tree. I went over – Lily of course didn't. She was afraid.' She really was determined to appear superior to her sister.

'When I came closer, I saw it was a little man. Very ugly he was – bright red face and a long white beard. The reason he was jumping up and down was that the end of his beard was stuck in a crevice of the tree and he was trying to pull it free. It was quite amusing.

'When he saw me, he began shouting at me. Oh, he was *so* foul-tempered! He said he'd been trying to split the tree to get some wood for cooking. He'd driven in his axe when suddenly, the trunk sprang asunder, caught the end of his beard and trapped him.' She looked up out of her memory. 'He really was an unpleasant person. He called me all sorts of names – "stupid senseless goose", that sort of thing. But even though he looked ridiculous I did feel sorry for him. So, I pulled his beard, pulled and pulled... I think it must have been an enchanted tree, hiding something from him perhaps. I thought it had trapped him on purpose.'

The bear's treasure, I wondered? For the creature was almost certainly the dwarf.

'He was making so much commotion that even timid Lily became curious. She stopped gathering wood, came over beside me, and seeing I wasn't getting anywhere she took out her scissors and snipped the beard so the little man was free.

'Was he grateful? No, he most certainly was not! Instead of thanking us, he just berated us for deforming his fine beard as he called it. He grabbed a sack of something shiny from the roots of the tree, called us uncouth, wished us bad luck, and ran off.'

Turning to me, 'Wasn't Lily foolish to cut his beard? It just made him even more angry.'

This was, I thought, a step too far. 'Well, I don't know. Were your efforts paying off?'

'Well, no...'

'What else could either of you have done?'

She didn't want to hear this. 'Well, maybe nothing else. But she did enrage him.'

I decided not to remind her of his wrath well before Lily came to his rescue. It was enough she'd admitted that Lily did the best thing.

'We went back to gathering the wood and went home without saying a word.' This appeared to sadden her. 'I know Lily was sad that the little man had shouted at her, and that I hadn't defended her. But she didn't say anything.'

For the first time she looked contrite. 'She didn't even say anything when I told Mother I was the one who'd freed the little man.' I let that go as well. She was already beginning to reorganise her opinion of Lily. I didn't need to weigh in.

'A few days later Mother sent us out to catch some fish for supper. As we neared the brook, we saw what looked like a huge grasshopper jumping near the water, then back away from it, over and over again. A few steps more, and we saw it was that little man again. Lily was less frightened this time, and asked him if he was in trouble.

'His reply wasn't pleasant. He called us all sorts of things, and couldn't we see it was obvious that his beard was tangled in the fishing line and the fish was pulling him to his death? I rushed to his aid, tried to disentangle his beard. But it was stuck fast. Then Lily pulled out her scissors and snipped the beard...'

She looked up at me, reorganising her memory, 'Carefully I will grant you. But she had to cut some of it to free him.'

This was definite progress. Lily was gaining some well-deserved credit.

'He was so rude! Called us both toadstools, said Lily had disfigured his face. After many more insults he suddenly seemed to remember something. He ran to the rushes, pulled out a large sack of heavy coins, or whatever was hidden down there and ran off, still cursing and swearing. It wasn't nice.' She shook her head. 'We didn't deserve that. Lily was only trying to help.'

I waited. Still, it wasn't yet the right time to say anything.

'The next week, Mother asked us if we would like to journey to the village at the edge of the forest because she needed some needles and thread, and more laces and ribbons. We loved going there! Mother always gave us an extra coin to buy a bag of sweets. On the way we had to cross a heath where there were some big rocks scattered across the path. There, above the largest rock, was a huge bird, hovering and watching something on the ground. As we approached it sank down, lower and lower until it disappeared behind the big rock. It was then we heard a piteous cry. I rushed over, and there...' She paused for her dramatic moment. 'There was the bird, its nasty long claws closed around that same little man. I think it was going to carry him off for a tasty dinner.'

She looked up, 'I didn't even stop to think if it was dangerous. I just rushed over and started trying to pull him away from the bird's grasp, pulling and pulling. Then Lily joined me, and together, with both of us pulling so hard, the bird let go and flew off.

'Well, you will never believe the thanks we did not get! Instead, the little man just screamed at us again, said we dragged at his coat and now it was torn and full of holes, and that it was all our fault. Still shouting, he fumbled under the rock, drew out a sack – this time I saw what was inside. It was full of precious jewels – and started to run off with it. But then...'

Another dramatic pause. I didn't have to pretend interest. This was fascinating.

'Please, go on!'

'You'll never guess who came roaring out of the woods.' I shook my head. 'It was the black bear, our friend! The little man tried to run away, but he was trapped because the rock was in his way. The bear walked straight up to him, towering over him. The little man was pleading, pleading, saying he'd give back all the treasures if only the bear would spare him.'

She leaned forward. 'And do you know what else he said? He told the bear to take us instead! He said we were fat as young quails and we would make a lovely meal! What a terrible, terrible man!

'The bear didn't say a thing. He just stared at the creature. Then he swung his paw...' She covered her eyes. Even the memory was too much. 'He struck him, and he fell. And he never moved again.

'Lily cried out, and she started to run away. But the bear called out to her, told her not to be afraid....'

I could sense the jealousy was about to come back. 'Why didn't he pay any attention to *me?* Just Lily, Lily, Lily. It was all about Lily. When I was the brave one!'

No, she didn't love him. She just wanted the spotlight. 'Well, maybe the bear saw how bold and strong you were, so he knew you were okay, but that Lily wasn't?'

That was better. 'Lily did stop running when she recognised his voice, and came back to where he was standing and sort of... he was sort of shaking. Then... the most amazing thing happened. His fur coat just... well, it just fell off from all the shaking! And there, instead of a bear, there was a man dressed all in gold! He had to be a nobleman. We just stared, which made him smile.

'He explained that he was a King's son, and he'd been bewitched by the dwarf who wanted to steal his treasures to keep them for himself. He'd been running around in the forest for two long years, he told us, trying to catch the dwarf, for only the little man's death could free him from the terrible spell.'

'How did you feel when he explained all that?' It was high time I stopped listening to story time and started acting like the therapist I was supposed to be.

'Really how did I feel?' I nodded. 'Well... I liked him better as a bear. He was more fun then, because he would play with us. When he was a Prince he was so serious.'

This made us both laugh.

'And Lily?'

A little contempt. 'Oh well. Lily. She was smitten. Her eyes were like moons, shining when she saw him and following his every move. It was pathetic really, the way she fawned on him.'

Did I dare say anything? Not quite yet.

'Anyway, he took Lily's hand,' sniff of indignation, 'but not mine, and he said he'd see us home safely. When he opened the cottage door and we stepped inside, Mother put down her sewing and looked up. "It's ended at last," she said. "And which one have you chosen?" How did Mother know all of this, before we told her?'

'I have no idea,' I said, but became even more certain the mother was a witch.

Rose shrugged her shoulders. 'Oh well, I was only hoping you might know, but I didn't expect it really. Anyway, the Prince told her he'd chosen Lily, and that he loved me, too, but as a sister.' She screwed up her face in distaste. 'So Lily gets to be Queen.'

When someone faces a situation they dislike but cannot change, there's only one positive way to deal with it. The situation must be reframed so it seems attractive. It can take some patients months to come around to that.

'Okay, sounds like that's definite.' She nodded, mournful now.

'It's not fair!'

'Rose, what's life like for a Queen in your world? Because I don't know.' Although I had a pretty good idea.

'Well, everybody adores the Queen. She gets to ride in an elegant carriage and wave at all the people, and they throw her beautiful flowers. And everyone talks about her and thinks about her.'

'And what if sometimes she doesn't want to ride in the carriage, or wave at the people? What if she'd rather... oh I don't know, what if she'd rather dress up in men's clothing?'

She burst out laughing. 'What a ridiculous idea! A Queen doesn't dress up in men's clothing!' She glanced down at what she was wearing. I could see the confusion. 'I mean she wouldn't *want* to anyway... would she?'

'But you enjoy dressing up and pretending?' She nodded. 'Does Lily?'

She didn't like this much. 'Lily's such a pleaser. She just does what other people want, all the time.'

'Like Queens have to do? Can a Queen choose how to spend her day?'

'Well... perhaps not. There are lots of things she has to do, and those things probably take most of the day. And I guess... she'd have to do what her husband tells her.'

She looked up, regarded me cautiously. 'I don't think I would like that much.'

'Do you think Lily would?'

'Oh yes! Definitely!'

We sat in silence while she reflected.

At last, 'I guess... I guess... well, in a funny way maybe what's happened is fair after all. I mean, if I were to become Queen, I'd have to do lots of things I don't want to do. No time to be me. But Lily will love pleasing everyone, taking orders, following rules.' She looked at me with a big grin, the light dawning. 'I guess I got off lightly, didn't I? Can you imagine me as a dutiful Queen?'

'Come to think of it, no, not really.'

'I can't either.'

We sat together in compatible silence for a few moments. Then she picked up the tricorne, placed it back on her head and tucked her beautiful mane underneath.

Picking up her coat, 'Well, I think I'll be going now. I need to get back and congratulate Lily and her...bear.' She stood up, smiling at herself. 'And I need to start enjoying myself, enjoying *not* being the Queen!'

'Goodbye, Rose.'

But she'd already vanished, through the window and deep into the forest.

The Wolf and the Seven Kids

Seventeenth November; Alex's birthday.

Waking well before any suggestion of sunrise, I'd allowed myself a delicious moment to pretend he was still alive, and imagine how we'd spend this special day. Bad idea. I hurried out of bed despite the cold, turned the radio on top volume, and forced myself to focus on the early morning news bulletin. Spooned some stinky cat food into Molly's bowl, switched on the kettle. It was still dark.

As I cycled to work, for some reason my mind kept returning to the day I had my twenty-four-week scan, the moment the doctor told me I was having a boy. I remembered the disappointment. I'd so hoped for a girl. Since then, I can't count the number of times I've looked back and regretted that moment. It made me feel so cold, so ungrateful. How could I have wished for anything besides Alex? Is it just me, or do we all yearn for something different or something more, rather than valuing what we already have, accepting it gratefully? If it is human nature to be plagued by this desire for more, the need for something other, I was beginning to appreciate the power behind the mindfulness movement, and why it's attracted such a huge following. Freedom from dissatisfaction.

This train of thought drifted away as I turned into the clinic parking lot, just as the first watery sunlight filtered through the trees. I dearly hoped to find Emma had booked a full clinic, with some really tough cases to distract and challenge me, take me through this day.

I was nearly granted my wish. A full clinic, yes. Challenging, on the whole, yes. But there were two cancellations, two hours when I was forced to remember, regret, mourn. I'd half expected Jane to cancel – her chronic fatigue means she's cancelled almost as many sessions as she's attended. But Josh, the seventeen-year-old suffering from anxiety, cutting his arms and refusing to leave the house, was more of a concern. Despite his parents' insistence that I see him on his own, I was beginning to think we should start meeting as a family. I sensed his mother was ambivalent about letting go of her boy, sending him mixed messages that only made his symptoms worse. I knew I'd been avoiding making that decision, worrying whether I could maintain the objectivity necessary to help a mother who was reluctant to part with her son, or allow him to grow up...

Once the last client left, I decided to leave straight away rather than hang around hoping for possible arrivals through the window. I was just too exhausted. So, as soon as I heard the front door close, I snapped on my cycle clips, zipped up my anorak, and slung on my backpack – not even taking time to write up the day's notes. I wanted to get out before anyone tried their luck with the window.

Too late. Just before I reached up to switch off the lights I heard the whistle of wind behind me, felt the sharp blast, heard the clunk as someone heavy landed on the floor just inside. But instead of the sounds of a dusting off followed by footsteps, I heard the clatter of hooves. I turned around.

A huge white mountain goat was trotting towards me with a no-nonsense look about it. Long shaggy white coat, perfect balance on those two-toed hooves, all lean muscle without an ounce of fat. Hardly any beard – must be a nanny. My hand dropped from the light switch.

'I'm not late, am I?' I shook my head, slightly nervous. Her long, curved horns looked sharp, and the eyes... I've never liked goats' eyes, those slits for pupils. Impossible to read their mood.

'Well, if I'm not late then you must have forgotten. Not a very good start, is it? Maaah!'

She certainly didn't lack self-confidence. But I wasn't about to start the session with a goat in charge. 'No, I hadn't forgotten. I was just going out to the car park...' She tilted her head inquisitively. '...I was going outside to where I left my cycle, to bring it closer to the surgery so I can see to get on it properly when we've finished.' Good lie. I congratulated myself.

'Well, go on then. But be quick about it!'

'No, never mind. Actually it's fine.' I removed my gear. I wasn't going to take orders from this creature.

'Well then, where are we supposed to sit? Do hurry! I have a great deal to tell you and I must find my children! Even now it could be too late!'

Another mother concerned about her children. The theme of the day, or so it seemed.

I gestured to the patient's chair. 'You're here. I'll sit opposite so we can see each other, just there,' pointing across the table to my black leather desk chair.

'I see you get to sit in the more comfortable chair.'

I felt my irritation rising. Stop it, Helen. The need to be in control might be the root of her problem, if back home she no longer was in charge for some reason. Or maybe she was tortured by envy, wanting anything others have. I sat down carefully, took my time extracting some sheets of A4 and a biro from my backpack, refusing to look up until I'd done so. Shuffled the papers unnecessarily, tested the biro. I sensed her fidgeting. Good. Deep breath. Then looking up with my therapeutic smile of non-judgementa kindly interest, 'And now, if you're comfortable, do tell me what brought you here this evening.'

'I already told you. You should have listened! My children! They're gone. Despite my careful instructions. They're gone, gone. And I... I fear the wolf has...'

The bravado broke at this point. Tears, and more noisy 'maahs'. How small I felt for disliking her. Her bossiness was merely a front, her way of keeping her distress from overwhelming her. Poor thing!

'Let me get you some tissues. And please, give yourself a bit of time. It's much better if you wait until... until the tears pass. We'll get to the bottom of things more quickly that way.'

She nodded and gratefully accepted the box of tissues which she examined on all sides, and then began to eat. I hadn't the heart to correct her. Once she'd finished it, box and tissues all, she looked up. 'Thank you. I feel much better now.'

'Good. I'm glad.' She didn't reply, just looked at me with what I thought was an expectant gaze. I was in charge now – first round to the therapist. 'Why don't you start by telling me about your children – their ages, and whether they're twins?' By 'children' I assumed she meant two. Goats usually give birth to one or to twins, very occasionally to triplets.

She nodded, sat up tall before beginning. 'I am the proud mother of seven wonderful kids.'

'Seven? But I thought...' She grinned mischievously. I wasn't as much in charge as I'd thought.

'That's right. Seven. I have twins, Billy and Lam. Since they were born, we shared our lives with six other mothers and their kids...' She paused, looked down, and took a deep controlled breath. 'Until one night this last month... we were right at the end of winter, before food was plentiful again for the wolves...' I could see this was hard.

'Don't hurry. You're being really brave.'

'The wolves... they must have been desperate. It was in full daylight – not even under cover of night – when three of them attacked our herd. We managed to surround the kids and face the wolves. We thought they would only go for the kids. But instead, they turned their snarls on us. Then they went straight for the three smallest nannies – each of those monsters grabbed one in their terrible jaws – and carried them away. They were screaming. It was... unbearable.'

I wondered fleetingly if she was suffering from PTSD after such a trauma, imagining the kids had also now been taken by the wolves. Surely, she wouldn't come to a psychologist if the only issue was child recovery. That would be a job for a child protection officer or the police, or whatever equivalents they have in their world.

'Once they'd gone, once we'd calmed the poor kids, we had to decide what to do. As I am the largest and the eldest, it was decided that I should take on the poor... orphans.' Pause for another noisy bout of sobbing and braying. I withheld more tissues, fearing that even a goat's digestive system might find two boxes of absorbent tissues a bit of a challenge.

Presently she took a deep breath, exhaled slowly and then looked up pleadingly. I noticed with quiet pride how quickly I was learning to recognise goat emotions.

'I have tried my very, very best to look after them. Honestly I have!'

'I'm sure you have. You must be remarkable, even for agreeing to take them all on in the first place. I've never even heard of a nanny looking after seven kids!' That helped.

'Thank you. But I failed. Failed.'

'Please, try not to judge yourself. Just let me know the facts so we can try to figure out the best thing to do. After all, they're only missing. You have no proof they're... no longer alive.' Even though I'd tried to soften that last statement, she still had to work hard to control another torrent of tears.

'After only a few days with such a large family, we ran short of food. I hadn't reckoned on so many mouths to feed. I explained to the kids that I would have to go out to gather some early spring plants and grasses, and that I'd not be gone long. But before I left, I warned them that the wolves might come back. I told them they would recognise a wolf because of its rough voice, and anyway, on no account should they let anyone into the shelter I'd found for us in the hillside.'

Her gaze was far away now, remembering. 'On my return I found them all hiding at the back, whimpering pitifully. You can imagine my worry, and of course I wanted to know at once what happened. Snowy, the eldest, told me someone had come calling. He'd said he was me, and asked if we would show him the opening to our shelter. But my Billy remembered my warning,' Here she paused for a moment of motherly pride. '...so he told the stranger to go away, because his rough voice proved he was the wolf and not our mother.'

'So I guess that means the wolf – it was a wolf, wasn't it?' She nodded vigorously. 'The wolf now knew he had to disguise his voice if he wanted to fool the kids?'

Another vigorous shake of her shaggy head. 'That's right. So next time I had to go out to gather food – and it was only a few days later, because those kids all have such appetites as you'd never believe. I told them again not to let anyone in. No one. Not even if they have a soft voice, because it might be a tricky wolf, not me. I told them to check the visitor's feet before they even think of opening the door.'

She was in full bossy mother mode now, gesticulating with her hooves and bouncing up and down in the chair. 'I said check their feet. If they have black feet, do not open the door.' She paused, satisfied with herself. 'Well, when I returned at sunset, they were all hiding again and making such pitiful sounds! I just knew things had gone wrong, and I asked Snowy to tell me what happened. He said someone did call not long after I left, someone with the loveliest soft voice, who said it was our mother returning with lots of tasty food. But little Pan had crawled under the hedge, and he could see the creature's feet. They were black. Black! Snowy told him to go away, because his black feet proved he was the wolf and not our mother.'

These little goats really weren't very bright, was all I could think. Talk about handing secrets to the enemy. No doubt the wolf had found a way to soften his voice, and now he knew he also had to whiten his feet. The information he needed was handed to him on a plate, excuse the bad joke. All he had to do was wait for the mother to go out foraging again. 'So what happened next?'

'I tried to make our grasses last, I really did. But in less than a week I knew I would have to go out again for more. This time I gathered all seven of them together. Even Almond the hopeless one.'

The hopeless one? What had made her decide this one kid was hopeless? But now was not the time to ask. 'After you'd gathered them all together, what did you tell them?'

'I was as clear as clear water. I told them they were not to open the door to anyone with a rough voice or black feet. Then I set out with my basket. I was gone all day and even just a little past sunset – longer than I'd intended – trying to gather enough food to last us, so I wouldn't have to go out again for a long time.

'But when I returned...oh what a terrible sight met my eyes! The entrance to our shelter was badly disturbed, the door wide open with a big crack in the middle, as if a large creature had bashed it and trampled the earth. And when I went into the shelter...' She began sobbing again, shoulders shaking and with much maahing.

'This must have been such a dreadful moment! You poor, poor thing.' And I meant it. I felt so sorry for her, sensing what she was about to tell me. She carried on sobbing and snorting for some time, but at last she looked up, the suffering in her eyes so heart-breaking.

'They were all gone! My children, gone! The wolf had disguised his voice and whitened his feet. The kids believed it was me, and Pan opened the door to him. Then the monster charged in, grabbed them and carried them off. He'll eat them all for sure if I don't find him! But where will I find them? Where would a wolf take so many, too many to eat at once? There could still be time to save them! Help me, please help me!'

'Whoa! Hold on there!' I spoke sharply to regain her attention, for she'd risen from her chair and was beating her front hooves against her face and stamping her back hooves in agitation. She looked to be in danger of blinding herself. 'Stop right now! You're making far too many assumptions. You don't know the wolf came in, or that he carried them off. Maybe they just ran out to play and got lost?' I knew that was too far-fetched because she eyed me suspiciously.

'You're wrong. I know it was the wolf. I know it, because Almond told me.'

'*Almond told you*? How is that possible? I thought you said the wolf came in and carried all the kids off?'

She didn't look so pitiful now. Sullen, defensive, and angry were better descriptors. 'He did. He carried of all the ones that count, that is. He didn't find Almond because she scrambled under a rock where he couldn't see her.'

More like Almond definitely did count. She was the smartest of the lot by the sound of it. Why wasn't this mother overjoyed that at least one kid had been spared? And if Almond witnessed what happened, she might be able to lead her mother to the rest of them. And if that was so, why did she come to see me? This wasn't a psychological matter; it was just plain common sense; if anything, it was a job for a detective. I was so taken aback I wasn't sure what to say next. More details might help, and it might give me time to figure out the best approach.

'So, Almond told you what happened, that's why you know?' She nodded. 'And she told you the wolf didn't... kill them?' Another nod.

'She said the monster stuffed them into a large sack and carried them off. Laughing he was, talking to himself. He said he was going to the lakeside and have a rest, and then....' She bent her head. 'No, I can't say it!'

I waited. I needed to know.

She took a deep breath. 'Yes I *can* say it. I have to, so you can help. The wolf said after his rest he would build a big fire and then he would... roast the kids for his dinner!'

'Almond told you all that?' Another nod. I wanted to shake her, but what good would that do her, or her kids? 'Then why are you here talking to me instead of letting Almond show you the path the wolf took to the lake, so you can rescue your other children?'

The distressed pitiful look melted. She stared at me, now sullen and defensive once more. In a cold voice, 'That's what the other nannies told me. They said I must listen to Almond. But Almond is a nanny. I never wanted to raise a nanny, because nannies are useless. My other children are all billies. And they're white. She's not even white.'

The poor little creature. Just because she wasn't the preferred gender or the 'right' colour, her mother had rejected her.

But she was clever. The cleverest of the lot. She'd had the sense to hide. At least the other nannies recognised her worth.

'Did Almond say anything else?'

'Well...she did say the wolf would probably be too tired to... build the fire straight away when he finally got to the lake. She said he'd most likely fall asleep first...'

'And?'

'And that if we went together to the lake – Almond said she'd peeped out from the rock and saw the way the wolf went, so she could show me. If we took some scissors, she said, we could cut the kids free while the wolf was still asleep.'

'That's genius! Surely she's right! That's what you need to do, isn't it?' I couldn't help myself, but I could sense her defensiveness coming to the fore once again. Slow down, Helen.

'I mean, Almond may not be the colour you dreamed of, and she may not be a boy, the gender you prefer... but hey, is that all there is to a... a goat? I mean, you're not a boy either, are you?' The frown softened, and for the first time I detected what must be a goaty smile. 'Almond seems to me to be very clever. And I think her plan is genius.'

I could see at last that she was beginning to reconsider. 'Maybe she is... a little bit clever. That's what the other nannies say. That's why I'm here. They told me my... opinions... my opinions were getting in the way of... being sensible. They said I need to learn to listen, not just be bossy all the time. It's not healthy, they said. Go talk to the psychologist, they said.' She looked down, ashamed. This was a big admission for her.

I could almost see her changing her attitude as she reconstructed that evening, bringing to mind details she'd deliberately overlooked.

'Almond said if we went together, she would put some rocks in the sack after she cut the billies out so they could run to you and be safe. She said she would sew the sack back up herself, and the wolf would think the goats were still in there. Because she's so small, she said, the wolf wouldn't even notice what she was doing. And she said she would be very quiet. Then when the wolf wakes up and tries to move the sack, Almond thinks the weight of it will unbalance him, and he'll probably fall into the lake.' She looked up, respect dawning for her little nanny. 'She told me wolves can't swim.'

'I think this little goat is very precious indeed, and I think you've recognised that now. Good for you! She nodded wearily and let out a sigh of relief. 'I also think you need to hurry back to Almond. You two nannies have a job to do. It needs both of you, and it needs doing quickly.'

She stared at me hard. It felt as if her steely resolve was flowing back. Suddenly, she jumped out of the chair and in one leap – I'm sure it was a single twelve-foot leap, although I still can't believe it – there she was, standing at the window.

But before gathering herself for a second stupendous jump, she paused and turned her head to look back at me. 'You're right. How wrong I've been to judge others only by their appearance. How wrong not to listen to someone because I'd already dismissed them. How small-minded to let my prejudices get in the way of... of figuring out what needs to be done. How foolish I've been!'

She turned back to the window, gathering her hooves underneath her and calling loudly into the darkness, 'I'm on my way, dear Almond! We'll rescue them. You were right all along. We can do it if we do it together!'

And with a mighty leap she sailed out the window, deep into the night.

The Valiant Little Tailor

I didn't mean to appear rude. I must have been completely absorbed in my note-taking, which wasn't surprising. My last client suffers from bipolar disorder, so it's vital for him to continue taking his mood stabilising medication. He'd come to me originally when he was high as high, full of ideas about some sort of plot against him, and his own plans for revenge. With the help of an excellent psychiatrist, we'd found the right medication in the right dose to stabilise but not over-sedate him, and he'd been stable and content for over two months now.

But I'd known from the moment he stepped into the consulting room today that he'd stopped taking the medication. He was talking non-stop and gesticulating wildly as he pushed open the door, and had changed the topic three times before he even sat down. Somehow I'd managed to convince him of the need to see the psychiatrist for an immediate review of his medication, and I knew my letter had to reflect the urgency I was feeling, but without sounding arrogant or high-handed. After all, unlike the psychiatrist,

I had no medical training.

I signed off the letter with a flourish – handwritten for Emma to deliver in person first thing in the morning – and looked up to congratulate myself on the careful wording.

However, instead of an empty room, it was quite a shock to find myself facing someone in the patient chair across the table. Someone arrogant and high-handed, impatient and annoyed.

'About time you looked up. Have you quite finished?'

'Oh I am so sorry! I... I didn't hear you come in.'

'Well, that's pretty surprising, given that all your papers except the one you're writing on went everywhere when I flew in through the window.'

I looked around, acknowledged the scattered papers on the floor. 'I really am sorry.'

He was clearly not prepared to let me off easily. 'I should think you could do better than that. You are, may I inform you, addressing the Sovereign of the realm of Lippstadt.' He stared, waiting for something. What?

'You may kneel.'

No way. I returned the stare, comfortable as therapists are trained to be, just to wait him out in silence.

He was magnificent, I had to admit. He sprawled lazily, pushed back from the table so I had a good view of his crimson silk breeches, generously cut and buttoned at the sides of the knees. Crimson silk stockings rose just above the breeches, finishing with carmine satin knee bands. The shoes were white leather fastened with intricately carved silver buckles. He wore a blue velvet coat – lapis lazuli described the shade more precisely – decorated with rich gold embroidery, a matching silk vest beneath.

The coat sleeves, also heavily embroidered, ended above the wrists, which allowed a good view of the full white linen shirt and lace cuffs. The decorated hilt of a ceremonial sword showed on his right side at the waist, which might explain why he had to sit so far back from the table. A crimson sash was draped across his chest from the left shoulder, secured at the waist just above the sword. Over it all he wore absolutely the most beautiful cloak I have ever seen. Full length red velvet, embroidered in gold and lined with soft white fur, held together at his breast with a silver clasp. In his left hand he held some sort of walking stick or rod – I couldn't really make it out.

He was clean shaven, hard haughty features and glittering dark eyes, a crafty intelligence woven into the arrogance. He sported a white carefully coiffed wig, the tail held securely by a black satin bow. I could smell the orange flower starch from where I was sitting. He continued to hold me with his stare, taking in my measure. I returned his gaze evenly, a current of challenge connecting us.

A moment more. Then suddenly he smiled, and seamlessly, without losing face, 'Perhaps in your world you do not bow. I will forgive you.'

Thank heavens for that. I returned the smile, nodded and waited.

'No doubt you would like to know what brings me here to this...' glancing round, 'simple establishment.' I let that pass, smiled and nodded yet again.

He lifted the walking stick – or whatever it was – onto the table, pulled off a sort of cap that covered one end of it, and extracted a piece of thick parchment which he carefully unrolled.

'I wish to create a document that enables me to annul the marriage between my daughter and her... husband.' He spat out the last word. 'I need you to help me create the wording, so there will be no questioning, no argument.'

Why me? I'm not a lawyer. Maybe he misunderstands my profession. 'I'm not trained to create legal documents.'

'I am well aware of what you're trained to do. That is not what I am asking. I have legal experts who will assist me with the wording. Your job is to come up with an incontrovertible reason to end the marriage.'

I felt as if I'd been thrown far into the middle of the ocean. Where to start?

'Has their union been consummated?'

He reddened, but with anger or perhaps disgust rather than embarrassment. 'No doubt it has.'

'Does your daughter wish the marriage to end?'

If he was angry before, he was enraged now. He leaned

forward, fury boring into me. 'How dare you ask such a question? We are talking about what I wish. My daughter's wishes in the matter are irrelevant.'

'Why?'

'Because she is but a *woman!*' He bashed the table with his fist to add emphasis. I waited a little, time for him to regard me a little more carefully.

Then, 'So am I. Perhaps therefore you should seek a man to help you, someone whose mind is more... relevant.' I locked into his gaze once more, and we sat together, unmoving, for several long minutes. At last he dropped his eyes, let go his grip on the scroll case, allowed his shoulders to relax.

'You are as clever as I was told you are. I am prepared to forgive you for living in such a strange world, a place where I see women are considered to be the equal of men. Because...' He looked up at me, no longer challenging, '...I really do need your help. My daughter may be... a mere woman...' He permitted me to smile with him. To my surprise I was beginning to like him. 'But I love her. She is my only child. I want the best for her. And I have now discovered... that I offered her in marriage to a... fraudster. A no-good liar.'

At last we were getting somewhere. Furthermore, he needed some recognition for his efforts. It couldn't have been easy for him to accept me as an equal.

'Thank you for your honesty and clarity. I will try to help you.' Another winning smile. 'But first, I need more information – quite a lot more in fact.' He nodded gratefully. 'Let's start with how you discovered that your son-in-law isn't... the man you thought he was.'

'That's easily done. The servants who guard the couple's bedchamber at night have heard him talking in his sleep. On several occasions he has called out, "Make me the doublet, boy, and bring me the needle and thread that I may patch the pantaloons." You know of course what that means?'

'I'm afraid I don't.'

'Ah well, I will tell you then. It means he is a tailor. A simple tailor. A common man, rather than the great warrior he claims to be. A liar and a fraudster, unworthy of my daughter's hand.'

'I see. So when you first encountered him, he told you he was a warrior?'

'He had no need to tell me. My servants found him asleep on the grass just outside the castle gates. He was wearing a girdle that read, "Seven at one stroke."'

'Seven what?'

He looked astonished. 'Seven warriors of course. It seems he slayed seven of them at one stroke.'

'He specifically told you that?' I'd unwittingly stoked his ready temper. His face reddened and he gripped the table. I chided myself. Slow down, Helen. Soften your approach. 'I mean, of course you would assume that's what the inscription meant. Anyone would think that.' That helped. He relaxed, normal colour returning to his face.

'Of course. When my servants informed me, I ordered them to bring the man to me, that I might meet such a mighty lord. When he was presented to me, I saw no reason to doubt the words on his girdle. A fine and able fellow he appeared, although slight of build and not as tall as I'd expected. I offered him military service and an excellent commission on the spot. He accepted, pleased of course to enter the King's service. He quickly proved to be a natural leader, and although he incited fear with the words on his girdle, he also commanded great respect. He rose quickly to the highest rank.'

'And that is why you offered him your daughter's hand in marriage?'

Another blunder. He looked at me pityingly.

'What an unsophisticated world you must inhabit! To consider military acumen sufficient to make someone worthy of a Princess? Impossible! He had to be tested. So, I created three trials and summoned him forth.' He paused for dramatic effect. He knew I was hooked now, that I wanted to hear more. After examining his fingernails carefully, he looked up at me, prepared now to continue his narrative. During this time my Kingdom was plagued by the presence of two giants in the forest where I most desire to hunt. These two brutes caused great distress, robbing, murdering, ravaging and burning, and no one could approach them without putting himself in grave danger. Eliminating these monsters, I decided, would be his first test.

'I described to him the whereabouts of these two giants and informed him that if he killed them, I would consider giving him the hand of my only daughter in marriage, and half my Kingdom as a dowry. As the task was so daunting, I offered him one hundred horsemen to assist him, but he refused their help. Looking back, it is fortunate they followed him.'

'Go on.' I really was fascinated.

'When he came to the edge of the forest he commanded the horsemen to wait, telling them he preferred to slay the giants himself. Then he set off alone – on foot no less. He was gone a mere three hours. When he returned to the waiting troops he appeared totally unscathed. Brandishing a bloody dagger, he told them the job was done, that he had given both brutes their finishing stroke, and that the troops were free to enter the forest safely now to view his handiwork. Of course, they entered at once, and to their astonishment they found the two giants stone dead, swimming in their own blood, with trees uprooted all around them. They rode back post haste to report to me, full of awe and fear of this valiant warrior.'

'Wow, that's really something! And I guess with the soldiers as witnesses, there was no doubt about his courage and ferocity?'

'Ah, now you are thinking more clearly! I noted, when my soldiers returned, that there were only ninety-nine of them. At the time I assumed I had miscounted and thought no more of it. However, when the warrior returned much later that day and in high spirits, I felt something was... odd...' His voice trailed off.

'You sensed all was not as it had been told to you?'

He nodded vigorously. 'I did indeed feel uncomfortable, although I wasn't able to say why.'

'We call that instinct, or a sixth sense. It's when we've learned or sensed more than is in our awareness. Instinct is always to be trusted.'

He smiled broadly. 'And I did trust that... instinct, as you call it. I summoned him to my throne once again. Praised him for his valour, but said that there was no greater gift than my daughter's pledge to him, so I would require a second test.' He paused, considering. 'I'm not certain, looking back, whether he was glad to face another challenge or not.'

'It doesn't really matter,' I said. 'I don't suppose it would tell us much.'

Another nod of approval before he continued. 'I told him that in an adjacent forest there roamed another foul creature, this one a unicorn which, rather than being a benign and magical creature, had caused us great harm.'

He paused to regard me, thinking carefully. 'I don't suppose you are familiar with unicorns?'

'Not really.'

'I thought not. Unicorns are magical creatures, pure and defenceless – even if, as in our forest, they are ill-tempered. It is perilous, to say the least, to slay a unicorn, even to order it slain, for he who does so is doomed henceforward to live a cursed life, to live half alive.'

He was undoubtedly the most fascinating client ever to sit across from me. I realised that once again, I was leaning so far towards him that my head was almost half-way across the table. How ridiculous I must have looked! I sat back as unobtrusively as I could manage. 'So what did you ask of the warrior?'

'I told him he must catch the creature – alive.' He shook his head so hard that even the wig trembled, some of the starch powder enveloping him like a halo. 'His response was too audacious. He said he feared one unicorn even less than two giants, that seven of them rather than just one would have been a challenge more appropriate for him.

'He asked only for a rope and an axe, and again refused the help of my one hundred soldiers whom I ordered to accompany him. He bade them wait outside the entrance to the forest, and again he entered alone and on foot. Only two hours later he re-emerged, leading the unicorn by a rope tied round its neck. It was most subdued, its horn cut at the tip. He handed the rope to the waiting soldiers, who could scarcely believe their eyes, and commanded them to take the beast to me.'

'When they did, were there ninety-nine or one hundred of them?'

His eyes twinkled. 'Clever you! There were ninety-nine again.' And then more seriously, 'Even though I marvelled at the sight of the unicorn, I felt unease. I decided to set him one further task.

'When he answered my summons next morning I will admit that he appeared totally unscathed, fresh as a spring flower. But rather than generating awe and wonder, this made me feel even more unsure of him.'

He regarded me, head cocked to one side. 'Instinct again?' I nodded, and he continued with a smile.

'I had been thinking all night about the final task to set him. I knew it must be the greatest of all challenges. By daybreak I knew what to ask. In yet another of my forests there dwelt a wild boar. He had gored many a huntsman, and many a horse, with his huge tusks. Everyone lived in fear of him. I told the warrior he had to capture this boar. I set not the easier of tasks. I did not ask him to kill the creature. Oh no! I commanded him to capture it alive. He laughed upon hearing my request. *Laughed!* He said such a task was mere child's play to him, and that to make it more challenging he would go forth without any weaponry or defence whatsoever!'

'But you sent the soldiers again anyway?'

'I did. Something kept urging me to do so, even though he always refused their help.'

'That wonderful instinct of yours yet again.'

He beamed at my praise. 'The soldiers watched as he trotted gaily into the forest, assuming they'd never see him emerge alive. But less than one hour later out he strode, fresh as the morning dew, not a hair out of place. He told the soldiers to approach the chapel that lies just inside the forest, and to look within it. Once there they spied the brute, kicking and butting the walls and door in his furious but futile efforts to escape.'

'And ninety-nine of them returned to tell you of this?'

'Just so. And thus it was that, despite the... discomfort on my part... I knew I had to honour my word. The wedding was held the next week, with great pomp and circumstance, and I bequeathed the couple half my Kingdom.'

'You are a man of your word.'

To my surprise, he frowned. 'I *was* a man of my word. Until... until one of the soldiers who guards their bedchamber came forth to tell me what really happened.' Looking up, 'Now I am compelled to break my word. I have never done so before. Never.'

What complicated creatures we all are! He was haughty, proud, arrogant, demanding. But at the same time, he was a man of high principles, someone who kept his word. And a man who loved his daughter – even though she was a female.

'Thank you for relating this tale so clearly. You face a complex dilemma indeed! May I ask leave to consider what you have told me?'

'Of course. I would have disregarded a glib response.'

'Thanks.'

I stood up, walked to the window where there was a clear run between the two walls, and began pacing. I always think more clearly when I'm moving, and his problem needed a lot of thought.

Two giants, a unicorn and a wild boar all submitted to this warrior. Yet despite his relatively slight build, despite carrying no weapons and entering the forests on foot, he emerged from each encounter totally unscathed. That suggested to me he'd conquered the creatures by wit rather than by using his muscles.

And what about the 'seven at one blow' claim? He'd never said seven what. Could be a bluff. Could be seven flies, for all anyone knew. But how could we find out?

Numbers hold the key.

Where did that thought come from? I smiled to myself. My instinct was now at work. I remembered thinking how curious it was that at the outset of each task one hundred soldiers set out with the warrior, but only ninety-nine returned. Did that one soldier hold the key? I returned to my chair.

'Important question.'

'I am ready.'

'If you counted correctly, on each occasion one soldier somehow disappeared around the time the warrior entered the forest.'

'That's correct.' He was loving this.

'I'm guessing now... but I think... he followed the warrior – unseen – and witnessed what happened.'

'That is exactly what he told me.'

I felt a little disappointed. I'd hoped to unscramble this all myself, but he was way ahead of me. 'Then I guess he told you how the warrior achieved his... amazing feats each time?' I looked across, the disappointment no doubt showing in my expression. 'So if you know all this already, and if what you know means he's a fraudster, why do you need my help?'

He reddened slightly. I should have put that more gently, hidden my disappointment. This is about him, not me, I reminded myself sternly.

'What I mean is, don't you have the evidence you need to annul the marriage already?'

'Yes, but also no. That is why I am here.'

'Explain please.'

'One soldier did indeed follow the warrior into the forest on all three occasions, and he did witness what happened each time. And it was the same soldier every time.'

'But he never told you?'

He shook his head, frowning. 'Not until he heard the... heard the warrior speaking in his sleep.'

He paused, then continued, 'You see, that soldier was one of the two that guards my daughter's bedchamber, that which is now her marriage chamber. He does so, just as he has always watched over her since she was a child.' He paused, thoughtful. 'He loves my daughter as... a sister.' Looking up sharply, 'Although of course he would never *dare* consider himself an equal with a royal!'

Here we go again. The belief that worth is accrued according to birth or gender, whether you're born into royalty, born a boy instead of a girl. Much more important than what you accomplish. How unfair...

He interrupted my wanderings. 'This is what he told me; on the first occasion, the warrior did not slay the giants. He stabbed them, true, but only after they had already felled each other, just to make sure the job was done. When he first came upon the two of them they were asleep. He climbed a tree nearby and threw rocks down on them, one at a time, so as to make each think he was being pelted by the other. Eventually they became so enraged with one another that they began a vicious fight. They tore up trees and belaboured each other for so long that at last they both fell down dead amidst the strewn branches of the trees. Then the warrior simply hopped down from the tree, stabbed each of them, and returned to the waiting troop of soldiers.

'Then there was the challenge of capturing the unicorn. On that occasion, according to my informant, as soon as the warrior entered the forest – and he did so loudly, whistling and singing so as to attract attention – the unicorn appeared and rushed directly towards him, lowering his horn to spit and kill him. But he is a nimble man. At the last moment, just in front of a large oak tree he sprang aside, too late for the unicorn to change course. The creature ran against the tree with all its strength, and the horn stuck so fast into the trunk that he could not draw it out again. The warrior waited for the creature to tire himself, then came out from behind the tree and put the rope round its neck. With his axe he then hewed the horn from the tree, cutting it slightly at the tip. Finally, he led the exhausted beast back to the waiting soldiers, who brought the unicorn to me.

'And now for the third challenge. The warrior must have known this forest already according to my witness, because he headed straight away for the only building within it, a small chapel. My informant had climbed the first tree he could find lest the boar run for him, and as a result he could not see what happened as clearly as he had done on the previous two occasions. But from what he surmised, the warrior ran directly into the chapel. The beast, who'd already spotted him, followed close behind, terrible to see with foaming mouth and whetted tusks. The next thing my informant knew, the warrior appeared at the chapel window, pushing hard against it and springing out through the opening he'd evidently created. Immediately he ran round the side of the chapel, and slammed and bolted the door. The boar was of course much too heavy and awkward to leap out of the window as the warrior was done, and not strong enough to break down the door, so he was caught.'

It was all so clear now. And so clever.

'But you say your faithful informant never told you what he'd seen?'

'Not until he heard the sleep talk.'

'Why then? And why, oh why, did he not tell you before?'

'He is a strange character I grant you.' He was thinking hard now. 'Loyal and trustworthy, but his way of thinking... does not make sense to me. He told me he had not come forward before because... because he believed the warrior had done nothing wrong, that he had in fact acted in good faith.' His thoughtfulness faded as anger overtook him. *'In good faith!* Had he not been such a faithful servant I might have had him put to death for saying that, for to me that seems blasphemous!'

He'd reddened again, pushing his chair back and preparing to bash the table with his fist, as hard as possible so he could emphasise his point. I felt the need to slow things down.

'Whoa! Hold on there, and bear with me just a moment, will you please?'

Mercifully I'd spoken soon enough and my table was spared. He stood upright, straightened his magnificent cloak, took three deep breaths, then slowly eased back down. He looked up at me, reawakening his steely stare.

'This better be good.'

A challenge. I loved it. 'Okay, what did you ask him to do for the first task?'

'That he rids us of the giants.'

'Did he do so?'

He didn't like that. Reluctantly, sullenly, 'I suppose he did.'

'And the second time, what was your demand?'

'That he captures the unicorn.'

'And?'

He lowered his head. 'He did so.'

'And finally, what did you ask?'

'That he captures the boar – alive.' He didn't wait for my humiliating question, 'And that is what he did.'

'So...I'm guessing here... but is that not what your faithful servant...'

'Thomas. He is called Thomas.'

'Is that not what Thomas concluded?'

He nodded, weary now rather than defensive. 'He told me he'd not come before, because on each occasion the warrior had fulfilled my demand. He said he had thought much about it, and because I had not specified how he was to accomplish the tasks, he concluded that the warrior deserved to be accorded honour and reward, even if his strength was ingenuity rather than physical might.'

'But you don't agree?'

'He is a *soldier!* A soldier uses his body not his mind!'

I decided not to argue – yet. 'But then, when Thomas heard the warrior speaking like a... tailor... why did that make him come to you?'

'Because then he knew the warrior had lied! He had told us he was a warrior, when in truth he is a tailor.'

I knew I had to be careful. 'I have to ask you some tricky questions. Please, try to remain calm. Okay?' Caught off guard, he was surprised and curious rather than angry. He nodded his agreement.

'Did the warrior ever actually call himself a warrior?'

Evidently he wasn't expecting that one. He thought hard, fidgeting, clasping and unclasping his hands. At last, 'No, I cannot recall that he did.'

'And – please stay calm – did he ever say he'd used physical strength to accomplish any of the three tasks?'

'I suppose... no, he did not.'

'So would it be possible to conclude that he never actually told a lie?'

'Well, he...no I suppose he never did.'

The final nail. Careful, Helen. Proceed slowly. 'And the inscription, "seven at one blow"...I know you didn't like me asking you this before...but did you ever ask him what the seven in the inscription was referring to?'

He shook his head and sighed.

'So it might have been... oh I don't know... seven mice? Or seven flies, perhaps?'

To my astonishment and delight he burst out laughing. 'Oh, what a clever chap he is! He made fools of us all!'

'No. You are not a fool.' He accepted the compliment almost greedily. 'He simply allowed you to infer what you wished. He built on your assumptions, true, but he never actually lied.'

I let him consider this. Then, 'One more difficult question. Really difficult for you, I know. But I have to ask it, because you told me you love your daughter.'

'And I do.'

'Okay, does she love her... tailor husband?'

Did I detect a tear in his eye?

'She loves him...absolutely.'

'Then does it really matter that he was not born with royal blood?'

I watched him wrestling with himself. It was so much to ask. Could he rework his entire value system? Could he consider someone an equal merely because of their efforts, rather than because of the characteristics with which they were born? Finally, he spoke.

'They are happy. My daughter has never been happier. And he... tailor that he is...' he smiled at himself, 'tailor that he is, he loves my daughter with all his heart.'

He squared himself, looked at me directly, chin held high. 'You know, I think he will make a fine king after I die. He would be able to outwit any enemy. He... he would probably spare many soldiers a needless death in... hasty battles.'

Wow! Such generosity, such humility. I would not have expected this an hour ago. But regarding him, I saw a new softness, a sort of tranquility about him.

He sat quietly for another moment. Then he glanced down at the scroll. To my surprise, he picked it up and squashed it, then replaced it in the container, and pushed the cap back in place. 'I won't be needing this now, thanks to you.'

Without another word he strode purposely to the window, turned briefly to nod, smile and tip his rod towards me respectively. Then he turned and vanished.

The Golden Goose

All I could think was that it must be group therapy night. The procession that flew through the window this Tuesday evening was unlike anything I had ever seen. When psychologists choose individuals to attend for a course of group therapy sessions, most of us base our decisions on a common theme. The theme might concern the type of therapy offered – for example, that all of these people would benefit if they learned the principles of Cognitive Behaviour Therapy.

Or we might put together individuals with similar issues – these people are all suffering from high anxiety, depression or panic attacks; or these couples are all experiencing difficulties in their relationship. But what commonality might run through this motley crew? I couldn't begin to imagine.

They were, nonetheless, connected. Literally. They'd come in as a queue, each clutching the waist of the person ahead of them, and each hurling insults at the person whose waist they grasped. They had been silent as the procession flew in, but as soon as their feet touched the ground the noise began – angry confused chatter. I could only pick out snatches of what they were saying, but everything I heard was about ownership or possession. 'It's mine, not yours.' 'I saw it first.' 'I deserve it more than you do!'

At the head of the queue was a delightful-looking youth, presumably a farmer's son. He had an unkempt mop of blond hair, a splattering of freckles, big blue eyes, upturned nose and a ready smile beneath a wide-brimmed straw hat. Below he sported plain woollen trousers, white stockings to the knee, and unadorned black leather shoes. He wore a rough cotton shirt starched to whiteness, full in the chest and sleeves, with a simple collar and thin cuffs held together by a single button at each wrist. He wore what looked like an extremely warm maroon vest over the shirt, probably made from wool, buttoned at the front – at least I think it was buttoned. I couldn't see his chest clearly because he was holding a goose.

The goose was amazing. Utterly serene, untouched by the chaos behind it, it had feathers of the purest gold. I felt a desperate urge to reach out and touch those feathers, to pluck one to keep. The boy, however, seemed unaware that the creature he was holding was unusual in any way. He was clearly fond of it, but to him it was just a goose. Nor did he seem particularly bothered by the rabble trailing behind him.

There were seven in the queue. The first three had to be sisters. The eldest, the one just behind the boy, had long strawberry blonde curls and blue eyes framed by long black lashes. Her features were petite and regular, and she might have been pretty had she not worn such a sour expression, her lips pursed tight, nose wrinkled in disdain. She was the only one besides the boy to be touching that exquisite goose – one hand was on the boy's waist, while the other appeared to be stuck fast just behind the goose's left wing.

Her sister – she had to be her sister – was dark haired and paler but with similar facial features. From what I could see her hands appeared to be glued to her sister's waist.

The youngest, a carbon copy of her big sister including the disdainful expression, was attached in a similar manner to the middle sibling. I guessed they must be serving maids of some sort, probably bar maids. All three were dressed alike, identical white chemises with short very full sleeves – almost a puff – ending above the elbows. Each wore a full skirt over her chemise, two of them maroon and one a nut brown, which must have been accompanied by some sort of bustle underneath, no doubt intended to accentuate their hips but instead giving the appearance of a dropped curtain. A tightly laced bodice of cheap indigo satin pushed up their young breasts. Plain black slippers completed the ensemble. I noticed a beer tankard tied by a string around the waist of the eldest maid.

Hanging on tightly to the youngest sister's waist – in an inappropriate manner in my opinion – was a parson. His profession was more than apparent, but it didn't seem to have stopped him fondling the bar maid, a lascivious smile on his reddened face. Spectacles perched on his nose, a tricorne in black with an upturned brim perched atop long grey curls, probably a wig. He wore a generous linen shirt with full sleeves typical of the late Eighteenth Century. Under his collar sprouted a white cravat, the two ends extending straight onto his chest rather than forming the base of a ruffle. Below the waist I could see knee breeches, fine silk stockings, and black leather shoes heavily polished with plain silver buckles in the centre. His long heavy black greatcoat, the top of a Bible visible in the left side pocket, extended behind him and almost totally obscured the face of the man clinging to his waist.

That man had to be a sexton. Although his linen shirt was white, everything else he wore was a dull matte black: the round wide-brimmed hat, long greatcoat, vest, woollen trousers, thick gloves and heavy muddy boots. Only one of his hands was attached to the parson's waist; in the other he clutched a spade. Small clods of earth fell off it when he landed on my office floor.

Two labourers completed this extraordinary queue. Both were good examples of the results of a strenuous outdoor life – roughened ruddy skin, dirty matted greying locks and unkempt moustaches. No fine greatcoats, silk stockings or shoes with silver buckles for these two. Instead, they wore short brown leather jackets, heavily used, marked and worn, over brown woollen vests fastened with roughly made mismatching buttons. Wide fawn-coloured woollen trousers – at least, fawn where the mud had failed to obscure the fabric. Heavy black boots, not unlike those the sexton was wearing covered their large wide feet. Heavy woollen scarves wrapped round their necks offered the only sartorial interest, some sort of pattern in brown and cream. Both sported brown cloth caps with smallish brims. The man in front had an open straw basket hanging from the crook of his left elbow with some sort of vegetation – carrot tops? – draping limply over the sides. The other, like the sexton, had only one hand glued to his companion's waist, while in the other hand he clutched a scythe.

Despite their obvious distress for which I felt I should sympathise, the queue struck me as ridiculously funny. It was a parody, a stage set for a 'guess my occupation' competition. But what, besides hands fastened to waists, could connect the assembled miscellany?

The boy, like the goose he held so carefully, remained oblivious to the rabble trailing behind even when they'd begun shouting. He walked purposefully towards me, then round the table to the patient's chair. 'May I sit down?'

He was polite, the beaming smile never absent. I guessed he was maybe sixteen, seventeen – his voice sounded as if it hadn't long broken. I found him delightful.

'Of course. Be my guest.'

With the greatest of care he placed the goose, still serene but now looking around with quiet interest, on the floor beside him. I noticed he had no trouble detaching his hands from the bird.

The transformation in the room was extraordinary. There was immediate and total silence. All seven individuals had become as statues, stopped exactly as they'd been the moment the boy let go of the goose. Not a sound, no movement whatsoever, not even breath.

My astonishment must have been evident, because he laughed heartily. 'Yes, it is odd, is it not? It happens every time like that.' He turned around to regard the statues behind him. When he turned back, the smile had vanished. 'But they... they are my problem. I dearly wish they would go away, go away and leave us alone.'

He glanced down fondly at the goose. It was cleaning one of

its resplendent wings, apparently unmoved by its followers or the boy's distress. 'I intend to take this wonderful bird to the palace, to give it to the King and his daughter. But how can I... with... with *them* following behind? If they come along as well, what an unwelcome gift I would bring.'

'You are giving this... this amazing creature *away?*' I couldn't help myself.

He sighed sadly. 'I suppose you wish to possess her as well?'

How unprofessional of me. 'I'm so sorry! That was totally out of line. No, I do not wish to possess your goose. I was just surprised you could think of... giving her away.'

'She is valuable.'

That went without saying. I waited.

'What need have I of the sort of value she can provide?' He spoke simply and sincerely. Wow!

This time I took a deep breath before I spoke, to hide my astonishment at his last remark. 'Could you not use the... gold?' I looked again at the shimmering bird. 'I've never seen such a...beautiful creature.' He looked at me warily, so I hurried on, turning back to him and ignoring the goose. 'What I meant is, each feather must be worth a... fortune, don't you think?'

The broad smile returned. 'I believe that to be so. And that is exactly why I wish to give her to someone who will use the wealth she affords wisely.' Noting my quizzical look, he went on, 'Our King is a wise and generous man. He will distribute the wealth to those who need it most. And I know he will take of her offerings sensitively, without causing her undue distress.' He smiled fondly at the goose who seemed totally oblivious to what was going on. In fact, she appeared to be about to fall asleep. 'And who knows? Perhaps it will bring some cheer to his heartbroken daughter, for she has recently lost her mother to a dreadful illness.'

We sat quietly as I gathered my thoughts. This goose must be magical, not only because of its exquisite appearance and the endless treasure it could provide – here I found myself longing to touch those feathers again – but also because it appeared to cast a spell on anyone who tried to possess it.

Yet the goose had cast no such spell on this boy. I thought I knew why, but first I needed to find out how he came by this treasure.

'I will try to help you free yourself of this... crowd. But first, I think it would help me if you would explain how you came to possess the goose.'

'It will be my pleasure.' He broke into a winning smile again. Such a delightful person, so guileless, so charitable. I live on a small farm with my father and my two older brothers... now.' I sensed a deep sadness. 'Our dear mother... last winter our mother died of an affliction similar to that suffered by our poor Queen.'

It was clearer now why he wanted to give the goose to the bereaved King and his daughter. He understood their suffering. When we can't stench our own wound, it can ease the pain a bit if we can offer solace to someone else. What a generous and sensitive young man he was! And clearly indifferent to material wealth.

'Besides, I came by the goose through luck. I did not earn her.'

'Would you be willing to tell me a bit about that?'

He nodded obligingly, removed the straw hat, checked to make sure the goose was comfortable – she was sound asleep now – and settled back into the chair to tell his tale.

'A fortnight passed; my father sent my eldest brother into the forest near our farm to hew wood. Winter is coming, the nights are growing colder, and soon we will need to keep a fire burning. Before he set out, Father gave him one of the beautiful, sweet cakes our mother had made...' The reminder hurt. He paused, wiped at a forming tear. 'Father gave him a sweet cake and a bottle of wine in order that he might not suffer hunger or thirst while he laboured.

'He was not gone all day as we had expected, but returned home at midday. He'd cut his arm with his axe, he said, and needed father to bind it up. That evening at supper, he related to us his encounter with a little old man with a long grey beard – a dwarf he supposed – who had, as he remarked, the audacity to ask him to share some of his cake and wine. He dismissed the creature, telling him the meal was his and his alone.

'I thought nothing of the encounter at the time. But the next day, Father asked my other brother to go into the forest and try his luck hewing wood, for we needed our winter supply of firewood more than ever. Father gave him a cake and a bottle of wine just as he had done for my eldest brother.

'He, too, returned early and without firewood, limping, with a deep cut on his leg. He said he'd made a false stroke with the axe and needed Father to bind up the wound. Later, he told us he, too, had met the little old man in the forest, and had – as his brother – refused to share his meal with him. He said the man told him things would not go well for him because of his selfishness, and then he'd laughed.' He paused again, then broke off from the story and leaned forward. They were selfish and unkind, don't you think? Surely there was enough cake and wine for two? Mother always baked generous cakes.'

The memory of his mother stopped him once more, made him turn away briefly. When he looked back, I nodded my agreement.

'Do go on.'

'The next day I asked Father if I might go into the woods and try my luck with the axe. My brothers laughed when they heard my request. They reminded me I had no experience hewing wood, so surely I would cut myself, if even they had not managed to return unscathed.

'At first Father agreed with them. But I kept asking, begging after a time. I did so want to help! At last, nearing midday, Father relented.

'But now there was but one cake left, and it was the spare one, the end of her batch. It was much smaller than the other cakes, just some dough she did not choose to waste. But I insisted that it would do.

'Father said I should have no wine as I am too young, only some beer. But I accepted the drink gladly. I did so wish to help our family. Because it was quite late by then, I didn't expect to encounter the old man. But not long after I entered the forest, I spied him coming towards me. He hailed me at once, and just as my brothers had said, he asked to share my cake and wine. I had to tell him that I had no wine, only beer, and that my cake was very small, but that I would be happy to share everything with him.

'Then, when we sat down to eat, a most remarkable thing happened. I reached into my knapsack, and instead of a small cake and a bottle of old beer, I found a large, sweet cake full of delicious fruits and nuts, and a bottle of the finest wine. You can be sure we enjoyed ourselves!'

He was far away, back in the forest now, that broad smile dominating his kind youthful face. It was a pleasure just to look at him. After a while he left his memory and looked up at me gratefully. 'Thank you for allowing me that memory again. It was the finest meal I have ever enjoyed.

'When we'd both eaten and drunk our fill, I rose to bid the old man goodbye, for I had work to do. He tipped his tall, pointed cap, bowed, and thanked me. Then he said – I remember his words exactly – "Since you have a good heart, and you were willing to divide what you have, I will give you some good luck. There stands an old tree," – he gestured across the glade where we had been sitting – "go and cut it down, and you will find something wonderful at the roots."'

He paused his narrative to look down lovingly at the sleeping goose. 'She is of course what I discovered among the roots of that old tree.'

'You must have been so delighted!'

'Indeed I was. I chopped enough wood to fill my knapsack while the goose watched me, quiet as she is now. But by then it was late, too near dark to find the path home. Besides, as I chopped the wood, I had formulated a plan, a way for the goose to share her gifts with those most in need.'

'And that plan was to give her to the King?'

He nodded. I knew my mother would approve of such a plan – and besides, I thought, what need have I of gold? I would only miss her gentle presence.' He looked down at her again and stroked her lightly. She shook her wing feathers in response, but remained deeply asleep.

'I knew, too, that if I returned home first...' He paused, turned around and gestured to the silent figures behind him. 'Well, you see what effect she has on people.'

Except you.

'I decided therefore to go to the King's castle early the next morning to present him with the goose. But first I needed to sleep. I knew of an inn nearby, so I walked there as the light faded, and asked if I might stay the night. I had a few coins with me to pay for my stay, as well as enough for a bite of supper. But... that's when the trouble began.'

'Trouble?'

'Yes. I ordered pie and an ale. The serving maid who brought my supper,' he pointed directly behind him. 'That maiden spied the goose sitting under the table when I threw her a bit of pastry. She put down her tray at once, and bold as bold addressed me. She said she desired greatly to touch the golden feathers. I begged her not to disturb the goose, for she was tired after our journey. But she insisted. It was as if a spell had been cast upon her. She was absolutely determined to stroke my poor tired goose,'

The goose did cast a spell – on the greedy. There was no doubt about it.

'No sooner had she laid a hand on the sleeping creature than the maid was stuck fast. She was angry, crying out that she deserved the goose for her own, in repayment for bringing me my supper. Her two sisters heard her shouting and came running in. The first grabbed at the goose but misjudged her aim, her hand landing instead on her sister's waist and sticking fast. The youngest then tried to pull her sisters away, that she might have the goose to herself, and she was stuck likewise.

'I dreaded the night, lest I was awake throughout with their bitter quarrelling, for they could not free themselves. Up we all trailed to my chamber.

'But the moment I set the goose down...' He gestured again to the silent figures. 'This same thing happened as you see now.' He shrugged his shoulders. 'There was nothing for it. I did not understand what was happening, but at least I enjoyed a good night's sleep.

'The next morning, as soon as I picked up the goose, the girls sprang to life again. I had to endure their arguing all the way to the King's castle.'

'And I guess you met the others on your way there?'

'That's right. Soon after I set out a parson spied us from across the way. He came running towards us – perhaps he thought I had kidnapped the maidens?' He laughed, but then sobered as he recalled the scene. 'But as soon as he saw my goose... "Out of my way!" he shouted, most uncharacteristically for a parson. "Out of my way! I shall have that golden bird for my own!" And as he tried to push the maidens away... well, you know what happened then.'

I nodded. 'And then the sexton?'

'When the sexton saw the parson behaving in... what he thought was an inappropriate manner, he called out. "Your Reverence! Have you quite forgotten that we have a christening today?" He ran quickly over and caught up with us. That's when he spied the goose, and...'

'I know. The evidence stands behind us.'

That made him laugh.

'Indeed so. By this time, thankfully, we were in sight of the castle. I had but one more field to cross. But no sooner had I stepped into that field than the two men labouring there, hearing the angry shouts behind me, looked up. They saw me first... and so of course they also spied my dear goose, and began running with all speed towards us. I turned to escape them, and managed to gain a bit of ground before they reached the sexton. But they were determined to push him and the others out of the way and to take the goose away from me.'

'And that's how you acquired all seven of them,' I pointed at the statues.

'That's right. And now I'm feeling so helpless, so downcast. How can I bring this... this confusion to the King and his daughter, when I only wished them to have this wonderful goose?

'I considered my situation with such attention that presently I realised I was no longer heading towards the castle, but facing our magic forest.' He stood up and pointed to the window. 'That forest.' He sat back down. The goose stirred sleepily, flicked its feathers. 'I needed advice and help, and I had been told of you.'

'I'm so glad you came, although I must admit, I've never had to deal with anything like... like this! Please, allow me to reflect for a few moments.'

'Of course.'

Never had I needed reflection time more. Clearly the boy was impervious to the goose's spell, a spell that affected anyone motivated by greed, anyone who wanted to have the goose to him or herself. The result, it appeared, was to give that person what they desired, but not in the manner they expected. A fitting punishment for the greedy. After all, greed means you can never be free of that which you desire.

The boy, on the other hand, had no desire to keep the goose – at least, not to keep her for the promise of the material wealth she offered. True, he delighted in her, but he wanted only to share his delight, rather than to keep her for himself. I knew he was safe from the spell and would remain free.

But how to get rid of the others? I thought, I imagined, I brain-stormed. Nothing, not a single idea came to mind. I looked down at the sleeping goose, then behind her at the seven absurd statues. Suddenly I felt an overwhelming urge to burst out laughing. They looked truly ridiculous.

Wait a minute! That's the solution! He didn't have to get rid of that crowd. instead of being a burden, they might just enhance the gift he was proposing to give. Hadn't he told me that the King and his daughter were grieving their Queen? Perhaps something as ridiculous as this motley crew would make them laugh, help them forget their troubles for a bit. They'd enjoy not just a valuable goose, but a laugh as well.

I looked up. 'I think I have an idea. It's only a thought, but...'

'Go on!' He was leaning forward eagerly.

'Well, you told me the King and his daughter are unhappy, didn't you?'

'They are! Especially the Princess, she misses her mother so much. In fact, the King is so distressed that he has issued a proclamation to say that anyone who can make his daughter laugh will be given her hand in marriage. He is that desperate to see his daughter happy again.'

This was even better than I could have imagined. This goose will bring this lad good luck indeed, just as the little man had foretold.

'I suggest you take the goose to the King, just as she is. He will be kind to her – you told me that yourself – and he'll use her golden gifts sensitively, never taking too many feathers until she replenishes what he takes.'

He nodded. 'I am sure of it. He is a just and kindly man. He loves all creatures, and in turn he is loved by all his subjects.'

'Good. But at the moment we also know he and his daughter are suffering.' I paused for dramatic effect. I was, I have to admit, rather proud of my idea.

'Look at that crowd.' I pointed, giving him ample time to turn around and regard them with care. 'Have you ever seen a more ridiculous sight?'

He turned back around to me slowly, eyes sparkling with amusement. 'You're right! They do look ridiculous!'

'The sight of them is most entertaining. Don't you think they'll bring a smile to the faces of the King and his daughter, help them forget their distress, if even just for a little while?'

He jumped up and clapped his hands in delight, startling the poor goose out of her slumbers. Immediately he bent to soothe her. 'I am so sorry, dear goose! I didn't mean to frighten you! But do you know what? We have a job to do! We are off to cheer up a King and his daughter!'

He bent down to pick her up, but then he stopped, straightened up and solemnly crossed the room to where I was sitting. Bending over, he picked up my hand in his young ones and kissed it. 'I thank you. Thank you for restoring joy to our land.'

Before I could think what to reply he'd straightened up again, hurried back to the goose and scooped her up. Instantly the din in the room was so great I wouldn't be heard if I had tried to say anything, so I simply waved to him with my kissed hand.

He returned my wave, made sure the majestic golden bird was comfortable, then leapt up and out of the window, the angry crowd trailing helplessly behind him.

The Elves and the Shoemaker

When I had wished for a real challenge this evening, I hadn't meant one that would upend the very foundations of my therapeutic training.

It had been such a routine, boring day in clinic. I felt I might just as well have handed each client my training manual with the relevant page earmarked right at the start of their session, leave the room, and let them get on with it.

No lovely twists and turns at all today. No one had discovered their mother was really their sister; no one told me their partner had left them to establish a same-gender relationship. None of the sorts of confessions that make you think creatively, rather than just dole out the usual formulaic suggestions.

That's not an excuse by the way; merely my justification, an explanation for my wish.

Only seconds after Emma switched off the lights in reception and closed the front door, I heard a rustling at the window behind me and felt it open ever so slightly – despite the wild night, with hardly a whisper of breeze accompanying. If whoever it is can fit through that sliver of night, then the person who's visiting me tonight must be very small.

They were indeed small. In fact, they were the tiniest people I'd ever seen. And for the first time since the fairytale visits began, there were two of them. What were they? Little men? Or boys? It was impossible to tell.

'Please Miss, may we sit down?' Crystal voices.

'Of course you can. Most... people... sit here, across from me,' gesturing across the table. 'I'll just fetch a second chair for you.'

Merry laughter, so infectious I found myself laughing as well. 'No need! No need! Plenty of room for both of us on the black chair.' They danced – or flew, I wasn't sure – across the room, did a neat somersault and landed on the chair simultaneously, accompanied by more laughter.

The only problem now was that I could no longer see them. The tip of one little golden cap was visible just along the line of the table, but that was it. However, before I could say a word, one of them addressed the other: 'We need a taller chair, do we not, Finnar?'

'No sooner said than done, dear Freyr!' And at once they were fully visible, sitting on the chair seat which had become larger – big enough to accommodate a half dozen of them – and now sited about an inch above the table. Incredible.

They were still laughing merrily. One was busy adjusting the ruffles of his shirt cuffs while the other flicked something I couldn't see off his waistcoat. Their clothing was exquisite. Both were wearing long silk coats, one magenta and the other a rich gold. Metal braid accentuated the collar, neckline and generous pockets. The coats were knee-length, and must have a vent at the back because the little men were sitting comfortably, their coats spread generously across the chair seat.

Beneath the coat, matching silk waistcoats buttoned half-way up allowed a good view of full linen shirts with ruffles at cuffs and collars. At the neck creamy linen cravats. Their matching magenta and gold knee breeches were, like the shirt and coat, full and generous of cut, closed at the sides of the knee with buttons, and finished with a buckle. White stockings were held in place with satin knee bands. Shoes of black leather adorned their tiny feet, the shoes fastened by gleaming silver buckles. Tiny ceremonial swords with jewelled hilts rose above the coat's side vents. Caps, magenta or gold to match each suit, completed the ensemble. Who could blame them for fussing with such exquisite garments? They were astonishingly beautiful, and they fit the little men perfectly. I was mesmerised.

'Of course you are admiring our garments. We've never worn clothing until we found these on the tailor's work bench.' I wasn't sure whether I was listening to Finnar or Freyr, but the speaker must have read my mind. 'I am Freyr, and this, is my companion Finnar.' They doffed their caps in unison. Utterly adorable.

But wait. Surely they hadn't come here simply for me to admire their garments! Get professional, Helen.

'It's wonderful to meet you both. I'm Helen. How may I help you boys?'

Uproarious laughter at what I thought was a polite and appropriate opening remark. Maybe they had come here merely to receive praise after all.

'Boys? We are not boys! We are *elves!'*

I couldn't yet read their facial expressions well enough to know if I'd offended, but thought it best to take umbrage. 'I'm so sorry! Of course you are elves! I see that now. And... you're both boys?'

They shook their heads vigorously in unison, then turned towards one another and said something in a most extraordinary language, one I couldn't begin to identify. Then they turned together to face me once more, a bit more serious now. They looked at me as if I were a bit backward.

'We are *elves.* Elves are merely that. We are all equal, without qualification.'

'You... you... there are no boys or girls, no males or females, among elves?'

Repeating, this time together, 'We are elves. Elves are all created equal.'

'Thank you.' I took a deep breath, trying to let this sink in.

'Could you give me just a moment here? We humans are accustomed to categorising creatures according to gender.'

I needed time. The information had slammed hard against a wall in my training, and I needed desperately to reframe the assumptions I'd already made. I would reflect later at the woeful rigidity of psychological assumptions and theories, based as they are on notions of gender – and binary at that.

'You are elves. Thank you. And... are you... the same age?' A rather random question, but I was still trying to get a grip on the situation, having lost one anchor in the first moment. Another blunder. More sad shaking of heads and another conversation.

This time Finnar addressed me. 'We are elves. Elves do not define themselves according to age.'

Now what? That was all I could think. 'So you don't know... how long ago you were born?'

More musical conversation. Then Finnar spoke once more, 'Elves are not born. We become.'

'You... *become?* Just like that,' I snapped my fingers, 'You are here?'

The laughter this time was a bit less light-hearted. I think they were getting a little exasperated with my ignorance. They regarded one another, exchanged nods, and turned back. Evidently it was now Freyr's turn to try to enlighten the untutored human.

'Allow me to answer your question. Yes, one of us simply appears each time a human shows kindness, just like that,' He tried snapping his fingers as I had done but failed, which made them both laugh merrily again, thank heavens. 'We appear whenever a human offers a great kindness to another creature, purely out of love or concern for that creature, without gain to themselves.' He paused, but went on without any apparent distress, 'And one of us disappears whenever a human chooses to be cruel to another living creature.'

I figured I could come back to their concept of time in a minute. This was far too compelling. I couldn't help asking, 'Does that mean your numbers are increasing... or (I shivered slightly, because I figured I knew the answer already) or decreasing?'

'In our world our numbers are increasing. In your world, our numbers are decreasing steadily.'

I was afraid of that.

'Can we go back to my question about age, please? If you... become... which of you... became... first?'

I was glad to hear more merry laughter. Finnar this time, 'Just as we do not measure by age, we do not measure ourselves by time.'

I felt myself inching ever closer towards the edge of a cliff. 'You have no measure of time? None at all?' Inside I begged that that was not the case.

'We know darkness from light of course. We work in darkness and we hide in the light.'

Somewhere in the back of mind I heard the words of Gibran's Prophet when he was asked to explain the concept of time:

'You would measure time the measureless and the immeasurable.

'You would adjust your conduct and even direct the course of your spirit according to hours and seasons.

'Of time you would make a stream upon whose bank you would sit and watch its flowing.

'Yet the timeless in you is aware of life's timelessness.'

At that moment I didn't feel at all aware of life's timelessness. I only felt as if I was drifting farther and farther out to sea, leaving all the frameworks I use to allow me to understand my clients far behind me.

'So you're just... here while you're here?' Two nodding heads. 'Never young, nor ever growing older?' More nodding.

'I see.' Well, actually I didn't see. I didn't see how it was possible to unthink the basis of all the psychological theories I knew, to throw out the idea of life stages, of progression of knowing according to experience, of maturing and growing 'wise' as a result of that experience. Nor did I know how to proceed if I couldn't infer the likely psychological challenges someone might face once I learned their age.

Childhood, self-sufficiency. Adolescence, identity and independence. Adulthood, vocation and procreation. Old age, making sense of one's existence. All gone if I didn't have time as my guide. Nor could I rely on gender stereotypes. I was sinking, and fast.

Try something else, Helen. Quick, before you panic. 'Perhaps you could tell me a bit about your families.'

Blank expressions. 'What do you mean, families?'

'Oh, I know you said you just... become. But surely you need a bit of guidance at first? Surely you need some others of your kind who... consider you... special? Who look after you, care for you, teach you things, as you adjust to the world?' I was desperate for one of them to say yes.

United head shaking and furrowed brows, followed by another elfin conversation.

Finnar spoke once more. 'I think we are not skilled at speaking to humans. You see, we almost never do so.' I felt privileged, despite my growing sense of helplessness. 'Let me explain again. We are elves. Elves are equal. No elf is more special than any other. We are perhaps each different,' he regarded his gold attire proudly, glanced at Freyr's magenta garments. 'But even so, we are all equal. We simply do our work in darkness and hide in the light, for the time that we exist. That is what it is to be an elf.'

No gender stereotypes to guide me. No birth order factors. No parental influences or family history. No life stages with accompanying predictable challenges. I prayed for inspiration.

'OK... Finnar, Freyr. Thank you for being so patient with me. This is all... so... new.' Encouraging nods. Clearly my credentials had been over-egged, although I hoped they felt they'd made some headway at last. Then Finnar elbowed Freyr – clearly something had occurred to him. After another brief exchange and vigorous nodding of heads, they turned back. Freyr spoke.

'Finnar recalls a woman of your kind, a servant-girl who was most industrious and obedient. But despite her good work, her master was cruel to her; every day we lost many of our kind, and every day she became more unhappy.' I marvelled at the way he told me this evenly, without any apparent distress.

'Finnar decided to help her. He wrote a note to her, asked her if she would like to visit our world, told her it was a place of laughter and joy. She accepted eagerly, so he and two others of our kind came to her and escorted her to a hollow mountain wherein a number of us dwelt. They entreated her to stay a while, and she – like you – asked us to measure the time. How long was she to stay? We told her three days, because we had heard her master once speak this phrase. "I shall be away three days. Clean everything while I am gone," he had told her. So we said three days, and she seemed content.

'After a very little time in our midst she began to dance and sing and feast on berries and nuts with us. She was so merry! At last she said she thought it was time to go home, that her time with us had come to an end. So, we filled her pockets with gold and led her out of the mountain back to her place of work.'

Finnar took up the story, 'From a hiding place we watched her approach her old quarters. She looked high and low, but she could not find her broom and brush. She was startled when a kindly couple, strangers to her, came out of the house and asked her who she was and what business she had there.' He regarded me thoughtfully, then looked away again, back into his tale. She asked the whereabouts of her master from whom, she told them, she had departed three days past. They seemed surprised, and explained that her master and mistress had both died over six years ago.'

He looked back at me, kindly now. 'It is no wonder you, like she, ask us about the concept you call time. You measure it, while we merely dwell within it.

We measure it according to hours and seasons, I thought. Measures we've invented, measures we rely on to create structure to order and organise our world. But now I thought about it, time could just as well be measured as moving slowly – when you're miserable – or quickly – when you're having fun. Or by light and darkness, or by warmth and chill.

I suddenly realised I'd been looking away, nodding to myself, lost in this completely new way of looking at life. How remiss! How self-centred of me!

'I'm so sorry! I was... thinking... hard.' They both smiled acknowledgment. 'But I've not asked what brings you here. I feel as if you have taught me so much already, so it's more than time I help you – if I can.' Which at this point I doubted.

Smiles. With an almost imperceptible nod from Finnar, Freyr began.

'We told you that we work in the dark and hide in the light. This is how it has always been.' Long pause. I could tell this next bit was difficult for him. There is a reason for this pattern.' He looked so ashamed. 'For a time, it was a custom for some of us...' Regarding me, 'I and Finnar among them, to find amusement stealing small humans, replacing them with changelings, ugly creatures with glaring eyes and a fat head. A changeling will only eat and drink and... scream. They cause the humans around them great distress. It was perhaps unkind, we think now.' They exchanged sober glances.

'On one such occasion the two of us were not careful. We took a small human from the house of two larger humans, forgetting first to ensure that no witches lived nearby. Alas, a witch dwelt in the next cottage, and after we exchanged the creatures, the human consulted the witch about this terrible turn of events. Of course, the witch knew it was the work of elves. She also knew how to break the spell cast upon the changeling.

'Acting on the witch's instructions, the human carried the changeling into the kitchen, put it down on the hearth, lit the fire and boiled water in two egg shells. This made the changeling laugh, and as soon as it did so, we were compelled to appear – both of us – before the human. Then we were forced to confess our deed, and take the changeling away after first returning their small human.' He hung his head.

I felt both for the human – presumably the mother of a child, if I was right about the 'small human'. But I also felt sorry for these two elves. After all, they only regarded it as a bit of fun. They didn't understand families, or a mother's love. I dearly hoped I wouldn't be asked to pass judgement on them.

'Do go on. I am listening to you, and I sense there is more to your tale.' Freyr looked up, grateful I'd not been critical.

'There is indeed more. We told you we elves are all equal. Nonetheless, there is among us one who is eternal. That is Erlkonig. Our... mischief, our misdeeds, our unkindness...came to the ears of Erlkonig, and he summoned us at once to his abode.' Two hanging heads now. Always until that moment, we had played in darkness, and only performed acts of kindness when we so desired. As punishment for our... misconduct, Erlkonig decreed we must thenceforward cease playing, and only toil throughout the darkness, helping any human who was in need through no fault of their own.'

Freyr sat up now with pride. 'Since his pronouncement, we have honoured Erlkonig's decree. But...'

I couldn't help interjecting. 'But then you must both feel very proud of yourselves.'

They glanced at one another, slightly nervous. Finnar spoke, 'That is not all. Erlkonig said we would be released from his decree once we discovered the secret of happiness, and that we must seek it out without rest until we find it.'

If you discover that, mates, please tell the rest of the world. What a sting in the tail for these two! Just seek the Holy Grail without resting until you find it, and then you can play again. I waited, hoping they weren't going to ask me for the answer, because I, like every other human, definitely didn't know what it was.

They exchanged looks once again, then Finnar continued. 'You see, we think we may have discovered that secret. But before we return to Erlkonig, we thought it wise to consult you, just to make sure.'

So, they were asking me after all. Asking me to confirm their discovery, which they hoped was the answer to one of Life's most elusive questions. Find happiness and find meaning. The twin dreams we all seek. Find those and you'll never need a psychologist, that's for sure.

Okay, look at it another way, Helen. They think they've found the answer to happiness, and they want to talk it through with you. What a privilege! I should feel honoured. And if our discussion is fruitful, it could be the most wonderful discovery of my life. After they'd succeeded in destroying every premise on which I'd come to rely when I tried to understand someone, I felt this encounter might at last yield something positive. No, something more than positive. Something unspeakably precious. After all, why does anyone consult a psychologist? To find a way out of suffering, a route back to happiness, a meaningful path through life. What a chance this was! I tried to keep my tone calm, even.

'Okay, why don't you tell me about your discovery?'

Two smiles, and Finnar began. 'Many darknesses past we heard of the misfortunes of a shoemaker. This human had become so poor there was only enough leather left for a single pair of shoes. With great sadness, the shoemaker cut out his last piece of leather to make it into one more pair of shoes. Then he retired for the night. Once he and his wife had fallen asleep, Freyr and I entered the workshop.' Finnar glanced back at the closed window behind us with a grin, 'Then we crafted a beautiful pair of shoes from the leather. On discovering the shoes when he woke, the shoemaker was delighted. He placed them in the shop window at once. A customer came in soon after and paid so well for the shoes that the shoemaker was able to buy leather for two pairs of shoes. Again, the human cut out the leather and retired to sleep – and of course it was our delight to make two more pairs of shoes for him during darkness. At next light, the happy shoemaker placed both pairs in the shop window, and made enough money to buy leather for four more pairs.'

Seamlessly, Freyr took up the tale. 'This went on until the shoemaker had become a very wealthy man. Together with his wife, he purchased a larger shop, and soon customers were always to be found waiting outside their door at first light, eager to buy at least one pair of the wondrous shoes.' Freyr smiled, but then sighed heavily. 'But this was becoming hard work for us! Elves are always naked,' The little creature glanced at the silken sleeves of the beautiful coat and qualified, 'Well, we were always naked then. And it was becoming colder and colder in the shop, and we had more and more work to do each night. We were beginning to suffer badly with cold toes, and we often pricked our fingers in our efforts to sew the leather with hands made clumsy with cold.

'But then one darkness, the shop seemed different. I cannot explain why, but we felt as if someone was watching us.' Freyr turned to his companion who nodded confirmation. 'And the next darkness...' Here Freyr stopped speaking and stretched out both arms to regard the fine silk coat, the ruffled sleeves. He became lost in admiration for so long that Finnar decided to take up the story.

'We entered the shop as usual, at first darkness. But there, instead of a long shelf of leather pieces, there awaited us...' Now Finnar, too, stretched out both arms proudly. 'These magnificent garments. Made exactly to our size. Made just for us.'

Now this elf, too, was lost in wonder. We all sat quietly. I shared their joy and gratitude, enjoyed the time we shared, and which I did not attempt to measure. At last, they both looked up.

Freyr spoke, 'Is this then the secret to happiness, the one Erlkonig demanded we discover? Is happiness found when one receives?'

I tried to contain myself, but I felt like jumping up and hugging the two little creatures. They'd shown me a truth beyond price. But I wanted them to feel they'd made the discovery. It was always so much more delicious that way.

'Well, perhaps that's true. But let's think back to the changeling.' I saw their little faces drop. 'I know. It's not a happy memory. But just tell me something. When you took away the small human, were you happy then?'

'No! No, not at all!' This in unison. Then Finnar spoke, 'We weren't given the small one. We took it unasked. That sort of receiving is not the same.'

I agreed. 'So what made that different from receiving the clothes?'

'We were offered the clothes freely, out of kindness, without asking or taking.'

'Okay. So, for something to bring you happiness, it must be given freely, given because the individual simply wants to give?'

'Yes! Yes!' They jumped up and performed a merry jig on the chair seat.

'Hold on guys! We're not quite there yet.' Instantly they sat back down, all elfin ears.

'Now imagine you visited the shoemaker's shop every darkness, and each time there was a new beautiful outfit laid out ready for you to wear. Would that make you happy?'

This took some thinking, as well as another serious elfin discussion. I waited. At last they turned away from one another to face me, beaming. 'No, it would not make us happy. Oh, at first it would be... so wonderful! But after a time... so many garments. We could never wear them all. And they would feel... well, we think they would feel undeserved.'

'You two are brilliant! You hit the nail on the head, as we say in this world. I feel sure you're right. A happy life is about balance, about giving as well as receiving, in equal – or at least near equal – measures. You understood that right away.' Two proud little faces. 'But happiness is more than that. It's also about knowing *how* and *when* to give and receive.

'And always, you have to do it freely!' piped up Freyr.

'Voluntarily. Because you want to!' Finnar's contribution.

'You're absolutely right. Unless the exchanges, the giving and receiving, are done because of love and kindness rather than a desire for reward or power, they won't bring true joy.

'And no one will be happy!' With that they jumped up together. clapped a high five, and turned the chair seat into a dance floor for another happy jig and a couple of somersaults.

'Thank you! Thank you! We will return to Erlkonig. If you want to be happy, balance giving and taking. Give when and where you see a need, and take only that which is freely and lovingly given! We're already happy! Thank you!'

And off they danced – or flew – across my office, out the barely open window, deep into darkness.

The Last Chapter

Even as I write this, I'm finding it hard to believe what's happening.

It's the twenty-second of December. The Winter Solstice always used to be my favourite day of the year, because after that the days begin to lengthen, offering hope in the form of a little more daylight each day.

But this year it means that for the first time I'll be entirely on my own over the winter holidays. No Theo. No Alex. Just the cat, who merely tolerates me at the best of times.

Today is also my last day in clinic before Christmas, and on the bright side (I suppose) I can say I'm looking forward more than ever before to a break from seeing clients.

Ever since the elves made their appearance last week, my attitude to a once-loved profession has changed profoundly. Without realising it, I'm sure those two little beings knocked down almost every foundation on which I'd based my clinical assumptions and formed my suggestions and treatment plans. Since then I've questioned any suggestion I come up with in clinic, and it's often left me incapable of saying anything at all.

At times it's been so bad that one or two more perceptive clients had asked me if I was feeling unwell.

No, I can truthfully say I'm feeling fine. But I have started to wonder whether I can go on playing this game – whether, in fact, I'm cut out to be a therapist at all any more. The more I've thought about our profession, the more I've been reminded of snake oil. What we call 'science' is nothing more than a series of assumptions on which we've built what we airily refer to as 'laws' and 'truths'. The elves had caused me to question everything – the importance of gender, of age, of family relationships. What makes us so sure they are the things on which to build theories and cures?

Because it's a Tuesday I write my notes up slowly, waiting and hoping for a fairyland distraction. Sure enough, just as I finish the last sentence, I felt the now familiar gust of wind as the window flew open. Icy tonight. I heard a rustling as someone passed through into my office. On this occasion, however, there was no accompanying footfall. Just a sort of shimmer – if you can hear a shimmer. I did.

Something passed beside my right shoulder. I looked up to see a ball of the brightest, most beautiful wheel of colours – iridescent blue, shamrock green, deep crimson, shining gold, matte silver – more I'm sure. It was flickering and bobbing up and down, hovering just above the chair opposite me.

'Hello, Helen,' she'd said. The lightest of feminine voices. Staring harder, I could make out a tiny woman at the centre of the ball of lights, her lacy wings moving so fast I could barely discern them, rather like a hummingbird. She was wearing a gown that must have been woven from butterfly wings, so soft and delicate were the shapes and hues. Her features are perfect – long golden hair, big blue eyes, a generous smile. I know I'm right about these details because she's still here, waiting for me to finish writing.

I was most surprised that she referred to me by my name. None of the others had ever done that. How did she know?

I asked her why she had come, what was troubling her, as is my custom. To my surprise she laughed merrily. Told me she didn't have any problems; that she'd come with an invitation. I remember feeling hot and cold at the same time, sort of frightened but also deliciously excited.

She said she'd come tonight on behalf of the many creatures who'd visited me. They were grateful to me, she said, grateful that I'd helped so many of them see things differently, helped them solve problems they thought they could never solve. They knew, she added more solemnly, that I was going to be alone this Christmas. (How could they have known this?) And they wondered, would I like to come and be with them instead of spending the holidays alone in my rented cottage?

At first I didn't know what to think. Was this...fairy, or whatever she is?... real? But then, for that matter, had anyone who 'visited' me on Tuesday evenings been real? If I accepted her invitation, where would I go? Would I ever come back? Somehow I doubted it.

Then I began to think about how lonely I would be this Christmas. How much I would miss Alex, be unable to avoid thinking about him. How I wouldn't be able to stop myself thinking about Theo and Freya either, happy together. How no one would even know I was on my own. When I also recalled the grave reservations I was beginning to have about my profession... well, suddenly it felt like an easy decision.

I asked the fairy if, before we go, she wouldn't mind if I wrote down what had happened this evening, so I could leave it here in my desk drawer along with the rest of my detailed 'Tuesday case notes' and the straw. I explained that I thought it would make a fitting final chapter in the clinical notes I'd been keeping of my Tuesday evening visitors.

Of course, whether anyone ever learns of the visits depends on whether anyone ever finds these notes, and if so whether they bother to read them, I thought.

She laughed at my request – what a merry laugh! – and said of course it was okay, that I was welcome to do so, and to take my time. I think I'm going to like this place where we're going. I've finished writing now. I'll look up, smile and let her know. It's time to leave.

Afterword

I suspect you're wondering what happened to Helen. Did she take her life that night? Did she go mad and spend the rest of her days in an asylum?

After the fairy turned off the light that she is, what really happened is that Helen cycled home. Home to her cottage. Home to her grumpy cat. And there, at last, she did what she had been needing to do.

Helen grieved.

She grieved for the loss of her marriage. She grieved for the loss of her happy home and her job in London. And most of all, she grieved for the loss of Alex.

You see, no one, not even therapists – maybe *especially* not therapists – can hold back grief forever. The longer you wait, the more distorted your thinking becomes and the harder grief pushes, until finally it bursts through. Only after you let grief overtake you can you finally start to heal, create a new life that can contain and incorporate your loss.

It took Helen a long time. Days, then weeks, went by. She ate, bought food when necessary, slept after a fashion, even fed the cat. But all in a sort of haze of tears. Time meant little to her. It grew dark, then light, then dark again. And still she cried.

Gradually, slowly, she became more aware of the time of day, and what day it was. She began to notice the birds singing in the morning, for by then spring had arrived. She began to notice the cool dew on her feet when she walked outside in the early morning. She remembered to brush her hair. Sometimes she cuddled the cat. The food she cooked began to smell and taste delicious.

Then one morning in April, she knew it was time. The pain had mostly receded, only occasionally sharp again when the memories pushed into her awareness unbidden. Otherwise, they were now only a dull ache in the background.

Before she could think it through that April morning, Helen rang Emma, and to her astonishment she picked up the phone. In her office! 'It's Helen.' Emma knew that. 'What', she wanted to know, 'happened to my job? My clients?'

Emma sounded slightly surprised. Did Helen not remember contacting her just after Christmas, asking her to notify everyone and let them know she had to take extended sick leave? Did she not remember asking Emma to invite them to seek therapy elsewhere if they'd rather not wait?

But many had waited. Emma also had a list of recent enquiries. When, Emma wanted to know, would she like to return to work?

Next week. Tuesday. Why not Tuesday?